Death
– by the –
BOOK

A DREW
FARTHERING
MYSTERY

Death
-by the-
BOOK

JULIANNA
DEERING

BETHANYHOUSE
a division of Baker Publishing Group
Minneapolis, Minnesota

Published by Bethany House Publishers
11400 Hampshire Avenue South
Bloomington, Minnesota 55438
www.bethanyhouse.com

Bethany House Publishers is a division of
Baker Publishing Group, Grand Rapids, Michigan

Printed in the United States of America

Library of Congress Cataloging-in-Publication Data
Deering, Julianna.
    Death by the book / Julianna Deering.
        pages   cm. — (A Drew Farthering Mystery)
    Summary: "In the summer of 1932, when the family lawyer is murdered and discovered with an unusual clue, Drew Farthering and Madeline Parker need to solve the case before the hatpin murderer strikes again in the English village of Farthering St. John." — Provided by publisher.
    ISBN 978-0-7642-1096-9 (pbk.)
    1. Murder—Investigation—Fiction. 2. England—Fiction. I. Title.
PS3554.O3414D34 2014
813'.54—dc23   2013039240

Scripture quotations are from the King James Version of the Bible.

This is a work of historical reconstruction; the appearances of certain historical figures are therefore inevitable. All other characters, however, are products of the author's imagination, and any resemblance to actual persons, living or dead, is coincidental.

Cover design by Faceout Studio
Cover illustration by John Mattos

Author is represented by Books & Such Literary Agency

14   15   16   17   18   19   20   7   6   5   4   3   2   1

To the One who knows me
and loves me still

— One —

Drew Farthering dropped to one knee to get a closer look at the note.

It was a lovely thing really, written with an old-fashioned quill pen on thick, yellowed paper, the handwriting embellished with the generous loops and flourishes of Queen Elizabeth's day. In fact, it looked as if it could be from her time entirely. Sweet. Romantic. But it lost some of its charm when one read the terse message: *Advice to Jack*. The effect was further spoilt when one realized that the note was secured by means of an ornate Victorian hatpin driven into the heart of Quinton Colman Montford.

That Mr. Montford was in no position to be inconvenienced by this was largely due to the vigorous application of a marble bookend to the balding back of his head.

"Not much to go on." Drew stood and picked up the two halves of the bookend, a bust of Shakespeare only recently separated at the neck. "You did say this had been checked for fingerprints?"

"I did *not* say. But yes, it has. There aren't any." Chief Inspector Birdsong pursed his lips under his shaggy mustache. "Weren't any."

"Must have hit him awfully hard to crack it into pieces this way."

"Or it broke on the grate there when he fell."

Drew examined the hearth and then scanned the room. The Empire Hotel in Winchester exuded respectability and quality without ostentation. Just the image that would be prized by Whyland, Montford, Clifton and Russ of London. No doubt it would be Whyland, Clifton and Russ now.

"How long ago?"

Birdsong shrugged his stooped shoulders. "I'd say an hour, more or less. We'll have to let the coroner determine that."

"He couldn't have fallen this way. Not if he was clouted on the back of the head."

"Obviously the killer turned him over, the better to attach the message." The chief inspector peered at Drew. "And tell me again just how you happened to turn up at a fresh murder, young Farthering?"

"Appointment. Quarter past two. To discuss finalizing my, um, mother's and stepfather's estates and revising my own will." Drew looked at him expectantly.

"Right. So you said at first. And you didn't go to his office in London because . . . ?"

"He had other business to see to, as did I. I've been looking for someone competent to manage Farlinford Processing for me, so it was simpler for both of us just to meet here in Winchester."

"Did he tell you what his business was?"

Drew shook his head. "No, of course not."

"Of course not. And how long had Mr. Montford been your solicitor?"

"I believe my father put the firm on retainer about 1907 or 1908. Before I was born, at any rate, so a good twenty-five years or more now. So what's it mean? 'Advice to Jack.' Who's Jack?"

"No idea as yet," Birdsong admitted, the expression on his craggy face as world-weary as any old bloodhound's. "Bring anyone to your mind?"

"I'm afraid not, Chief Inspector. A client of the firm, perhaps?"

"Yes, well, we're checking that, though I expect there would be any number of Jacks or Johns or even Jonathans utilizing a law firm of any size. I wonder what advice our Mr. Montford could have given this Jack."

"Evidently, it wasn't very well received."

Drew looked down at the body. Montford was lying with his head thrown back, his mouth slackly open, one arm crumpled at an awkward angle beneath him.

"He couldn't have felt a thing. Thank God for that, poor fellow." Drew knelt once more, turning the head to study the wound on the back of the skull. "Looks rather like the killer was a tallish chap. My height or very nearly."

"Quite probably."

"I presume the pin was, ah, used after death?"

"It would seem so." Birdsong touched one callused fingertip to the small, dark stain on the front of the man's finely made shirt. "Stabbed through like that alive, I'd expect a good deal more blood than this. Clearly he was bludgeoned first."

The spatters on the grate and the hearth and the sticky reddish-brown that had soaked into the carpeting were testament enough to that.

Drew took careful hold of Montford's sleeve, lifting his hand. "Where's his ring?"

"Eh?"

"His wedding ring." Drew pointed out the pale band of flesh and slight indentation on the third finger of the left hand. "I don't suppose you chaps found it anywhere? Pocket perhaps?"

"No. All that was in his pockets were a few pound notes, some odd pence, ring of keys, nothing out of the ordinary."

Drew shook his head. "He was a nice chap. Always a kind word when I was a boy, even when I'm sure I was a dreadful nuisance. My father liked him very much. My stepfather, as well."

"Perhaps he wasn't quite what he seemed."

"I suppose there's always that possibility, Inspector. Ah, well. Is there any way I can be of help here?"

"No, I suppose not. If you happen to think of anything that might be useful, you know where to reach me."

"Certainly."

"At any rate, I don't expect that you will need to reach me." Birdsong looked at Drew from under his heavy brows, and his meaning was clear.

"No need to warn me off."

"True enough." Birdsong's scowl deepened. "Warning you off didn't do the slightest bit of good last time, either."

"Inspector, I assure you, I have no interest in this case. I was acquainted with the man, and I'm truly sorry to see he's dead, but I have no idea who could have killed him or why. I assume you and your men are best equipped to discover that."

"Quite right." Birdsong narrowed his eyes. "All the same, if you *were* to think of something, it's your duty to report it."

"You may rely upon me."

There was a tap on the door, and one of the uniformed officers came into the room. "They're here to collect the body now, sir, if you are done."

"All right, Barnes. We've just finished up." Birdsong turned to Drew. "If you'll excuse us now, sir . . ."

"Just leaving. Er, have they informed Mrs. Montford?"

"Someone is seeing to that, yes."

"Poor woman. I must send condolences to her. I met her a time or two when I was a boy. Charming lady."

Drew took the road past Farthering Place and into the village. He didn't want to think about murder anymore, unless of course it was written in the pages of a cracking mystery novel. It was about time for the latest release on the list from the Mystery Mavens' Newsletter if he had his dates in order. Perhaps Mrs. Harkness would take pity on him and let him buy a copy before she sent them out to everyone else. This time he'd be ahead of the game, and Madeline would be the one who had to wait.

Farthering St. John was comfortingly usual that afternoon. He waved as he drove past old Mrs. Beecham tending her roses, and sat smiling as Mr. Farnsworth drove his seemingly endless flock of sheep across the road in front of him. It was already early August and the spring lambs were getting big. Madeline would never forgive him if he didn't take her out to see them soon.

When the way was finally clear, Drew drove down the high street and pulled up in front of the Royal Elizabeth Inn, fondly known as the Queen Bess, the center of everything in the village and just down from the bookshop.

He got out of the Rolls and stepped into the street, only to jump back again as a bicycle whizzed past.

"Good afternoon, young Farthering!"

"And to you, Mr. Llewellyn!"

Drew laughed to himself. The old blighter had to be nearing

seventy, but there was no one who could discourage his vigorous jaunts on his two-wheeler. The people of Farthering St. John contented themselves with the knowledge that he hadn't yet run anyone down.

It was a good day, and Drew wasn't going to let the unpleasantness in Winchester spoil it for him. Now, if Mrs. Harkness would just be obliging, the day could turn out to be very fine, indeed.

He glanced up at the sign above her bookshop: *The Running Brooks*. Most people thought the name odd, but he'd always liked it. It played on a quotation from Shakespeare's *As You Like It*, and it suited Drew's mood most especially today to read again the words of the exiled duke painted on the shop's sign:

And this our life exempt from public haunt
Finds tongues in trees, books in the running brooks,
Sermons in stones and good in everything.

Yes, there were certainly worse things than the quiet of little Farthering St. John.

Drew pushed open the door to the shop, tripping the bell that hung above it, but there was no one in sight. He looked round for a moment.

"Hullo?"

"Oh, good afternoon, Mr. Farthering!" Mrs. Harkness came out from behind a stack of large boxes. "Do pardon the mess. I've just gotten in my latest shipment, and they've gotten it all wrong, I'm afraid."

"Oh, dear," Drew said. "Have you spoken to them?"

"They're supposed to send someone round this week, but you know how it is these days. No one ever seems to take the trouble to do things properly the first time." She smiled and brushed a strand of short, graying hair out of her face. "Now, how can I help you?"

"I, uh . . ." Drew gave her a sheepish shrug. "I know it's not due yet, but I thought I'd see if you had the newest book from the Mystery Mavens' Newsletter in."

"Now we are eager, aren't we?" Mrs. Harkness wagged one thin finger at him. "You know I'm not allowed to sell those yet. They're not officially released until Friday."

"Oh, but you know better than anyone how I like a good murder mystery."

Unbidden, the image of poor old Montford's battered body sprawled before him, but he pushed it out of his mind. That wasn't his case to solve. He much preferred the ones with handy answers contained within the covers of Mrs. Harkness's books.

He took a deep breath and then grinned at her. "I had hoped to collect the newest one from you directly. The last one was stolen from me, you know. Right out of the post."

Her eyebrows shot up under the sweat-dampened fringe of hair on her forehead. "Stolen? Did you report that to Mr. Pringle at the post office?"

"Not to worry. I know the perpetrator, and she returned the book to me directly after she'd finished reading it. And she was good enough not to spoil it by telling me the ending."

The indignation on Mrs. Harkness's face quickly turned to indulgence. "Ah, your young lady. Miss Parker."

"Miss Parker." He couldn't quite subdue the smile that tugged at his face. "Have you met her?"

"Not to speak to, no, but I've seen her about the village, and of course at her uncle's funeral. She's a lovely young lady."

"An intelligent one as well, and I'd sooner take a clever woman over a beautiful one. She was quite pleased with that volume of Shakespeare you suggested I give her. You know, I'm sure the two of you would get on famously. Madeline loves books. I daresay she'll be your best customer in time. Next to me, of course."

"I daresay. Though, if she reads your books, I don't suppose she'll be buying her own, now, will she?"

"No, I suppose not."

"So she's not going back to America?"

"Not if I have anything to say about it."

"Then she hasn't accepted you yet. Of course, you know I've always had hopes for you and my Annalee."

"Why, Mrs. Harkness!" He chuckled despite the flush he felt in his cheeks. "Annalee is married and has two children."

Mrs. Harkness's eyes sparkled with mischief, and she began unpacking one of her boxes. "Well, one never knows what lies ahead."

"Besides, I thought she'd moved away."

"Oh, yes. Marcus has been given a position at Lewis's in Liverpool."

"That must be a grand opportunity for him, though I suppose you didn't much care for him taking Annalee and the little ones along."

"Well, she couldn't very well have her husband go off without her, could she? But Annalee's just a girl yet. She's not yet twenty-five."

"I was sure of that much, seeing her mother's little more than a girl herself." He winked at her. "If only I were just a bit older . . ."

She turned bright pink and put a hand to her mouth, looking rather like a schoolgirl after all. "Now I *know* you're after something."

"Well, I do have an ulterior motive." He leaned closer to her and lowered his voice. "Are you *sure* I can't buy a copy of the new Mystery Mavens' book right away?"

"Now, now," she scolded, shaking her head and chuckling as she checked one of her packing lists.

"After all, I did risk life and limb to come see you."

She pursed her lips. "You did, did you?"

"Well, I was quite nearly run down by Mr. Llewellyn and his beloved bicycle."

Again her smile was indulgent. "He seems a nice old gentleman even if he is rather an odd duck."

"Is he? Odd, I mean."

"Well, really. A man of his years ought to slow down a bit. And he should have his people about him."

"Perhaps he hasn't any."

"Yes, perhaps you're right. And really, there's no harm in him. I'm sure he'll settle into our ways once he's been here awhile longer."

"Oh, no doubt." Drew looked about the stacks of new books once more. "Now about that new book . . ."

"You know I'm not allowed."

"But you do have them in, don't you?"

She tried to look stern. "I'm not supposed to say."

"But suppose I just happened on a copy." Drew looked into one of the open boxes. "Perhaps in here."

She shook her head, and he pointed out another box.

"Here?"

"Certainly not. Those are textbooks." She snatched up the box and put it on a side table. Then she began unpacking the books, setting them out on a high shelf.

"May I help you with that?"

"Oh, no. I can reach it just fine, thank you."

"Very well." He walked round to the front counter where her packing lists were awaiting verification. There was a freshly opened crate just beside it. "Now there's an interesting possibility. I suppose with something as popular as the books for the Mystery Mavens' Newsletter, there would be several copies coming in all at once. They wouldn't be in there, would they?"

She turned to face him, abandoning the task at hand. "I am absolutely not going to tell you where they are."

Again she tried to look stern, but she was softening, he could tell. And she hadn't said the books weren't in that one.

"No, of course not." He strolled over to the crate, peering sideways into it.

"Now, Mr. Farthering, if there's nothing else, you really must let me get on with my inventory. I have to sort through some of the boxes in the storeroom, and if I come back and count the books in that crate and find one missing, I'll just have to put it on your bill." She looked at him over her spectacles, her expression stern, but her eyes twinkling. "And you won't be getting one when I send the rest of them out."

He made his own expression humble, even abject. "That would be no more than right."

"Well, then, I must get to my inventory. Have a look round the shop if you like. I'm sure you can show yourself out."

With that, she gathered up her packing lists and went into the back room.

It was as much as an invitation.

Drew waited just another moment before reaching into the crate. The new book was by Dorothy L. Sayers, *Have His Carcase*. The latest exploits of Lord Peter, no doubt. Delicious.

He slipped a copy into his coat pocket and then, just to make sure, he left in its place money enough to pay for two or three of its kind. And if she added the price of the book to his account on top of it, that would be all right as well.

When he went out into the street, he made sure to give the bell above the door a good jingle so she'd know she could come back to the front of the shop.

He would have doubtless been swaggering on the way home if he had been walking, but since he was behind the wheel, he had to content himself with a certain smugness of expression.

"Well, my fine Miss Parker, you'll not be getting those dainty little hands on this one before I've had a go at it. The further adventures of Lord Peter and Harriet Vane, including the romantic ones, no doubt, and I won't be giving you so much as a peek at it till I've finished the whole thing, bat those lovely blue eyes as you will."

The scene from earlier in the afternoon tried once more to force its way into his thoughts, but he again drove it off. He would occupy his mind with Detective Lord Peter Wimsey and not solicitor Quinton Montford. No doubt Chief Inspector Birdsong would thank him for it, too.

With a determined smile, he turned toward Farthering Place and then slowed, puzzled at what he saw. Unless he was mistaken, that was Nick standing there at the side of the road, waving his arms like the flagman for a railway, his sandy hair sticking up and his hazel eyes wide. Drew pulled over.

"Nick, old man, what in the world—?"

"I just managed to slip out the back way." Nick jumped into the car and wiped his sweating face with his handkerchief. "Madeline. She said I had to warn you."

"What's happened? Is she all right?"

"No, no, she's fine," Nick panted. "Perfectly fine. It's you she's worried about."

Drew let out the air that was pent up in his lungs and put the car back into gear. "Why don't you tell me what's going on without all the melodrama?"

"I've just had the tongue-lashing of my life, I can tell you that much."

"Really? Why?"

"Accusations of a rather forceful nature, I must admit, and insinuating all manner of impropriety."

Drew chuckled. "What exactly have you been up to?"

"Yes, go on and laugh now, but you might want to turn round, you know. Before it's too late."

They were at Farthering Place by then, and Drew pulled up at the steps, glad to see his family's ancestral home was still standing in the grove of oaks at the end of the drive in all her imposing, respectable glory. From what Nick had said, Drew had half expected to find the old manor house nothing but rubble around his feet.

"Hadn't you better—?"

"Too late," Nick breathed, nodding toward the formidable middle-aged woman dressed entirely in black, who, despite her cane, came sailing along the garden path round to the front of the house like an ocean liner in open water.

"There you are!" Steely eyes blazing, she pointed one accusing finger at Drew. "Finally man enough to show your face, are you?"

Drew blinked at her. "I beg your pardon?"

"And well you should, young man. Stand to your feet when addressing your elders. Now, where have you been hiding yourself?"

"Hiding?"

"Stand up, I say!"

She thumped her cane against one of the tires. Drew scrambled out of the car, removing his hat and feeling horribly guilty. Guilty of what, he did not know.

"I was just at the bookshop and—"

"A very likely story. Now, what do you have to say for yourself?" She turned her head sideways, peering at him over her wire-rimmed spectacles as if she were some enormous parrot in full mourning.

"I, uh—"

"Yes, of course. There is no excuse you could possibly offer. I'm glad we can agree on that much. I hope you realize that the situation cannot continue as it is."

"I don't—"

"Well, I didn't think you would, but that doesn't matter."

"Look here—"

She put up a hand to silence him, looking the perfect image of saintlike patience in the face of great provocation.

"No amount of contrition will be sufficient at this late hour. I have already arranged for a taxi to come take us to the train station and told one of your housemaids to have everything packed up before he gets here. This little episode will soon be nothing more than a shameful memory. For you and for Madeline, I trust."

"Me and—" Then it all made sense. Drew smiled. "Aunt Ruth, it must be. How lovely to meet you at last."

"Oh, dear," Nick murmured, and he slunk out of the car and toward the house.

"Don't you Aunt Ruth me, young man!" she roared. "I'm not your aunt, and don't hold your breath waiting for me to be."

"Again, I beg your pardon." Hat over his heart and determined to keep hold of his affable demeanor, Drew made a slight bow in her direction. "Shall we go into the house, Miss Jansen? I'm sure Madeline will be delighted to see you."

"She has seen me already. And no, she was not delighted." Aunt Ruth swept up to the top of the steps, then turned to glare at Drew once more. "I will go into the house only because I have never been one to air dirty laundry in public."

Nick scurried up to the door and opened it for her.

She vouchsafed him a nod of thanks. "I apologize for what I said to you earlier, young man. I had no way of knowing you were not this Farthering fellow, but we sometimes suffer for making poor choices in the company we keep, don't we? Let that be a lesson to you."

"Indeed, ma'am. I certainly will."

With a derisive snort, she sailed into the house.

Drew stood at the foot of the steps for a moment more and then glanced longingly back at the car. It wasn't too late for a quick getaway.

Nick gave him a half-dazed smile. "Coming inside, old man?"

"Good heavens. No wonder you looked as if you'd been hit by a train."

Nick laughed, and a touch of color crept back into his face. "I believe the only thing she didn't accuse me of was sacrificing Christian maidens to my pagan gods out here on the front lawn."

"Sorry about that. Obviously that was all intended for me. What exactly am I meant to have done?"

"Evidently you've led one Miss Madeline Parker astray with your silver tongue and modern ideas, not to mention forever soiling the family honor."

Drew chuckled. "Oh, is that all."

"Apparently, it's enough."

"Well, that's easily cleared up. I'll just explain to her that

Madeline has been living at Rose Cottage since her uncle died. Even the old hens in the village haven't quite figured out how to be scandalized at that."

"Explain away, my friend, for all the good it will do you. When the dear auntie came in earlier, she found Madeline sleeping—sleeping, mind you!—on the divan in the library. And she had her shoes off." Nick grinned. "If that doesn't tell the whole sordid story, I don't know what would."

"But surely Madeline told her—"

"You've seen what it's like to try to get a word in edgeways, haven't you? I daresay Madeline gave up trying to be heard ages ago."

"Well, the lady has got to take a breath sometime, hasn't she? I will just wait for a lull in the storm."

— Two —

Well, I've hunted him down at last."

Aunt Ruth stormed into the library, and Madeline stood up, her shoes decently on both feet.

"Aunt Ruth—"

"And why didn't that other boy tell me he isn't who I thought he was?"

"That's Nick Dennison. He's learning to manage the estate. His father is the butler here."

"With all these people to do his work for him, no wonder this Farthering fellow has time for mischief. He tried to give me some cock-and-bull story about being at a bookstore." The older woman raised one graying eyebrow. "I can guess the kind of books."

"If you guess Shakespeare and a lot of the other classics, you'd be right. Drew's a very well-educated man."

"Educated in mischief, I'll be bound."

Aunt Ruth's lips were pressed into that tight line Madeline knew so well. Over the years, the expression had etched vertical creases into Aunt Ruth's forehead and upper lip, advertising her displeasure with the world and all it had to offer.

"I wish you would just give him a chance. Talk to him for a little while and see. He's got a lot of good qualities."

"I suppose he does. Lots of money, fancy friends, a big house, the latest automobile, fashionable clothes and a handsome frame to display them, what else could a girl want?"

"It's not—"

"Oh, I know. I know." Aunt Ruth waived one hand in its black glove. "It's not that way with you. You love him for his warm heart and his generous spirit and his kindly soul. Let me tell you, young lady, in the short time you've been here, you know nothing about his heart, spirit, or soul but what he's wanted you to see. It's easy for a man like that, one of these men of the world you hear about, to fool an innocent little girl like you. No telling what he's talked you into already."

"But Aunt Ruth—"

"Don't you Aunt Ruth me, miss. Didn't I see you with my own eyes exhibiting yourself here on this sofa half dressed?"

Madeline bit her lip. "I was just reading a book and fell asleep. Drew wasn't even here for me to *exhibit myself* to. And I was completely dressed except for my shoes."

"Well, bare feet are just the beginning if you ask me."

Madeline fought the urge to scream. "Why don't you sit down for a while and we can talk about this?"

"There's nothing to talk about. Go see that that maid has packed all your things. I'll make sure the cab driver is still outside. He's driven off with all the luggage, like as not."

Aunt Ruth bustled out of the room, and Madeline sank down onto the couch and dropped her head into her hands.

"All clear?"

She looked up to see Drew peeking around the door and flung herself into his arms.

"Oh, Drew, I'm so sorry."

"For what, darling?"

"I don't know. For what she must have said to you outside."

He gave her a wink, and there was warmth in his gray eyes. "She is a bit of a pepper pot, isn't she?"

Madeline smiled in spite of herself and smoothed the dark hair off his forehead. "She really doesn't mean any harm. She thinks she's protecting me."

He squeezed her tightly against him. "That's my job now, isn't it?"

"Drew. Drew." She buried her face against the fresh linen of his shirt and burst into tears. "I don't want to go home now. I don't."

"It's all right, darling."

He had such a wonderful voice, soothing and sure, as if he could make anything all right.

"I don't know what to do." She lifted her head and smiled again. "I guess I'd better make up my mind one way or other."

"That's the preferred method, of course."

She sat on the sofa and pulled him down beside her. "I can't believe she's come all this way. I don't think she'd ever left Illinois or even Chicago in her life."

"She seems rather determined nonetheless. It's good of her to wear mourning for your uncle. I didn't think they were all that close."

"They weren't. She never liked him at all. But she always wears black, at least ever since I've been alive. She was engaged to a man who died a few days before their wedding. I suppose she never got over it."

He looked around the room and then lowered his voice. "You don't suppose he took the coward's way out and made away with himself, do you?"

Madeline stifled a laugh. "You are *very* bad. Besides, Aunt Ruth was quite the beauty in her day. I should show you some photographs."

"So who was he, this chap who died? Must have been quite something."

"That's just it. I don't know anything about him. She's worn mourning for him ever since he passed away, but she never speaks of him. I mean, except to say how different things would have been if her Bertie had lived. I'd never dare ask her about him."

Drew frowned. "Just because she's been unhappy, it doesn't follow she should want you to be."

She squeezed his hand. "No, it doesn't. And I don't think that's what she wants. Not really. She just has that way about her. My uncle Cal says she'd scowl at a sunrise and bark at a bluebird. Of course, he doesn't say it where she can hear him."

"I daresay."

He grinned at her with that little spark of mischief in his eyes that she had already come to know so well. Surely even Aunt Ruth couldn't dislike him for long. In the weeks Madeline had been here in Hampshire, she had seen him with the older ladies in the village—well, with all the women to be honest. He didn't intentionally flirt, not really, but he was never lacking in charm, charm that was all the more attractive for its artlessness, charm that made them girlish and indulgent whenever he was around.

But Aunt Ruth was right, even though she had only meant to be sarcastic. Madeline did love him for his warm heart and his generous spirit and his kindly soul. She loved his wit and his intelligence, his protectiveness and his coolness through the worst of situations. She wouldn't lie to herself, either. She loved the look of him and the sound of him, the touch and the taste and the smell of him. Oh, why did he always have to smell so good? So many men reeked of liquor and cigarettes, but he always smelled like freshly laundered linen, new books, and tea and honey.

She was unable to resist pressing her face against his neck and breathing in his clean, masculine scent. He did nothing more than slip one arm around her waist and lay his cheek against her hair, but she felt that instant electricity between them, that quickening in her blood that made her want to kick off caution and restraint like a pair of too-tight shoes.

But that wasn't going to happen. They'd already talked about having no regrets between them and being careful to stay out of situations that might make it too easy to slip.

She pressed a little closer, breathed a little more deeply. It wasn't going to happen, but it would be easy, oh, so easy—

"Madeline!"

Madeline shoved herself away from Drew, and he sprang to his feet.

"Exactly what I suspected." Nostrils flaring, eyes snapping, Aunt Ruth stormed into the room, the picture of delighted righteous indignation. "Get up this minute, young lady. The sooner we're away from here, the better."

Madeline stood, anger, embarrassment, and irritation fighting for supremacy inside her.

"I beg your pardon, Miss Jansen, and with all due respect, but Madeline is of age." Despite the touch of color in his face, Drew managed to keep his tone and his temper cool. "She ought to be able to make such decisions for herself, don't you think?"

Aunt Ruth snorted. "She never could make a sound decision.

And how could she be expected to? She may be twenty-two, but she's really just a child. How else could she have been so easily seduced into staying on here so long?"

Drew's tolerant smile tightened. "Seduced? Now, really—"

"She was raised up to be a good girl. I knew it was a mistake letting her tramp all over creation with a couple of flibbertigibbets for even a few weeks. Now they're who knows where and she goes and gets ideas in her head."

"Carrie and Muriel are back in Chicago now, Aunt Ruth. I wrote you about it. I couldn't just leave with everything that was happening here." A little tendril of grief tightened around Madeline's heart. "And then there was the funeral."

"You should have come home. I don't care what was happening." Aunt Ruth shook her finger in Madeline's face. "You listen to me, my fine lady. You may have your uncle's money now to do with as you please and no one to answer to, but it will do you little good if you lose your precious soul in the bargain."

Madeline merely looked down at her folded hands and said nothing. It was always this way. The more she tried to get Aunt Ruth to understand, the worse the situation became.

"You mistake my intentions, ma'am," Drew said. "I have made Madeline an honorable proposal of marriage."

"Hogwash."

Drew blinked. "I assure you—"

"If your intentions were anything but low down, you'd have asked permission from her family."

"And I would have, the moment she accepted me."

"Bah. A gentleman asks permission first."

"You're perfectly right, and for that I do apologize. But with everything that happened here when she arrived, I thought it would be best to have her answer before I presumed to contact you in America."

"Presumption it would have been." Aunt Ruth's eyes flashed. "And is still. How long have you known each other? A month now?"

"Nearly two," Madeline blurted, and then she wilted under her aunt's glare.

"Two whole months, is it? Well, why have you waited so long? You could have saved yourself the trouble and moved in the moment you stepped onshore."

"Please, Aunt Ruth, I'm trying to do the right thing. That's why I haven't given him an answer yet. I thought if we waited a while, to get to know each other better, and—"

"Playing house in your little love nest the whole time, of course."

"No."

Madeline said nothing else in protest, but her face was hot, and mortified tears had sprung to her eyes. What must Drew think? Of her and her family? But if a sharp retort leapt to Drew's tongue, he kept it firmly subdued.

"You should congratulate yourself, ma'am, on a job well done." Smiling, Drew put his arm around Madeline. "As you say, you raised her to be a good girl, and she is just that. Through everything that's happened, she's conducted herself with courage and clear-headedness and absolute propriety. You've fashioned her into a young lady any man would be honored to have as his wife."

Dear Drew. Of course he'd use honey to catch Aunt Ruth. Madeline squeezed his hand, her eyes glowing, but her aunt merely crossed her arms over her broad bosom, peering at him again over her spectacles.

"I may have been born at night, young man, but it wasn't last night. Though I see how an innocent girl could be taken in by that glib tongue. Well, your foreign ways are no match for honest American truth, Mr. Farthering, and if Madeline is old enough to be in such a fix, she's old enough to hear it. I hope and trust that, as you say, she is a good girl. Yet whatever she has or hasn't done, she's coming back home with me and no more nonsense about it. I won't have her staying here for you to play upon her sweet, easily led nature."

He glanced at Madeline, and she could see him holding back a chuckle. Sweet, to be sure, the gleam in his eyes said, but easily led?

Aunt Ruth jerked her head toward the door. "Come along, Madeline. I'm sure that lazy girl has your things packed by now. The cab is waiting."

"No." Madeline tightened her hold on Drew's hand, but she didn't raise her eyes.

Aunt Ruth pursed her lips and glared at Drew. "Don't be stubborn, Madeline. We don't have time for it. Get up."

"I'm not going." Madeline lifted her head, her mouth set in a firm line. "I'm staying here."

"Darling." Drew pressed her hand to his lips. "I'm so glad. I can inquire into getting a special license—"

"I didn't say I'd marry you, either." She hoped her expression was cool and imperious, despite the tremor in her voice. "I'm not going to be rushed into or out of any decision as important as this one."

Drew kissed her hand again, a mingling of pride and disappointment in his eyes. "Nor should you be, darling. I've told you before, I want you to be sure of me. As sure as I am of you."

"Madeline Felicity Parker, if you think for one minute—"

This time Madeline looked the older woman in the eye. "I'm not going, Aunt Ruth."

Her hand trembled a bit in Drew's, but she didn't look away.

Aunt Ruth threatened, cajoled, warned, and pled, but it was all to no avail. Madeline wasn't going home. Not yet.

"Very well. You've taken the bit in your teeth. I suppose there's nothing else but to let you run with it." The older woman strode out of the parlor and, seeing Nick on the stairs, snapped her fingers at him as if he were the bellboy at New York's gleaming new Waldorf Astoria. "You there. Boy."

Nick came down with an obliging bow. "May I be of service, ma'am?"

"There is a taxicab waiting out front with our luggage. Tell the maid that Miss Parker will not be returning to America after all, and have her things returned to the cottage."

"At once, ma'am."

Madeline hurried over to her aunt and took her arm. "I know you're mad at me, but—"

"And," Aunt Ruth told Nick, "have them take mine there, too."

Madeline glanced, wide-eyed, at Drew and then back at her aunt. "You're . . . you're staying?"

Drew swallowed audibly. "Here?"

"I realize I can't force Madeline to come back home. Well, I don't suppose you can force me to leave, either." Aunt Ruth gave him a poisonous smile. "Unless you want to charge me with trespassing and have your police drag me off to whatever sort of prison you have in your town. Perhaps you people are used to that sort of scandal and wouldn't even notice."

Madeline glanced at Drew again. "No, of course he wouldn't do that, Aunt Ruth. But do you have clothes and everything for a stay? Won't Uncle Calvin and Aunt Emily be expecting you back?"

Aunt Ruth made a dismissive little hissing sound. "Em will do just fine as she is, and Calvin's her husband, not mine. She can see to him, too."

"But your clothes—"

"I guess they have wash buckets in this country? And even dress shops?"

"Well, yes, but—"

"Then I don't think that will be a problem. Now show me this cottage of yours."

"But Drew—"

Drew took Madeline's hand. "I think having your dear auntie to visit will be perfectly charming, darling. That way she and I can become great friends, and she'll see you're in no danger here whatsoever."

"No danger." Aunt Ruth smirked. "None besides the half-dozen murders, more or less, and who knows what other shenanigans that have gone on here."

Drew pressed his lips together, and a shadow passed over his gray eyes. It had been not even two months since Mason was killed, and Madeline knew Drew still felt pain in the loss. And then there was Constance, murdered just a few days before that. Drew had told her of the guilt and regret that goaded him at every memory of her. Did Aunt Ruth have to trample those still-raw remembrances?

The heat in Madeline's face intensified. "Please remember, Aunt Ruth, that besides being my uncle, Uncle Mason was Drew's stepfather. We were both very fond of him, and his death came as a great shock. I met his wife, Constance, only the one time, but she was Drew's mother. You can understand how he must feel. How we both feel."

Drew managed a gracious smile. "It was a difficult time for all of us, Miss Jansen, as I'm sure you can well imagine. Surely you wouldn't have wanted Madeline to travel all the way back to America on her own after such a loss."

Aunt Ruth pursed her lips. "I suppose not, not right away, but she could have come home anytime this past month. How long did you think I'd be put off with those letters, Madeline? And time passing and us wondering only the Lord knows what you might be doing over here." She sneered at Drew. "Society folk. I told your mother, God rest her, she had no business marrying a foreigner *and* an upper-crust bigwig to boot. At least your father, God rest him, didn't take her back over here where we'd never see her again. But that uncle of yours, and God rest him too, I suppose, I was always afraid he was going to turn your head with his fancy falderals and riding horses and high-toned finishing school. Now I see he did after all."

Madeline's eyes stung. "Uncle Mason was like a father to me, and you know he was. After Daddy died, he tried his best to look after me, even if he couldn't come see me that often."

"*We* looked after you, your aunt Emily and I, and it was only right that we did." Aunt Ruth looked away. "I'm sorry that wasn't good enough."

"I never said or thought any such thing. I know you both did everything in the world for me, and I'm more grateful than I can ever say."

"All Em and I ever wanted was for you to grow up a fine Christian girl, and this is the thanks we get."

Madeline sighed and didn't reply. Obviously Aunt Ruth had made up her mind and wasn't to be troubled with such paltry inconveniences as actual truth. Discretion being the better part of valor, Drew also said nothing.

Finally, Aunt Ruth rapped her cane on the marble floor. "Well, is there or is there not a cottage?"

Drew gave Aunt Ruth a determined smile. "Why don't you show your aunt down there, Madeline, and I'll see where Nick's got to with your luggage. How would that be?"

A few minutes later, the two women were standing on the doorstep of Rose Cottage. It was a charming place, picture-postcard perfect, and Madeline smiled as she opened the green-painted door to the quaint little front room.

Aunt Ruth peered inside. "Not very big."

"We won't need a lot of space." Madeline led her through to the bright kitchen. "I haven't done much cooking since they take care of that up at the house, but we can, anytime we want to. Isn't it sweet?"

"Humph." Aunt Ruth stomped back into the front room. "Where's the bedroom? Or do you not use the one here much, either?"

Madeline bit her lip, but whether it was to keep herself from crying or laughing, she wasn't sure. "I've been using this one." She pushed open the door to the room she'd been occupying, a nice airy space with a cozy bed and heaps of fresh down comforters and mullioned windows all along the back wall that flooded the place with light every morning. "But if you'd like, I can move to the other one."

The second bedroom was much like the first, clean and bright and cheerful. Evidently even Aunt Ruth could find no fault with it.

"No need for you to change now," the older woman grumbled. "I suppose the girl can put all your things back where they were until you come to your senses."

Madeline squeezed her aunt's hand. "You'll see. It really is lovely here." Then, without warning, she pulled her aunt into a tight hug. "I am glad to see you again. I am really."

Aunt Ruth stood stiff in her embrace, studying Madeline's face, her own expression severe. Then she softened and stroked Madeline's hair back from her temple.

"I just hope you don't end up being sorry you were ever mixed up with this Farthering boy. If you are, I'm certainly not one to say I told you so. Now go find out who's knocking at the door while I see what's what in here."

Madeline found Drew and Nick peering around the still-open front door. Nick looked especially wary.

"Is it safe?"

"Come in, you silly thing. Did you get it all?"

Nick nodded.

"All present and correct," Drew said as he and Nick set down their burdens of bags and boxes. "After much persuasion, Anna is on her way to unpack for you."

"Oh, good. Poor girl, Aunt Ruth must have scared her half out of her wits. And she's taken such good care of me here so far."

"I did have to give her a pound note to get her to come back." Seeing the older woman come into the room, he winked at Madeline and put one finger to his lips and whispered, "Not a word." He then turned and smiled at Aunt Ruth. "I trust everything is satisfactory, ma'am."

She granted him a nod. "It'll do. For now. I don't suppose there's such a thing as a telegraph office nearby."

"Of course. You may come up to the house and telephone your message, or if you'd prefer to write it out, I'll be happy to send someone down to the village with it."

"I'll take it myself." She narrowed her eyes. "Just to make sure."

"Certainly, ma'am. I'll have the car brought round for you."

She made a grudging little huff of acknowledgment. Then, seeing Anna had made a wary appearance, she began settling herself and her belongings into the cottage.

While Aunt Ruth was ordering Anna and Nick around, Madeline moved closer to Drew and lowered her voice. "It's very nice of you, you know. Putting up with all this."

"I'm a nice fellow. And as irrefutable proof, I brought you this, hot off the presses." He took a little book from his coat pocket and presented it to her. "Haven't even cracked the cover."

"Oh, Drew! It's the new Lord Peter."

"And Harriet Vane, as well."

Hugging the book to her chest, she leaned up and swiftly kissed his cheek. "And after I stole the last one from you."

"I told you I was a nice fellow."

"It might not do you any good, you know."

He smiled the warm, lazy smile she loved. "They say trials build character, so there's that at least."

"Madeline!" Aunt Ruth stood in the doorway, hands on hips. "Come and see that all your things are put where you want them. Then you'll be going to the village with me too, so say your goodbyes."

"Yes, ma'am."

Madeline sighed, and Drew squeezed her hand.

"Courage, darling. You've got Lord Peter to help you along for now." He raised his voice for her aunt to hear, "We would be delighted to have you to dinner this evening, Miss Jansen."

Aunt Ruth acknowledged the invitation and dismissed him with the same curt nod, and Madeline could only watch as he walked the path back toward the house. But before he disappeared, he turned and gave her that smile once more. It helped tremendously.

— Three —

To say that Drew's first dinner with the formidable Aunt Ruth was uncomfortable would be a rather mild assessment, but he gave thanks that it was little more than that. Between him and Nick and Madeline, they managed to keep the conversation pleasant, directed away from those subjects most likely to cause contention. So the topics of shifty-eyed foreigners, slick talkers, and morally bankrupt scoundrels being strictly off-limits, they were left to discuss the weather and Aunt Ruth's difficult and dangerous first-class passage across the Atlantic via luxury liner. Drew found himself only occasionally wondering about who had murdered Quinton Montford, and each time he banished those thoughts, they became less and less insistent. After all, he wasn't the police.

After three days, Aunt Ruth still managed to be only a little more than civil to Drew, but civility was an improvement nonetheless. Still, it was a bit wearing to feel like an intruder in one's own home, and Drew decided an afternoon of golf would be a welcome change.

Nick and Bunny hadn't arrived at the club by the time he got there. Roger's car was parked outside, but Drew hadn't yet seen the man himself. He decided to go ahead and change his clothes. He was early for their tee time after all. Perhaps a few practice shots wouldn't come amiss.

Just as he got out of the Rolls, one of the caddies hurried up to him.

"Mr. Farthering, sir?"

"Yes?"

"A man asked me to give you this."

Drew tossed the boy a half crown.

Would appreciate you joining me on the first green.

The words were scrawled across the back of the card the boy had handed him. On the front, along with the official seal, it said *J. T. BIRDSONG, Chief Inspector, Hampshire Constabulary.*

Drew walked through the clubhouse. There seemed to be a lot of people standing about the club in little groups, talking in low voices and glancing toward the course.

"Good morning, young Farthering!"

Drew turned to see Mr. Llewellyn from the village among the onlookers.

"Good morning, sir. I didn't know you played here."

"Don't play at all," he said, chuckling. "But I do ride my bicycle through this way quite often. Saw there'd been some sort of row, so I thought I'd find out about it."

"And?"

The old man scowled. "No one knows anything. People milling about, claiming a man was hit by a stray ball and killed outright. Shouldn't be allowed, talking when one hasn't a clue, yet they won't let anyone near enough to see what did happen.

I may as well pedal myself on back to the village, eh? Tomorrow's newspaper will be quicker than this."

"I daresay." Drew waved and made his way through to the course.

Several constables were holding back onlookers, and by the time Drew could see the first green, he didn't need Birdsong to tell him anything. There was a body lying not two feet from the hole.

Drew removed his hat, grieved once again to look upon death.

The chief inspector managed a grim smile. "Ah, Detective Farthering. Good of you to come."

"Not at all, Inspector. What's happened?"

"Act Two, it would seem, of our little drama in Winchester last week. I thought perhaps another pair of eyes that saw the aftermath of the Montford murder might help us here." Birdsong shrugged a little self-consciously. "Saw your car turn into the drive."

Like the last time, there was a note on the body, secured by a hatpin through the heart. Judging by the amount of blood on the shirtfront, Drew assumed the man had first been stabbed in the same area.

He knelt to get a closer look. The victim was a placid-looking middle-aged man with a sedentary paunch in his jowls and belly. Rather well-off too, judging by his clothing. There were tobacco stains on his fingers and tiny burn holes in his coat.

Drew scanned the neatly clipped grass at his feet. It seemed pristine still. The body must have fallen where it lay. There were no marks that would have indicated it was dragged or even shifted much. It would take nerves of steel to stab a man here on the green at the first hole at three o'clock in the afternoon with dozens of potential witnesses.

Drew looked about again. The trees were a good ten or fifteen yards away. The clubhouse was in plain view. He gave a quick wave to the men sitting up there with their gin and tonic, and they were obliging enough to wave back. He hadn't a clue who they were, but they could certainly see him.

How was it that no one seemed to have seen the murder?

"Do you have any idea what sort of weapon might have been used?" Drew asked.

"As best I can tell, something sharp and narrow-bladed," the chief inspector offered. "Most likely the letter opener we found in the victim's inside coat pocket. Common enough to be untraceable."

"And the body was lying this way?"

"No. It was facedown, a bit doubled over. Impossible to see the blood or the wounds from any distance."

Drew considered that and then the note itself.

Kentish wisdom would have him paid so.

It was the same graceful writing, the same aged parchment as was used on Montford in the hotel room, fastened by another antique hatpin. This one was larger than the first and looked to be silver with an amethyst set into it. Drew read the words again. What did the killer mean by *Kentish wisdom*? And what had that to do with the first murder?

"'Kentish wisdom would have him paid so,'" Drew murmured. "'Advice to Jack.'"

What was the connection?

"I don't know how I can help you, Inspector," Drew said.

"You were involved with the first murder. Your solicitor."

"I wouldn't exactly say 'involved.' I merely had an appointment with the man. He was dead well before I arrived."

"Fair enough," Birdsong said. "But you were some little help in that matter at Farthering Place. I thought perhaps you might have some observations on these current cases."

Drew smiled faintly. "I see."

Birdsong drew himself up with a sniff. "It's part of my job to make use of any source of information as may become available in an investigation."

"No need to be defensive, Inspector. If you want my help, all you need do is ask."

Birdsong scowled. "No, I do *not* want your help, *Detective* Farthering. I do *not* want you mucking about interfering with my official duties. No, nor your friend, Nick Dennison. Nor your young lady. All I want is for you to tell me if you've noticed anything besides these blasted bits of writing that would con-nect the two murders."

"The hatpins, of course." Drew dropped to one knee again and peered at the body. "Both men middle-aged. Both appear to be professional men."

"You didn't know the man?"

"No. Should I have?"

"It's your club, isn't it?"

"Well, yes, but that doesn't assume an acquaintance with each and every member, does it?"

"I suppose not." Birdsong consulted his notes. "He was a doctor. Name of Corneau. Ever hear of him?"

Drew shook his head. "Do you know anything else about him? Where he lived? Where he had his surgery?"

"He lived in Chilcomb and practiced in Winchester."

Drew frowned. "And no one here saw anything?"

"What they saw was Dr. Corneau playing the hole with his caddy. Next thing they knew, Corneau was on the ground and the caddy was running for the clubhouse, calling for a doctor. Claimed it was the man's heart."

"Have you talked to the caddy?"

"The man's not to be found. Corneau's regular boy was called away on some family urgency, and evidently this one took his place. No one at the clubhouse seems to know anything about him, and the manager claims all of his regulars are accounted for. None of them was out here with the doctor."

Drew's frown deepened. "So this unknown boy comes out to the clubhouse, waits until Corneau needs a caddy, gets himself hired on, and before the doctor can sink his first putt, stabs him through the heart and disappears. Why?"

Birdsong shook his head.

"And I suppose no one thought to detain the caddy." Drew looked up at the clubhouse again, squinting against the afternoon sun. "The sun would have been behind anyone who was looking this way, so he'd have had a clear look. Did you get a description?"

"Not anything specific. Evidently no one really looks at a caddy. 'Thin, tallish chap' is all anyone's said."

"No one saw him when he came running into the clubhouse?"

Again the chief inspector shook his head. "Seems all the attention was on Corneau. This fellow ran in shouting and ran out again. Perfectly natural to think he was going after some help. By the time they all realized the doctor had been stabbed, the caddy was well away."

"So no one could tell you what he looked like? What he was wearing? What he sounded like?"

"Not anything helpful," Birdsong admitted. "He had a cap on, dressed like any of the other fellows who caddy here. Seems he had darkish hair, but no one's overly certain about that. One of the men who saw him leave said he had a rather low voice. 'Husky,' he said it was, as if he'd had a sore throat or congestion."

"Or didn't want to be recognized."

"There is that."

Drew thought for a moment. "I suppose you've turned out his pockets. Might I see?"

"Griffiths," the chief inspector called. "Bring me what you have."

One of Birdsong's men came up to them with a few small items bundled into a gentleman's handkerchief.

"This is everything, sir." He spread the handkerchief over the chief inspector's outstretched hand, displaying the dead man's possessions. "Certain he wasn't robbed."

Birdsong prodded a stack of three five-pound notes. "No, I'd say whoever did it wasn't after money. Has Tompkins photographed this lot?"

"Yes, sir."

"All right then. Clear all these people away from here. I want everybody who's not on police business back in the clubhouse."

"Right away, sir." The constable turned to the onlookers, shooing them away from the crime scene with both hands as if they were barnyard fowl. "That will be all, ladies and gentlemen. You'll all have to go back inside now. Everyone, if you please."

Birdsong turned his attention back to the items in hand. "Besides the notes, a pocket watch, a few shillings, matches, wedding ring, couple of tees, penknife, bit of pocket lint. Not much help."

"No cigarettes?" Drew asked. "Or cigarette case?"

"Not that we found."

Drew nodded, then turned his attention to the plain gold band. "I thought . . ." He looked down at the corpse. "I thought he had a ring on already."

The band on the dead man's left hand was similar to the one found in his pocket—of high quality but not ostentatious.

Birdsong narrowed his eyes. "You don't reckon this was Montford's, do you?"

"Might have been. Did his ever turn up?"

"No. No, it didn't."

Drew shrugged. "It's obvious the two killings are connected.
The messages, the hatpins." He paused. "You don't suppose
this man, this doctor—"

"Corneau."

"Right, Dr. Corneau. You don't suppose he might have taken
Montford's ring for some reason."

"You think he could be our Winchester killer?"

Drew shrugged. "It's not out of the realm of possibility, is
it? Then someone might have done for the good doctor to get
vengeance."

"A bit fanciful, don't you think? Granted, if the doctor *is* a
murderer, it stands to reason someone may want to kill him as
a measure of payback. But why would he have killed Montford
in the first place?"

"I don't know, Inspector. But no, that doesn't seem right at
all. The notes are written in the same hand, I'd lay odds on that,
and the same paper. Corneau couldn't have written them both.
More likely our killer brought Montford's ring from Winchester
and left it on Corneau."

"But why?"

There was no humor in Drew's low laugh. "We don't even
know for certain if it actually is Montford's ring. Worth inquir-
ing into, I expect." He looked round and saw the men were there
with the stretcher, waiting expectantly. "I suppose that's all
there is for now, but I'll certainly keep my eyes and ears open,
Inspector, and my mind working. Any flashes of brilliance will
be immediately reported to you."

Birdsong's dour expression did not change. "I'll have an extra man put on just to take your telephone calls. We really haven't enough to keep us busy as it is."

Drew gave him a sarcastic smile in return and then sobered as he looked down at Dr. Corneau for the final time, watching as the men carefully lifted his body onto the stretcher and covered it with a sheet. It was now just a sad, empty shell without the spirit it had housed. *God have mercy.*

Drew turned back to Birdsong. "What else do you know about the doctor? Did he have family?"

"According to one of club members here, he had a wife and three children, all grown, and a number of young grandchildren." Birdsong hesitated. "Would you like to come to his surgery with me? Hear what his staff have to say?"

Drew nodded, trying not to look too surprised. "Yes, if I might."

"Best come along, then." Birdsong shook his head, watching the men with the body. "Always devilish sudden, aren't they, these killings?"

"Devilish," Drew murmured, and then Dr. Corneau was carried away as if he had never been.

There would be no more golf today.

"I say, that was quite a shocker at the golf course, wasn't it?" Nick removed Drew's clubs from the Rolls and slung them over his shoulder. "And we just missed it."

Drew got out of the car, and the two of them walked up the path from the garage to the house.

"What happened to all of you anyway?" Drew asked.

"Bunny's new motor car punked out on him, and by the

time he had it going again and we got to the course, the police wouldn't let anyone in." Nick grinned. "Bunny was so distraught about his precious car, Roger had to take him round to Barbie Chalfont's for drinks. I made them drop me here first so I could get the details right off."

"I'm afraid I haven't many details on the case so far. I even went with Birdsong to the doctor's surgery to see if anyone working for him knew of any reason he'd be murdered. It was just the one nurse and a girl at reception, and they neither of them had any clue. So, such as it is, you know Madeline is going to want to know every detail so far too, and I'd as lief tell you two vampires both at the same time."

"I don't know if that's such a good idea." Nick looked round and then lowered his voice. "It seems dear Auntie isn't letting Madeline out of her sight these days, and I doubt it would increase her fondness of you if you were to bring such lurid tales to her niece's attention."

"I suppose you're right, though I did want to talk to both of you about what's happened. There's certainly something odd going on, and I had hoped that, between the three of us, we might make some sense of it."

Nick's eyes narrowed. "They said there was a note on this one, too."

"Yes. It said, 'Kentish wisdom would have him paid so.'"

"That's worse than the first one. Any ideas on what it means?"

"No." Drew shoved his hands into his pockets. "I don't suppose Auntie is feeling any more charitably toward me, is she?"

"She's been relatively quiet as far as I can tell. She's in the library with Madeline. Knitting or crocheting or whatever it is old ladies do."

"Crocheting lace, I expect. Was it white?"

Nick nodded. "What I saw of it."

"Crocheting, I should think. Madeline's learning it. I didn't really know what it was either, but she seems to enjoy it. Best not bring up that bit about old ladies, though."

Nick smirked. "I see you've already made that mistake."

By then they had reached the French doors that led to the library. Open doors. Drew put one finger to his lips and then, removing his hat, went inside.

"Good afternoon, ladies. Hard at work, I see."

Madeline and Aunt Ruth both glanced up from their spools of white thread and tiny metal crochet hooks. Madeline looked particularly fetching, her dark hair a soft frame for her lovely face, her long legs tucked gracefully under her, and her slender hands nimble and skillful as they worked.

There was a sparkle in her periwinkle-blue eyes as she set down the lacy little piece of fluff in her hands. "Hello there."

Aunt Ruth continued counting for another few seconds. Then she too stopped work and peered at Drew over her steel-rimmed glasses.

"We weren't expecting you back until later this afternoon."

"Didn't end up playing actually, ma'am. The course was closed suddenly."

"So that's what they do when there's a murder, eh?"

Drew glanced at Madeline. "You've heard about it, I see."

"It's all the talk evidently." Madeline shrugged in helpless apology. "Anna heard it from the grocery boy, who had the story from one of the caddies out there who was kind of put out because he doesn't make any money when the course is closed. Anyway, Anna was telling Beryl about it, and Aunt Ruth heard them talking."

"Good thing I did, too." Aunt Ruth came to what was apparently a stopping point and set down her work. "I don't suppose you were going to bother to tell us there is a killer at large? I say it's an insult to your guests to make them get important news from the help."

"I didn't want to worry you," Drew said. "Either of you. And it's nothing to be worried about. The police are seeing to everything, and I'm sure they'll catch whoever's done it before long."

Aunt Ruth snorted. "What kind of a place is this? I haven't been here a week and already you're involved in two murders." She arched one eyebrow at him. "That we know of."

"Not involved actually."

"Not involved? Hah. They seem to follow you around. If you ask me, there's something—"

She broke off with a muffled shriek as her crocheted lace, hook, and ball of thread careened off the coffee table and disappeared under the sofa.

"Oh, dear." Drew tossed his hat onto the table and dropped down to his hands and knees. "Nick, cut him off before he gets out the door with it."

Aunt Ruth drew her feet up off the floor. "What is it?"

"It's all right, ma'am. Nick, get the thread and other things. Be careful, you idiot."

"What *is* it?" Aunt Ruth demanded, and Drew finally managed to pull a struggling Mr. Chambers out from under the sofa by the scruff of his neck. The little white kitten squirmed, batting his paws in midair, claws extended, emerald eyes wild.

"I'm terribly sorry, Miss Jansen. He doesn't mean any—"

"Give him to me."

Before Drew could protest, she snatched Mr. Chambers from his hands and sat him on the sofa beside her. Then, before the rascal could leap away, she tickled the back of his head with a black tassel from her jacket. He attacked it with his entire little body, holding it in his front paws as he kicked it, rapid fire, with the back.

Still on his knees, Drew could only watch in amazement as Madeline's formidable maiden aunt played with the kitten. He glanced at Madeline, but she was smiling on the unlikely pair too and didn't notice. With Aunt Ruth's face softened that way, Drew could see something of a resemblance between her and her niece. Perhaps she really had been lovely in her day.

Abruptly the woman glared at him. "Well?"

He scrambled to his feet. "I, uh—"

"I'm terribly sorry about your lace, ma'am." Nick offered up the wadded tangle of thread he had rescued.

Aunt Ruth merely pursed her lips. "Oh, just put it down there on the table. It won't take a minute to fix it." She looked down at Mr. Chambers, her face softening once more. "He didn't hurt anything, did he? No. No, he didn't."

She wiggled her fingers under his fuzzy chin, and he immediately abandoned the tassel and wrapped all four paws round her wrist. She made some little clicking noises with her tongue and started scratching his neck. After a few halfhearted kicks, the kitten closed his eyes and began to purr.

Drew shook his head. "I've never seen him take to anyone quite that way, ma'am. You're a wonder."

"How is it I've been here a week and didn't know you had a kitten in the house?"

Drew shrugged. "I suppose I didn't want him inconveniencing anyone."

"Poppycock. As if the angel could be an inconvenience." She narrowed her eyes at Drew. "I thought all you Englishmen had huge, slobbery dogs running around everywhere."

"We have them in the stables and about the estate. The gardener has one too, but we don't typically keep them inside. My mother didn't care for them in the house."

"She must have been a sensible woman."

Drew and Nick exchanged glances. Before her death, Constance had been described in a variety of ways, but *sensible* was not a word that was commonly used. Still, since her policy regarding the estate's dogs was one of the few things of which Aunt Ruth seemed to approve, Drew did not contradict the notion. Aunt Ruth seemed to have given her wholehearted approval of Mr. Chambers as well, despite his destruction of her lacework, and Drew silently blessed the fuzzy little beggar for it.

"He's a darling." Madeline beamed at the kitten as it basked in her aunt's attentions. "He was born the day I came here. Isn't that sweet?"

"I didn't suppose he dropped out of the sky," Aunt Ruth said. "Where's his mother?"

"Oh, she's about the grounds somewhere," Drew assured her. "Now that the kittens are weaned, she stays out a bit more. She's quite a hunter."

"And the rest of the little ones?"

"In good homes nearby, but I just couldn't part with old Chambers here."

"Chambers?" The old lady scowled at him. "What kind of a name is that?"

"Mr. Chambers, actually. I named him after my old Latin professor."

Aunt Ruth shook her head. "Not a very sensible name for a cat."

Drew wasn't quite sure how to make amends for his shortcomings in feline appellations, but he was rescued when Denny appeared in the doorway with a decorous cough.

"Are you at home to a Mrs. Montford, sir?"

He presented Drew with a silver tray containing a tasteful, engraved calling card. *Mrs. Q. C. Montford.*

Drew glanced at Madeline and then nodded. "By all means, Denny. Show her in."

"Oh, I say!" Nick brightened and sat up straighter in his chair. "What do you suppose she wants with you?"

"I daresay we'll find out."

Overlooking Aunt Ruth's suspicious expression, Drew and Nick both stood at the appearance of a tall, bewildered-looking woman, slender and clad in solemn black.

"Mr. Farthering?"

She offered Drew her hand, and he clasped it briefly. It was a soft, womanly hand, a hand that showed little sign of hardship or toil.

"I don't know if you'll remember me—"

"Of course I do. You and Mr. Montford were always very kind to me when I was a boy. I'm so glad to see you again. May I introduce Miss Madeline Parker, her aunt Miss Jansen, and Mr. Nicholas Dennison?"

"Good afternoon." Mrs. Montford barely spared them a glance before turning her expressive brown eyes back to Drew. "Thank you for seeing me. I should have telephoned ahead, I know, but I just couldn't take the chance that you might not speak to me."

"Nonsense." He guided her to a chair and then sat down himself. "I would be quite pleased to know if there's any way I can be of help to you. I'm so sorry about what happened to Mr. Montford. It must have been a terrible shock to you."

"Oh, Mr. Farthering." She stopped for a moment, her eyes filling with tears, but she blotted them away. "No. I haven't

time for any silliness just now, and I'm certain you haven't."
She smiled, her mouth tight and her lips quivering, and then
she leaned a bit closer to Drew. "Do you think I might speak
to you in private for a few moments? I promise I won't take up
much of your time."

"Of course." Drew stood and held out his hand to Madeline.
"Darling, do you think you and Nick might take your aunt to
see to that matter we were discussing?"

"What matter?" Aunt Ruth demanded. "What are you talking about?"

"This way, ma'am. I'll explain everything."

Nick took Mr. Chambers from her, offered her his arm, and
hurried her out of the room before she could say anything more.

Madeline looked a bit vexed at having to leave, as well. No
doubt she was dying of curiosity just now, but she let him bring
her to her feet. "We're going to need your help, too."

He kissed her cheek. "Won't be long."

"Thank you, my dear," Mrs. Montford said to Madeline, her
smile wistful. It had to be painful, with her loss so fresh and
raw, to see a happy couple.

Once they were alone, Drew shut the library door and sat
down beside her once more.

"Now, what can I do for you?"

She folded her hands in her lap. "I want you to find out who
killed my husband."

It wasn't precisely what he had expected her to ask.

"You want me—"

"Please, Mr. Farthering, hear me out."

"Mrs. Montford, believe me, I would do anything in my power
to help you, but surely this is a matter for the police. They're
much better qualified—"

"But I read about you and that awful situation with Farlinford Processing and everything that happened here."

"That was hardly anything, really. I merely stumbled upon a clue or two. The police would have found out the villain in time, no doubt."

"That may be so, but he might have been in South America well before then and completely out of the reach of the law."

"I still think the police—"

"Bother the police." Her expression turned fierce. "They've got everything wrong as it is."

"Do they? In what way?"

"They suspect that my husband was meeting a woman there at the hotel. I know that's not true."

"What evidence do they have of that?"

"Nothing but their nasty little minds. I just know it's not true. Not of Quinton. He was a good Christian man."

Drew made his voice as gentle as he could. "Good Christian men have stumbled before. Presumably that's what makes a merciful God and a living Savior such a pressing need."

"I'm not saying he was perfect. I knew him too well for that. But I knew his heart as well as I know my own. Can't you make them see the truth?"

"I'm sorry, but I don't know anything about it. I don't know the truth of the matter. I hope for your sake that they're wrong, but I really can't interfere with their investigation."

"So you won't help me?"

"Mrs. Montford—"

"Can't you even consider that things might not be as they seem? Your poor stepfather, Mr. Parker, he was all but tried and convicted by the newspapers and the local gossip, and he was innocent, wasn't he?"

"Yes, but—"

"And would you have liked to see him buried with the name of murderer and embezzler blazoned over him?"

"But your husband—"

"My husband wasn't an adulterer. The police are content to let him be branded with that. The press love anything that adds spice to a story, I know that much." Her eyes pled for her, soft and doelike. Maybe it wasn't so surprising that Montford would have been still in love with her after so many years. "Won't you find out what really happened?"

"You know I'm not actually a detective or anything, Mrs. Montford."

"But you could talk to people. Ask questions. I know I'm asking a very great favor of you, but I don't know where else to turn. The police won't listen to me at all. They've already made up their minds about everything."

He looked at her for a long moment, and she put one tentative hand over his.

"Please, Mr. Farthering. You mentioned a merciful God and a living Savior. I presume you're a Christian man yourself."

Drew nodded.

"Won't you help me? For His sake?"

"Mrs. Montford—"

She pulled her hand back, a little flush of pink on her cheeks. "I'm sorry. I didn't mean to be quite so maudlin. But I've already lost my husband. I can't lose his good name, as well. Not for my sake alone, but for my son's, too. And because, as you have said, good Christian men have stumbled before. It's what the world expects of us, isn't it? Frailty and hypocrisy?"

That was true enough. The world was always waiting to exult over the failings of anyone who claimed the name of Christ. Did every man who tried to live his principles have to have a dirty little secret? Must he absolutely be a fraud?

Surely there were good men in the world, men who weren't perfect but who meant to be honest and true to their faith. Was it so very impossible that Montford hadn't betrayed his wife and his beliefs?

Drew nodded, smiling a little. "Maybe so. And maybe there's more yet to be known."

Tears sprang into her eyes once more. "Oh, thank you. Thank you."

"I can't promise anything." He stood up, bringing her with him. "I don't even know where I'll start, but I'll see what I can find out. Fair enough?"

"Bless you, Mr. Farthering."

— Four —

Once Mrs. Montford had gone, Drew made his apologies to Madeline and to her aunt and then excused himself for the afternoon. He wasn't quite sure where to start or what to do to shed light on the Montford murder, but he'd given Mrs. Montford his assurance that he would try. Best to start at the beginning, at any rate, and that meant at the Empire Hotel in Winchester.

He parked the Rolls round the corner from the hotel and, after making sure there was no obvious police presence, went inside. With a nod to the flame-haired boy lounging near the lift in brass-buttoned uniform and organ-grinder's-monkey cap, Drew rang the bell on the front desk. The clerk immediately appeared, a large, smiling, smooth-faced man with light hair that had been brilliantined into submission.

"Good afternoon, sir. May I help you?"

"Good afternoon, Mr. . . ." Drew peered at the little pin on the man's coat. "Mr. Leonard. How are you this afternoon?"

"Very well, thank you, sir. Did you wish to book a room?"

"Not just at the moment, thank you. Are you generally here on duty in the afternoon?"

"Generally, sir. Not on the weekends, of course, but during the weekdays, yes."

Drew leaned on the counter and lowered his voice. "Did you happen to be here the day Mr. Montford was killed?"

Mr. Leonard's accommodating smile faded. "Are you with the police?"

"Not strictly, no, though I do work in conjunction with Chief Inspector Birdsong. I presume he's questioned you already."

"He's cautioned all of the staff. We're not to discuss the incident with anyone besides the police."

"He couldn't have meant you weren't to talk to me, Mr. Leonard, I'm certain of it. When I last spoke to the inspector, he said he was going to have one of his men available for the sole purpose of taking my telephone calls whenever I have a breakthrough in the case. That sounds rather as though he'd want me to have whatever information you might be able to provide, don't you think?"

Mr. Leonard looked very prim. "Perhaps if you gave me your name, sir, I would know whether or not the chief inspector mentioned you specifically."

"Didn't I say? I beg your pardon. I'm Drew Farthering from Farthering St. John."

The lift boy grinned. "I remember taking you up on the lift that day."

The desk clerk gave the boy a reproving glance, but his expression was less guarded. "I read all about all the goings-on at Farthering Place in June and at your company, too. How terribly interesting that must have been." At a grim look from Drew, he cleared his throat, solemn and professional. "Of course, it must have been quite dreadful for you, as well."

"Quite."

Turning red in the face, Mr. Leonard looked round and then leaned closer to Drew. "I don't suppose I'd be telling tales out of school, then, if I were to answer whatever questions you have. Seeing as it *is* you, sir."

"I should be most grateful. What can you tell me about that day? Anything out of the ordinary?"

"I don't know, sir. There was a young lady called for him. For Mr. Montford. It was after the police had arrived, perhaps three o'clock. We told her no one was allowed up on the first floor. Then there was a telephone call. It was the same girl, I'm sure, asking to be connected to Mr. Montford's room. We told her we couldn't put any calls through at present, but she wouldn't leave a message."

"Do you know who she was?"

The desk clerk shook his head. "No, sir. I'd never seen her before, and she wasn't registered here. I'd remember."

"Begging your pardon, but I might know who she is, sir." The boy at the lift came over to the desk. "I mean, I think she's been here before a few times. Always comes in on her own for just the one night, but don't always stay till morning."

"Did you tell the police this?"

"No, sir, on account of they never asked me about any girl and I didn't think of it till now."

Drew frowned. "How is it you remember her and Mr. Leonard doesn't?"

"Mr. Leonard ain't been here as long as me. And this girl, well, she don't come round like she did earlier in the spring and summer."

"And her name?"

"Oh, I couldn't say that, sir. Wouldn't be proper, me striking up acquaintances as it were, though I might could pick it out if I heard it again."

"Do you remember the last time she was here? Before the murder, I mean."

The boy screwed up his face, thinking. "Not the last time particular, no, but I remember *a* time. It was my girl's birthday, and I remember I wanted to ask this lady what perfume she had on." He grinned. "I could tell it was real class. I thought I might get some for my Doris when I finished work that day."

"And did she tell you?"

"No, sir, 'cause I never asked her. Wouldn't be proper, as I said."

"And when is Doris's birthday?"

"May nineteenth. Wouldn't hardly forget that, not after I did last year."

"May nineteenth, is it?" Chief Inspector Birdsong walked up to the desk. "We'll need to see your register for that day."

The desk clerk's eyes widened. "Chief Inspector, how good to see you again, sir. We didn't know you were coming."

"I can see that. I hate to interrupt your little conference, Mr. Leonard, but perhaps I might join you? Not that I'd want to inconvenience Mr. Farthering here. I mean, we're just the police and that."

The lift boy whistled low. "Lumme."

Drew smiled. "Ah, the very man. Good afternoon, Chief Inspector. It is lovely out today, isn't it?"

"There's some would say so, Mr. Farthering." Birdsong rocked back on his heels, glumly contemplative. "There are others, those in charge of official murder investigations, who might have more to concern them."

"Oh, no doubt. No doubt. Must be an intolerable burden."

"I, uh, I hope I haven't done anything wrong, Inspector." Mr. Leonard rubbed his podgy hands together, his little eyes round and concerned. "He said he was working with the police and all, and I knew about what happened at Farthering Place before. I didn't think . . ."

Birdsong sighed. "No, that's all right, Mr. Leonard. The gentleman has been of some small help to us now and again. But mind you check with me the next time anyone wants to ask you questions, understand?"

"Certainly, sir."

"Now then." Birdsong turned to the lift boy. "Do you remember when this girl started coming to stay here at the hotel?"

"Dunno. Sometime in the spring, I reckon. Can't say exactly."

Birdsong studied the diminutive young man. "We spoke to you before, didn't we? Phipps, isn't it?"

"Yes, sir. Ronnie Phipps."

"All right, Phipps, what else do you remember about this girl?"

The boy glanced at Mr. Leonard and then shrugged. "Nothing."

"Perhaps Mr. Leonard could get the register for May nineteenth for you, Inspector." Drew smiled at the desk clerk. "If it wouldn't be too much trouble, of course."

"Oh, certainly. Right away. You mind things here, Phipps. Won't be a minute."

Mr. Leonard disappeared through a narrow door behind the desk. Drew then moved closer to the lift boy. "We haven't much time. What else do you know about the girl?"

Phipps shrugged. "I don't know nothing. I told you, I don't make acquaintances with the guests. Wouldn't be proper."

Birdsong fixed him with a baleful eye. "We can discuss this when Mr. Leonard comes back, if you like. Or maybe you'd prefer police headquarters?"

Phipps turned rather green under his freckles. "I don't want to lose my job here. Have a bit of pity, eh?"

Drew shook his head. "You're wasting time."

"All right, here it is. I told you I wanted to know about her perfume. Honest, that was all. I waited on the corner after my shift was done until she left that day and followed her back to the shop where she works."

Birdsong pursed his lips. "To ask about perfume?"

"That was all, and don't go saying it was anything else. Lumme, it was four o'clock in the afternoon!"

"All right, all right," Drew said. "What did she say?"

"I lost my nerve. I never did anything but walk on past. I was afraid she'd remember me and tell someone here and I'd be sacked."

"Where's the shop?"

"Two streets over. The toy shop on Southgate."

"And you'd know her again if you saw her?"

"Oh, sure. Tall, sort of thin girl. Dark-haired. All right enough, I expect, but nothing special."

"All right then." Birdsong leaned down until he was within a few inches of the little man's face. "You play us fair and there's no reason this needs to be official, understand?"

Phipps nodded.

"We'd like you to come round to the shop to identify the girl," Drew said. "She needn't see you at all. Afterwards you can come back here and Mr. Leonard will be none the wiser."

"But what about—?"

"Here we are." The desk clerk came back into the room with a large register book. "Of course, someone had mislaid it, but I did finally find it. May nineteenth, did you say?"

Birdsong took the book from him. "I'll have to put this into evidence for the time being, Mr. Leonard. I can give you a receipt, if you like."

"Well, yes, if you must, but—"

"And we'll need to borrow Mr. Phipps here for a few minutes." Drew smiled at Mr. Leonard. "You can manage without him for a bit, can't you? Yes, I thought so. Come along, Ronnie."

He escorted Phipps out through the front door, leaving the chief inspector to deal with a bewildered Mr. Leonard. Birdsong caught up to them beside the Rolls a couple of minutes later.

"Just what did you have in mind here, Detective Farthering?"

"A mere matter of identification. Simple, quick, and painless." Drew took his coat from the back seat of the car and handed it to Phipps. "If you'll just put this on over your uniform and give the chief inspector charge of your hat, we'll go into action. Can't give ourselves away at first glance, eh?"

Phipps put on the coat and was nearly swallowed by it. Then, looking defensively at Drew, he surrendered his cap to the inspector, who immediately turned it over to Drew, who stowed it safely in the boot of the car.

"Very good. Now, if you'll be so kind, you can take us round to the shop. You and the chief inspector can stand very inconspicuously across the street while I go inside and see if they have someone who fits your description of the girl we're looking for. I'll ask her to show me something they have in the front window, and you can tell us afterwards if I've found the right one. Then you pop right back here and no trouble. Agreed?"

"All right." Phipps grinned a little. "Sounds a bit of fun actually."

Drew gave him a hearty swat on the shoulder. "Good man. Seem like a sound plan to you, Inspector?"

Birdsong gave him a grudging nod, and the three of them

made quick work of the walk to Hirsch's Toy Shop on Southgate Street. Drew left his companions at a discreet distance across the way and, after a convincing few moments of examining the items in the store window, went inside.

"Good afternoon, sir. How may I help you?"

The girl who greeted him was dark-haired, tall and thin. All right enough, but nothing special. Drew removed his hat and had to force a bland, impersonal smile. At this point he couldn't allow a touch of triumph to glimmer in his eyes.

"Yes, good afternoon, Miss . . . ?"

"Miss Allen. May I show you something?"

She was young, a few years younger than Drew himself, he'd have bet.

"I was wondering if you might show me one of those dolls in the window."

"Certainly, sir. Which one did you have in mind?"

"I don't know how to describe it really. I'm not much of one for baby dolls, but it's the one in the very front of the window. In the center. It has on a long white dress."

"That'll be our Dy-Dee doll, the very latest thing just in from America. Isn't she darling?"

"Terribly attractive. If I were a five-year-old girl, I shouldn't leave off kicking and screaming until I had one, no matter the cost."

Miss Allen smiled politely and led him to the front window. As she leaned in to retrieve the doll, Drew glanced across the street to see if Phipps had a clear view. A discreet nod from Chief Inspector Birdsong told him their mission had been successfully accomplished.

"Here you are."

The girl put a white-clad bundle into his arms, prompting

a bleating coo from its puckered rose-colored lips. Startled, he nearly dropped the thing.

"It talks."

"Oh, yes, sir. Besides having eyes that open and close and movable arms and legs, the Dy-Dee doll coos, drinks, and wets."

Drew thrust the infant phenomenon back into her arms. "Perhaps something a bit less authentic."

"Very well." Miss Allen put the doll back into the window and brought out another, this one glancing sideways out of painted blue eyes, her bobbed hair and headband molded and painted on her composition head. "This is Patsy. She doesn't talk, drink or wet, but she has a large variety of clothes and accessories to choose from, and her—"

"It's quite lovely, really, but I don't think it's quite the thing."

"All right. If you'd prefer, we have some lovely French dolls from the eighties and nineties from the House of Bru." She picked up a fussily dressed doll in a lace cap. "The Bru dolls are all authentically outfitted."

Drew began to gracefully decline. "Actually, Miss Allen—"

"My grandmother has one of these and just adores it," the girl gushed. "You wouldn't think older ladies would care for dolls, but—"

Drew gave her a nod. "Come to think of it, Miss Allen, you have just made a sale. Wrap it as a gift, if you would, please."

A few minutes later, package in hand, Drew tipped his hat and hurried out the door and round the corner, where Birdsong and Phipps were waiting for him.

Ignoring their curious glances at his purchase, Drew looked at Phipps. "Well?"

"That's her, sir, the very one." Phipps was ecstatic. "I've seen her round the hotel half a dozen times if I've seen her once."

They walked back to the Rolls, where Drew reclaimed his coat, stowed his package in the boot of the car, and returned Phipps's hat to him with the utmost respect.

"You'd best get back to your job now before Mr. Leonard starts wondering what we're all up to."

"What should I tell him, sir? He'll want to know where I've been and all."

"You just tell him it was police business and you're not allowed to say." Birdsong gave the little man his most forbidding glare. "And see you don't say, understand me, Phipps?"

"Right, sir. Right. You can rely on me, sir."

Drew gave Phipps a pound note. "You've been a great help."

The lift boy touched his cap and sprinted back into the hotel.

"What now?" Drew asked.

The chief inspector's face displayed its usual scowl, but Drew could see a spark of excitement in his hound-dog eyes. "I'll send one of my men to stay out here in the street until the shop closes. Then he can ask her to come down to the station and have a bit of a chat with us."

"Excellent. Do you think I might . . ."

Birdsong pursed his lips, his scowl not all that convincing anymore. "I suppose you could come along and see what you make out of this register book until they bring the woman in. Never hurts to have another set of eyes, you know."

Drew smiled.

"Anything unusual?" Birdsong asked.

Drew closed the hotel register and rubbed his eyes. "Nothing really, Inspector. There were five unaccompanied women who engaged rooms there on May nineteenth. She could be any of them. But I don't see four of those names repeated any time before or after the nineteenth, and the other one, a Miss Josephine Chadwick from Sterling, stayed for two nights in May and four in July. Phipps said this girl only ever stayed one night at a time, if she even stayed the night."

One of the constables stuck his head in at the door of Birdsong's office. "The young lady is here, Inspector."

"Right. Send her in."

Drew stood up to leave, but Birdsong waved him back into the chair.

"May as well stay on now. A smooth talker like yourself may well get something out of her that we can't."

"Very well, Inspector. I'll do my best to stay out of the way."

A moment later, another police constable escorted the girl into the room. "Miss Allen, sir. This is Chief Inspector Birdsong, miss."

Drew stood, and Birdsong looked up from his desk. Without her familiar surroundings and professional cheerfulness, in just her plaid wool skirt and plain white blouse and without the navy jacket emblazoned with Hirsch's logo, she hardly looked seventeen, though Birdsong's records stated she was twenty-two. She gave Drew a puzzled smile.

"We appreciate you taking the time to come speak with us today," Birdsong said. "Have a seat, if you please."

Drew gave her his chair and seated himself on the edge of the chief inspector's battered desk.

Birdsong studied her for a long moment. "You are Miss Margaret Allen, is that right?"

"Yes." Her brown eyes grew round, and her voice became softer than it had been at the shop. "I've never been to a police station before. Have I done something wrong?"

"I don't know, miss." Birdsong peered at her. "Have you?"

Her lower lip trembled. "I . . . I don't think so. What is this about?"

He pushed the picture of Whyland, Montford, Clifton and Russ across the desk toward her. "Do you know these men?"

She glanced at Drew and again at Birdsong and then picked up the photograph. "No. No, I'm afraid I don't."

Birdsong's eyes narrowed. "None of them?"

She shook her head. "Should I? Who are they?"

"My name is Drew Farthering." Drew smiled, hoping a little warmth and understanding would coax her into cooperating. "I'm, uh, working with the police on a rather serious matter, and I was hoping you might be able to help."

"You were at the shop today. You didn't really want to buy a doll, did you?"

Drew shook his head. "I didn't start out to, I admit, but now I'm hoping it will help smooth over a rather bumpy relationship for me. But no, that wasn't why I went into your shop originally. We had to make sure we had the right person. You understand, I'm sure."

She looked at the chief inspector. "What's he say I've done? I never saw him until this afternoon, I'm positive, and I can't help who comes into the shop."

"Really, Miss Allen, no one's accusing you of anything. We're just trying to get some information." Drew put his hand over his heart. "You have my word on it."

"I'll try to help, but I really don't—"

"Give the photograph another look," Drew said. "Are you absolutely sure you've never seen any of them?"

She did as he asked, and again she shook her head. "No. I'm sorry, but I haven't."

Birdsong lit a cigarette, observing her until she became visibly uncomfortable. "Ever been to the Empire Hotel, miss?"

Something flickered in the girl's eyes. "Which hotel?"

"The Empire. On St. Peter Street. It's just two streets from your job." Birdsong took a drag on his cigarette and then released the smoke into the air above his head. "You were seen leaving there on the nineteenth of September. That was a Monday."

"I was . . ." She looked pleadingly at Drew. "But Mr. Farthering, I couldn't have . . ."

Drew kept his expression pleasant. "You were seen, you know."

She bit her lip. "Which hotel did you say?"

"The Empire Hotel," Birdsong supplied.

"Oh, yes. How silly of me. Yes, I did go there a while ago. I couldn't tell you the exact date. It had slipped my mind altogether."

"And the reason for your visit, miss?"

"I went to see a friend."

Drew glanced at Birdsong but said nothing.

"And who was this friend?" the chief inspector asked.

"It was, um, Grace. Grace Poole." Miss Allen smiled prettily. "I hadn't seen her in ages."

A smile tickled the corners of Drew's mouth. "And that was when you were both at Thornfield Hall, was it?"

Her face paled. "I don't know what you mean by that. She's from Torquay."

Birdsong consulted the register. "I don't see a Poole for that date."

"No, well . . ." The girl fidgeted for a moment and then brightened. "She would have been under her married name now, of course. She was Poole when we were at school together."

"And what is her married name?"

She gave Drew a look that was at once coy and pleading. "Oh, I have the most terrible time with names. It was nothing out of the ordinary, just a usual surname, as I recall. If I could just see the register, I know I could pick it out."

Drew couldn't help pitying her. He knew well enough that bland, skeptical expression on the chief inspector's face.

"The police will be talking to whomever you claim to have met that day, Miss Allen. You may as well just own up to whatever it was you were doing."

Apparently she was determined to carry it off.

"Now I know why she's not on the register. We met there for lunch, but I don't believe she was stopping there at all, come to think."

Birdsong merely looked at her. "You'll find yourself in considerably less trouble, miss, if you'll tell us the truth."

The girl's lower lip quivered again, but she held her head high. "I don't know what you mean."

"Do you have a solicitor, miss?"

"Wh-why?"

"You may wish to telephone him and let him know we'll likely be taking you into custody." Birdsong stood, looming over her. "On suspicion of willful murder."

"I didn't kill him."

"Kill who, miss?"

"Quinton Montford."

"And how do you know Montford is the subject of our inquiry?"

"He was killed at the Empire, wasn't he?" She calmed a little, again holding her head defiantly. "Who hasn't heard about that by now?"

"Then would you care to tell us what you know about that incident?"

"I don't know anything about it." She picked up the photograph once more and began to sob. "I just know I went to the hotel and they wouldn't let me upstairs. I heard afterwards that a man had been killed, and later I found out it was Quint."

A tear fell onto the picture, onto the face of the dead man, and she wiped it away with one tender finger.

Drew handed her his handkerchief. "So you did know him. Rather well, it seems."

She looked up, her eyes fierce. "We were in love! He was going to divorce his wife and marry me."

Birdsong sat down again, looking mildly disgusted. Drew could hardly blame him, even though this just confirmed what the police had already suspected. How many young girls, and not-so-young ones for that matter, had fallen for that old chestnut? But Montford? He hadn't at all seemed the type. Poor, trusting Mrs. Montford. Who could ever tell about people?

Drew gave the girl a moment for her fresh grief, and then he cleared his throat. "How long had you and Mr. Montford been meeting?"

"We, uh . . ." She took a deep breath. "Since March. He would tell me when he was coming, and I would book a room at the hotel. I always used different names and didn't ever speak to anyone, so they really couldn't find me. The staff never knew who Quint was either or really that he was there at all. I mean, as far as their records went."

"But this time was different?"

"This time he made the reservation." She blotted her wet face and then squeezed the handkerchief into a tight little ball. "He said he had some other business to take care of, but then I was to meet him afterwards."

Birdsong eyed the girl. "And what time was that meant to be?"

"At three o'clock."

Her face was blotched with crying, and she seemed more like a schoolgirl than ever.

"That was rather an odd time of day, wasn't it?" Drew asked. "Didn't you have to leave your work and all?"

The girl sighed. "Mrs. Hirsch didn't like it, of course, and Mr. Joseph had to promise he'd see to my work as well as his own while I was away before she'd let me go."

"So you usually didn't meet Mr. Montford in the afternoon?"

"No. This was only the second or third time."

"Were you there at three, miss?" Birdsong asked, and she nodded.

"And I was too late."

That brought on another torrent of tears, and there was nothing to do but wait it out.

The chief inspector shuffled through his notes for a moment. "How did you and Mr. Montford meet?"

"He, um, he came into the shop one afternoon. We sell a lot of different things, toys and games and such, and he wanted something for his son. For his birthday." Her lips trembled into a smile. "I don't remember what it was he said that first time, but he made me laugh. He came back a couple of weeks later and asked if I didn't want to take some supper with him after we closed. I didn't know then that he had a wife."

"And does Mrs. Montford know about you?"

She looked up at the ceiling, blinking rapidly. "I don't know. He was supposed to tell her. He promised he would." She pressed the crumpled handkerchief to her mouth, suppressing a small cry. "You don't think she . . . ? Oh, no. No. She couldn't. She just couldn't."

Birdsong drew his heavy brows together. "What are you saying, miss?"

She blinked again, calming somewhat. "I . . . I don't know what I'm saying. I've never met her. I don't know what she's like or what she might do. Oh, my poor Quint."

The girl was pretty cut up, and Drew gave her another moment to compose herself.

"When was he supposed to tell her?" he asked finally. "Did he say?"

"He said he would before he came back to Winchester. That was why he made the reservation himself. He said we didn't need to hide any longer."

"And that was your final conversation?"

She nodded at Drew, too choked up to speak.

"What did you do when you weren't allowed into the hotel?" Birdsong asked. "Did you know he was dead?"

"I went round to the tobacconist's, the one across the street and down at the corner, to telephone. But the man at reception told me he couldn't connect me to the room and he couldn't give out any information about any of the guests. I didn't know what to do or what to think, so I went back to my flat to see if he would call there. I didn't know what happened until I saw the next day's newspaper."

She wiped her face and said no more. Evidently she was done with crying for the time being.

Birdsong studied her for a while. Long enough, Drew suspected, to make her wonder how much the police knew.

"Do you know a doctor by the name of Corneau? Has his practice here in Winchester?"

She blinked rapidly. "Who?"

"Dr. Joseph Corneau. Did you ever have occasion to visit his surgery for any reason? Perhaps you knew him socially?"

"No. I don't have a regular doctor. I'm not much to go to one, to be honest, but if I did, I would most likely go down to the hospital. St. Cross's."

Birdsong questioned the girl a bit more, but she didn't have much to add. All she could say was that she got there too late to see Montford. Finally the chief inspector sighed.

"That'll be all for the time being, miss. If you'll give me your address and telephone number, you're free to go. See you don't stray too far from home until we give you leave, eh?"

She accepted the pencil and paper he pushed across the desk and did as he asked. Then she stood to go.

Drew rose when she did. "I'm so sorry to have upset you, Miss Allen." He gave her his card. "If there's ever any way I can be of help, do let me know."

She murmured her thanks and hurried away.

"So, Detective Farthering, what did you think of her?"

"I'm not quite sure. She doesn't at all seem the murdering type, but so few murderers do. She's not a very good liar, at any rate, but I'd take bets on one thing. She's sure she's lost the love of her life."

Birdsong sagged in his chair. "She's young, isn't she? A girl like that should have people looking after her, father or brothers or someone to warn the old lechers off. Of course, they won't let you look after them anymore. Not these modern girls. If I thought my Betty was carrying on with someone my age, why I'd . . ." He sat up straight again, fumbling with his notes and not looking Drew in the face. "But that's neither here nor there. The Allen girl had an appointment with Montford at three, and that was when—"

"Perhaps there is something in that line of thought, Inspector. Suppose there *is* a father or a brother, an uncle or even just a bloke she went round with before she met Montford. Maybe this protector, whoever he might be, felt the same way about her as you do about your daughter. It would be enough motive for murder, wouldn't it?"

"It would, I expect, except there isn't anyone. No family. But we'll do some investigating to see if she had a young man. As best we know at the moment, though, she's all on her own."

"Right. Any problem with my telling Mrs. Montford about this? I am in her employ in a manner of speaking."

"You think she'd want to know?"

"She claims she does. Whether or not she believes it is another matter."

The chief inspector shrugged. "Not very comforting news for a grieving widow, but do as you please, only no specifics. No need to give out the girl's name and that."

"You may rely on me, Inspector. And I'd like to hear about the boyfriend, if any such person exists."

"Fair enough. Er . . ."

Drew lifted an eyebrow, waiting for the chief inspector to continue.

"You don't think, well, the girl acted as though she were wondering about Montford's wife and all. You don't suppose—"

"I thought your men had spoken to Mrs. Montford already."

"Yes, of course. She has a reasonable alibi, neatly verified by the staff."

"Well, there you are. Of course, we can't rule anyone out as yet, eh?" Drew put his hands behind his back and rocked a little on his heels in imitation of the chief inspector. "It's early days yet. Early days."

Birdsong's expression held perhaps one part amusement to nine parts sour tolerance. "So it is."

"One last favor, Inspector, if you'd be so kind."

Birdsong narrowed his eyes, and Drew smiled.

"I'd like to use your telephone."

— Five —

The maid who answered the telephone at the Montford residence told Drew that Mrs. Montford would be pleased to receive him at any time that afternoon. He jotted down the address on the back of the envelope Birdsong had pushed helpfully toward him and was soon on his way. It wasn't an errand to which he looked forward. From what he had seen of Mrs. Montford to date, she wasn't likely to change her conviction that her husband had been always faithful to her and to his beliefs no matter what the police had uncovered.

The house was a gracious three-story Georgian, the last one in a long, quiet streetful of homes much like itself. Drew rang the bell, and the door was almost immediately opened by a simpering young girl in a maid's cap and apron. After he gave the girl his calling card, she showed him into a small sitting room that was as charming and feminine as its occupant.

He bent briefly over the hand the lady offered. "How are you this afternoon, Mrs. Montford?"

"I have my moments." She smiled unconvincingly and fingered the pink chiffon sleeve of her dress, a touch of pain and pleading in her doe's eyes. "Quint never liked me in black, you know, and I'm sure he'd hate seeing me in it now. He said it was a cruelty to widows to expect them to look grim when they already feel grim. I know that's terribly scandalous, and I would never appear in public like this, but you don't think it's too awful just at home, do you? This was always one of his favorites. Wearing it makes me feel as though he's just in the other room or on his way home from his office."

"That's perfectly understandable, ma'am. I only wish the information I have for you could be a comfort, as well."

"You've found out something? Oh, forgive me. Please do sit down."

He pulled up the delicate little Louis XVI chair she indicated, steeling himself for what he was about to do. "We've found the girl."

There was a flicker in her dark eyes, but her face betrayed nothing. "The girl?"

"She works in a shop in Winchester. She had been meeting Mr. Montford at the Empire since March."

Mrs. Montford's chin quivered, and Drew was certain she was going to crumple into tears, but she only took a trembling breath and looked steadily at him. "I know that couldn't have been the case."

Drew cringed inwardly. "Mrs. Montford, I know this can hardly be pleasant for you to come to terms with, but the police know—"

"The police know only what some shopgirl has told them. What evidence do they have?"

"Only what the girl told them and what the hotel staff claim to have seen. Are you saying he hadn't made regular visits to Winchester over the past several months?"

"No, I can't positively say he hadn't. But I can't say he had either. He never told me much about his work. He wanted to put that all behind him once he was at home with me. But I know he often met clients elsewhere if they were unable to come to his office. You were to have met him in Winchester yourself according to that Chief Inspector Birdsong. What's so odd about that?"

"Nothing at all. But it hardly proves he wasn't seeing the girl, does it?" Drew paused for a moment, then added, "Then again, I suppose it doesn't exactly prove he was either."

"No. It doesn't." Mrs. Montford let out a sigh. "You don't understand. Quinton loved me. We'd been sweethearts since we were children. He would never betray me. I know he wouldn't."

"Why do you suppose the girl would lie?"

She closed her eyes and shook her head. "Perhaps she thought it would be exciting, claiming to be a murdered man's mistress. Or she wants to be in the newspapers. I don't know."

Drew made his voice as gentle as he could. "I'm not saying your husband didn't love you. I'm only saying . . ." He struggled to find a way that would not add hurt to what she already had to bear. "We men can be a rather sorry lot at times. I know men, good men, who love their wives, and yet they strayed. I by no means excuse it, but it happens all the same. And I'm not saying this girl meant anything to him."

She lifted her eyes to his, and her mouth was a firm line. "And I'm saying you don't have any proof that he ever even met her. She says she knew him, that the two of them went to that place in Winchester several times over the past few months. Did anyone ever see them together? Do you even know what dates and times she claims they met?"

"I'll grant you that much. She says she doesn't remember the exact dates. And she says she used a variety of false names to register, so there's really no way to track them down. And no, as of yet there's no one who claims to have seen them together." He gave her an apologetic smile. "Rather suspect, isn't it, once you give it a hard look? I just don't know what this girl could hope to gain by lying other than a ruined reputation."

"Whatever her reason, she *is* lying. She is."

"That doesn't explain how she knows about your son."

She blinked. "My son?"

"She mentioned him when she was telling the chief inspector about Mr. Montford. If your husband didn't know her, how would she know about the boy?"

"I . . . I don't know. Perhaps she guessed. Most men Quinton's age have children. A great many of them have sons."

She dabbed her eyes with her lace handkerchief, and he felt very much the cad for having told her any of this.

"I'm very sorry, Mrs. Montford. I wish I had something more comforting to tell you."

"What else have you found out?" she asked after a moment. "Do they know why someone would have killed him?"

"Just guesses at this point, I'm afraid. Possibly someone who didn't like him seeing this girl. The police are still making inquiries."

"I want to know, Mr. Farthering. I want you to find out why. And why this girl is lying about my husband."

"Ma'am—"

"No, I won't hear anything more about this girl and my husband being involved with each other. If he was killed because of her, how do you explain this Dr. Corneau being killed, as well? I suppose he was her lover, too."

"They're not sure why the doctor was murdered. There's really nothing else I can—"

"Then give me the girl's name and address. I'll speak to her."

The woman was nothing if not single-minded. Would Madeline be like that after twenty or thirty years of marriage? Drew was almost certain she would be, gentle and womanly and boned with steel. Smiling a little, he shook his head.

"You know very well I can't do that, Mrs. Montford. If I were to tell you that, it would put an end to my already rather tenuous relationship with the police. They tolerate me, for the present at least, because I try not to interfere with their business and because I lend them a hand when I'm able. If I were to muck this up, as the chief inspector would say, that would be the last of it. No more inside information. No more viewing the evidence. No more being admitted to the scene of the crime. What good would I be to you then?"

She caught an eager little sobbing breath. "So you'll keep trying?"

How could he refuse her? "I'll find out what I can. If the girl is lying after all, I'll find out why. Provided—"

"Oh, thank you. Thank you so much."

"*Provided* you stay strictly out of it. Are we agreed?"

She nodded rapidly, but there was a brightness to her eyes that hadn't been there when he first came in. "And you'll tell me the moment you find out anything, no matter how small?"

He took the soft hand she held out to him. "The most monumentally infinitesimal item will be reported to you without delay."

She pressed his hand before she released it, and her eyes were made even brighter with a glimmer of tears. That was all the thanks she could manage and, for the little he'd accomplished so far, more than he felt he deserved.

Madeline turned from the shelf where Mrs. Harkness kept books on lace making and other traditional crafts.

"And just *why* couldn't she have done it?" She put her hands on her hips and looked up into Drew's face, a challenge in her periwinkle-blue eyes and a defiant set to her mouth that made it not a whit less captivating than usual. "You never think women are capable of real crime."

"That is not so. Just because I don't think Mrs. Montford committed murder doesn't mean I don't think she possibly could have, farfetched as it seems. All women are quite notorious, and you're the worst of the lot. I'm surprised old Birdsong hasn't had you in custody for theft well before now."

Madeline laughed. "Theft? What are you babbling about?"

He dropped his voice and leaned close enough to smell the light fragrance of her hair, glad to be with her now and not wrestling with questions about solicitors and shopgirls and golf-playing doctors. "I know you've stolen the heart of every man you've met here in Hampshire. In all of England, I'll be bound."

That brought a pretty color to her cheeks, but it took none of the contrariness out of her expression. "I mean it. You think every woman you meet is sweet and gentle and would never hurt anyone."

He shook his head. "Oh, no. I've been taught to know better. I have the scars to prove it."

He smiled when he said it, but in spite of his intended lightness, he knew there was a touch of rue in his face, in his voice, that she was quick to pick up on.

"I'll want to know someday."

It wasn't a demand. Her tender words held only a desire to know and console, and he felt certain he could trust her with those little raw places he carried inside.

"Someday," he said, and then he pulled away from her, coloring a little himself. "Ah, Mrs. Harkness, there you are."

"Do forgive me interrupting you and the young lady, Mr. Farthering, but I couldn't help overhearing just a bit of what you were discussing, and I thought this might interest you."

Mrs. Harkness handed him a rather thick, scholarly looking tome entitled *Leave Her to Heaven: Women and the Crimes They Commit.*

Drew looked at the book for a moment and then caught the older woman's eye. "I wouldn't have thought you'd stock such a thing here."

"Not usually, no. I ordered it for a gentleman who was writing a book of his own. Some lurid murder mystery with a kindly old grandmother slaughtering her neighbors right and left and for no reason I could figure out. Frightful stuff."

"Really? Someone from the village?"

She smiled faintly. "I told him I'd never say. You know how people talk, and he didn't want everyone thinking, well, that he wasn't quite right."

Drew couldn't help but laugh. "Did he ever have it published?"

"I think he's abandoned the idea. He took up a new hobby and never came to collect the book. But I hate to even let you look at the thing. His bloodthirsty stuff was nothing worse than what's in that book right there, and all of it from police files. I glanced at only a few pages, but it's a wonder I slept all the next month. Women bludgeoning their flat mates, stabbing the boss, smothering the kiddies, poisoning old mum or dad."

She shuddered. "If you want to know what all they did to their husbands, you'll have to read it for yourself."

"Sold." Drew grinned. "And never let anyone tell you that you don't tell a good tale."

"Now, Mr. Farthering, you know what they say. Truth is stranger." There was reproof in her expression, and a definite fondness, too. She turned to Madeline. "Did you find something you wanted, miss?"

"Yes, thank you. I think my aunt will enjoy this book on Irish lace making."

"Oh, that's a lovely one, isn't it? And such good photographs." Mrs. Harkness took the book from her as well as the one Drew was carrying. "I'll just put these on the counter for you until you've finished having a look round, shall I? You'd better get used to it, Mr. Farthering. I know when I see a young lady who enjoys shopping."

"I'll make sure and keep a close watch." Drew took Madeline's arm and strolled over to the shelf that housed crime fiction. "Now, you suspicious character, which of these should we take along with us this time?"

"Hello there."

They both turned at the decidedly American voice, and Madeline's face was all-over smiles.

"Well, hello to you. What are you doing here? Oh, let me introduce you to Drew Farthering. Drew, this is Freddie Bell. I met him yesterday when I was out."

Bell was one of those hearty-looking outdoor types, tall and blond and brashly good-natured. Drew offered his hand but not a smile.

"How do you do, Mr. Bell?"

"Call me Freddie." Grinning, Bell pumped Drew's arm as if

they were long-lost friends who hadn't had a falling out. "And how are you today, Miss Parker? I took your advice and came to buy some picture postcards and a guidebook."

"It's a pretty area, isn't it? Of course, Drew is always telling me there's nothing to see here."

"Tourists generally prefer somewhere a bit more exciting, don't they?" Drew shrugged. "What can I say about dear Farthering St. John? 'An ill-favored thing, sir, but mine own.'"

"You're too modest, Mr. Farthering." Bell had the audacity to wink at Madeline. "I'd say your little village has some very attractive features."

Drew managed not to sneer. "How long before you have to leave? I'm sure there are many things you've yet to see here in England, and I'd hate for you to miss any of them. York or the Lake District perhaps? Hadrian's Wall?"

Bell seemed unaware that these charming destinations were about as far from Farthering St. John as one could go and remain still in England. He only grinned.

"Oh, I'm in no hurry. My idea of a nice vacation is to go where you want when you feel like it and stay there as long as it's fun. I think I'm going to like Hampshire."

Madeline beamed at him. "Oh, I'm sure you will. I love it here."

Drew was certain she had absolutely no idea how perfectly intoxicating her smile could be. Obviously, Bell had noticed.

"Would you care to have lunch with me?" The American turned a little red. "Both of you, of course. Then you could tell me what I should see that's not in the guidebooks."

"Actually," Drew began, "we're due at—"

"We'd love to." Madeline looked up at both of them. "We don't really have to hurry off, do we, Drew? I'd love to hear some news from America. I've stayed here in Hampshire longer than I was expecting to, you know, and even though it's wonderful here, I can't help missing the States."

Drew knew when he'd been defeated. "If you like, darling. Far be it from me to part countrymen far from the shores of home."

"That's great," Bell said. "My treat, of course."

Typical American. He *would* try to impress Madeline with his money.

"I won't hear of it," Drew said. "You'll be our guest."

Bell shook his head. "Oh, no, I couldn't—"

"Of course you will." Madeline took each of them by an arm. "You're the visitor here, Mr. Bell."

"But I invited you," Bell protested.

"I know just the thing. Drew, you call over to the house and have Nick pick us up in the car, and then we can all go up to Winchester for lunch. Won't that be fun?"

"But, darling, suppose Mr. Bell has something—"

"He doesn't have something else to do. You don't, do you, Mr. Bell?"

"No, come to think of it, I don't." Again, Bell grinned. He seemed to do little else.

Drew managed a slight smile. "Well that's settled then. If you'll pardon me, I'll go ring up Nick and see if he's up for a bit of adventure. He may actually be doing some work for once, and I'd hate to interrupt that."

"Where are we going for lunch?" Madeline's expression was carefully innocuous. "They have some very nice hotels in Winchester, don't they? What was the one you were at last week?"

So that was it.

"There's absolutely nothing to see at the Empire anymore, darling," Drew said, giving her hand a squeeze. "Every bit of evidence has been photographed and cataloged and cleared away.

Her face fell. "Oh."

"That's kind of a shame," Bell said. "Miss Parker was telling me about those murders you're investigating. I wouldn't mind hearing about how that's going. Where do you usually go in the village for a bite? How's the food at your inn over there?"

"Very good, actually. Just plain English food, but wholesome and well served."

Drew led them both to the counter, where Mrs. Harkness waited with their purchases.

"There's always the Rose Garden," Mrs. Harkness offered as she wrapped the books. "But I suppose Miss Parker's gone there with Mr. Bell already."

Drew glanced at Madeline. "Oh, really? Well, we wouldn't want a repeat then, would we?"

Madeline turned a little pink. "We happened to meet at the post office the other day. I was telling him how good the trifle is there, and we decided to have some."

"Oh, dear." Mrs. Harkness bit her lip. "I just heard Mrs. Webster mention there was an American in town and that the two of you had gone to Mrs. Leicester's for tea. I hope I haven't spoken out of turn."

Drew laughed. "Certainly not. Miss Parker is perfectly capable of making an informed decision when it comes to trifle."

"It was pretty good cake anyhow," Bell added, "but kind of a ladylike place for my taste."

"In that case, I think the Queen Bess would suit very well." Drew took the paper-wrapped parcel from Mrs. Harkness. "Thank you. Will you put these on my bill?"

"Certainly, Mr. Farthering. I hope you enjoy them." She made a brief note in her account book and then looked up, smiling. "So nice to see you again, Miss Parker, and to meet your friend Mr. Bell. Do come again."

They walked across the street to the inn and quickly found a table. Bell rushed over to pull out a chair for Madeline, and Drew could do nothing but stand politely aside until she was seated. He deposited his parcel of books in the unused fourth chair at the square table, and then he and Bell sat down facing each other across the board. It was the perfect arrangement for adversaries.

Adversaries? All the man had done was pull out a chair for a lady. No doubt he would have done as much for his female cousin or maiden aunt. And let's not forget the trifle. Trifle indeed.

Drew covered a smile with a polite cough. He had it bad, as they said in the cinema, and there was no denying it. For him, Madeline and rational thought didn't seem to be able to exist in the same place at the same time. Well, it didn't mean he had to be a churlish host.

"How's your appetite, Bell?" Drew smiled again, and this time the smile managed to be friendly. "You'll find the fare here plain but filling."

"What do you recommend? I don't want something I can get any time when I'm back home. What says 'Hampshire' more than anything else I could order?"

Drew considered for a moment. "You could always try—"

"That's Mr. Farthering there."

Hearing his name from one of the waitresses, Drew looked up and saw a lanky young man stalking toward the table.

Drew stood. "I'm Drew Farthering. Is there something I can do for you?"

"My name is Daniel Montford."

"Ah, yes. How do you do? I'm so sorry about your father."

Young Montford sneered at the hand Drew offered him.

"I want you to leave my mother alone, do you understand? This business with my father has come near to killing her, and I won't have ill-bred little weasels like you making it worse."

His face had gone all red and patchy and his Adam's apple bobbed at an alarming rate. For some reason, grief seemed to make young people look younger and old people look older. Drew didn't know why that was, but it certainly mucked about with people's appearances and not at all kindly. He'd noticed it with the Allen girl, and Daniel Montford was no exception. He was probably no more than three or four years Drew's junior, but just now he looked as if he should still be studying his Latin verbs and beginning algebra.

Still, he couldn't have had an easy time of it. Bad enough losing one's father at all without losing the image of him at the same time. Couldn't fault the chap for wanting to protect his mother.

"Look here, I wouldn't upset you or your mother for the world. And believe me, I know how you're feeling with all this, but I *am* trying to help. Truly. What if you and I had a little chat. Man to man and all. What do you say? I'm sure Mrs. Burrell has a private room we could use for a few minutes." Drew turned briefly to Madeline. "If you and Mr. Bell will excuse me, darling."

Madeline nodded.

"Sure, sure," said Bell, looking as if he were at the cinema and very much enjoying the production.

Montford's lip curled. "And just how would you know how I feel?"

"There's no good to be had from airing all this in public," Drew said. "Come along."

A few words to Mrs. Burrell, and Drew and young Montford were shown into a sitting room at the back of the inn. Drew made sure to shut the door.

"This is much cozier, don't you think? Shall I send for some tea or something?"

Montford's only answer was a belligerent shake of the head.

"All right," Drew said. "Suppose we don't waste time with chitchat. How about you telling me—"

"I want to know."

"What?"

"I want to know how you'd know how I feel about all this?" Montford's voice quavered. "Was your father murdered? Was he keeping some cheap little tart on the side while telling you he wanted you to grow up to be a fine Christian man who always did the honorable thing? Did he sit there in the pew singing hymns and holding your mother's hand as if they'd been married two weeks instead of two decades?" His eyes welled with tears, but he dashed them away. "You tell me how you know."

Poor fellow. It was hard enough when one's father died peacefully in his bed. Murder was another thing entirely.

"All right, perhaps I don't know. Not really. But even if your father took a rather relaxed view toward his marriage vows, he didn't deserve to die the way he did." Drew steered the boy to a chair and sat him down. "Let's try not to condemn anyone until we've found out exactly what's happened here, shall we?"

"Seems rather obvious to me. They had a quarrel, and she killed him."

"You mean the other woman."

"Of course she did it. Who else would?"

Drew sat down opposite him. "Now that's the first sensible thing you've said yet. And, not coincidentally, that's precisely what I'd like to ask you. Who else do you think would want your father put out of the way? Who would profit by his death?"

Young Montford glared at him. "The police have already accused me, so there's no use starting that all over again."

Drew lifted one eyebrow. "And why would they think something like that?"

"I came into a rather tidy inheritance, if you must know, apart from a life estate for Mother."

"I'd have thought you'd need to wait. Until you had reached majority."

Again the young man sneered. "I turned twenty-one two months ago."

"I see. Well, man to man then. Your mother has asked my help in finding out who killed your father. I told her I would. You wouldn't want me to break my promise to her, would you?"

Montford narrowed his eyes. "If you upset my mother again, if you embarrass my family, I'll kill you, do you hear? I don't care who knows it, I'll kill you and hang the upshot."

He said it with a little tremor of emotion in his voice, a bit of youthful bluster that might have been amusing under other circumstances, but Drew did not doubt his earnestness.

"No need for threats. The question had to be asked. Now that we're certain who didn't kill him, how about we consider who might have done it? So, apart from your unimpeachable self, who would have profited from your father's death?"

Montford managed to look human again. "Nobody really. Dad left everything to Mother and me, apart from a bit for his sister, my aunt Maude, and some remembrances for my cousins. Their part couldn't amount to a thousand pounds as far as I'm given to understand."

"What about the firm? I understand the other partners wouldn't benefit from his death?"

"No. I suppose they may earn some extra fees taking over his current cases, but they all have more than they can see to as it is. It'll actually be a hardship for them until they can get things sorted out."

"So, we're back to you."

"I tell you I've been over this already with the police. I don't have to tell you anything."

"Don't you want to know what happened to your father?"

"I believe I already do."

"But not for certain. Wouldn't you rather know for certain?"

"The police can see to things. You're not with them. You're not even a proper detective. It's ridiculous to think you can do more than they. You muddled about in those murders at your company and at your house, and now you think that means you know everything. Well, it doesn't, so just keep your nose out of this, do you hear?"

"Your mother was the one who asked for my help. Such as it is, I promised it to her. It would be up to her to release me from that promise, and frankly, it has nothing in the world to do with you."

Young Montford spat out a rather choice epithet, and Drew couldn't suppress a grin.

"I remember several of the boys at my prep school had to write five-hundred-word essays on the proper use of language when they started flinging that one around. Of course, most ten-year-olds would rather have a sound caning than that sort of punishment."

Montford's face reddened. "All right, clever. All right. You're not so much older than I am."

"No, I don't suppose I am. How about we both act like grown-ups then and leave the nonsense for the schoolyard?"

Montford stood up. "Very well. I see we have nothing more to say to one another. I will speak to my mother about this, you can be sure. If she asked for your help, it was only because all this has been terrible for her and she didn't know what to do. I'm sure she's already thought better of it. I'm the head of the family now, and I can see to things in the future."

"She knows how to reach me if she needs to. I am at her service anytime." Standing, Drew smiled and offered his hand once more. "And no hard feelings, eh?"

Montford merely snorted his contempt and stalked out of the room.

Drew went back to Madeline and Freddie Bell, a bemused look on his face. "Do pardon the interruption."

As usual, Bell grinned. "Sure. Angry cuss, wasn't he?"

"Perhaps a bit too angry, given the circumstances." Drew sat down and put his napkin in his lap. "Now what have we decided on?"

Madeline frowned. "What do you mean 'too angry'?"

"Oh, I don't know really. He just seems awfully fierce. Defensive when there was really no need."

"You don't think he knows something, do you?"

"If he does, he's not telling. Or he's not telling me, at any rate. I'll have to see if the chief inspector has been any more successful."

Bell looked at Drew. "This inspector guy, he lets you in on things? About the case, I mean."

Drew shrugged. "He tolerates me. I suppose, if nothing else, I'm a change from the drudgery of his regular police work. Though I expect his real feelings are more along the lines of something I read in the latest Campion mystery, a comment about no amateur jiggery-pokery ever doing anybody any good."

"Miss Parker told me you were the one who solved that case at your company," Bell said. "I think that's swell. I like to consider myself a little bit of a sleuth, too. Mind telling me how you figured it all out?"

— Six —

The meal turned out to be rather enjoyable after all. Bell insisted on hearing every detail about the incidents at Farthering Place, and then he told about his wanderings throughout the States and in Europe. A few of his tales may even have been true.

As far as his flirting with Madeline went, Drew came to realize that it was more of a habit with the man than a personal interest, and possibly even more of a general friendliness than actual flirting. The realization that he had the same tendency himself, Madeline most definitely excepted, made the American nearly tolerable. Even so, Drew was rather relieved when lunch was over and they parted ways.

Madeline slipped her hand into his as they walked out of the village and up the path through the meadow toward home.

"I'm sorry."

"Whatever for?" Drew asked.

"For not telling you about meeting Freddie before now."

"Any reason why you should?"

"No, I don't suppose there is, but there's no reason I shouldn't, either. There really wasn't much to it. He was in the post office when I went to buy stamps. He was trying to buy some too and couldn't figure out the money right, so I helped him."

"And I suppose you had a nice chat about how American money is so much simpler."

"Well, yes. Then we introduced ourselves, and he asked me what he should see in Farthering St. John. I happened to mention the trifle at the Rose Garden, and he asked me to go with him. We had a nice talk and that was it. To be honest, I didn't think about him again until he showed up today. I mean, I did like talking to him, but I don't want you to think I'm hiding anything from you."

"You know, even though I can't help having murderous thoughts toward any man who looks at you, I never worry about being deceived by you. Should you, as you Americans say, decide to slip me the mitten some dreary November day, I fully expect you'll come straight to me and tell me plainly that, though you have the fondest regard for me, you could never be truly happy with anyone but the Nubian trapeze artist you've lived next door to all your life and whom, until he very recently and tearfully confessed his passionate yet honorable feelings for you, you had never looked upon as more than a brother." He sighed and spread one hand across his chest. "Though heartbroken, I could never stand in the way of your happiness."

She shook her head, laughing. "I think you may rival even Lord Peter Wimsey himself for talking piffle."

"Never underestimate the power of piffle, my girl. I expect that even the strong-minded Harriet Vane shan't be able to resist it forever."

"I'll keep that in mind. Though I'm more than halfway through the book and she shows no sign of wavering."

She took a firmer hold on his arm as they stepped from stone to stone in crossing the little brook that ran just below Rose Cottage. "I hope Aunt Ruth likes the lace-making book."

"It seems just the thing. Just don't give her the one on women and crime by mistake."

Madeline put her hand over her mouth, stifling a giggle. "I can't believe you actually bought it anyway."

"It is a bit grim, isn't it? I may not even read it, you know, but Mrs. Harkness seemed so eager to be rid of it."

"See? That's my point exactly." Madeline shook her head and made little *tsk-tsk* noises with her tongue. "You thought you were being nice and taking it off her hands, and all she was doing was giving you a sales pitch."

"Bah. Just for that, I'm going to read every grisly page of it and then tell you about it in minute detail just before you go to bed every night."

"That won't bother me. My mind will be completely occupied with the dinner party we're having tomorrow night. What I'll wear, how I'll do my hair—"

"Which sparklingly witty comments you'll make and to whom."

She bestowed on him a gracious nod. "That will certainly be something to consider, though I mostly leave that to you."

"Wise choice." He sobered. "You don't suppose it's too soon yet, do you, darling? After all that's happened."

"It's just dinner, isn't it? And if Aunt Ruth is going to be staying for a while, it seems only polite to have an occasion to introduce her to everyone."

"True. A nice, quiet dinner isn't exactly scandalous, is it?" She gave his hand a squeeze. "I'm sure it will be fine."

The evening of the dinner party was clear and balmy, a night that in other times would have been ideal for fireworks and a dance band. It was too soon, of course, to host the sort of gala evening for which Farthering Place had been known when Constance was alive, but a quiet dinner party for some friends would be just the thing.

Drew straightened his tie, smoothed his hair back, and then turned as Madeline came into the parlor.

"You're ravishing as always."

She made a slight curtsy, as much as the sleek-fitting pale-blue satin of her gown would allow. "Thank you, kind sir."

He put his hands around her slender waist, pulling her closer to him. "Tonight would be a lovely opportunity to make a very special announcement."

Madeline twined her arms around his neck, her eyes glowing. "Really? You want to tell everybody I'm going back to Chicago?"

"Ah. Point taken, darling. Point taken." He took her arms from around his neck and bowed formally over her hand. "I ask nothing more than the honor of your company."

She laughed and gave him a peck on the cheek.

"Ahem."

Madeline stepped away from Drew with a determined smile. "Hello, Aunt Ruth. Don't you look nice."

Aunt Ruth was clad in black as always, but her gown was a watered silk with full sleeves and a sequined bodice, as tastefully fashionable as any Drew had seen that season. Her hair was upswept, the Gibson Girl look that had been out of fashion for nearly two decades but which flattered her much more than would any of the bobbed styles that were the current rage.

Drew smiled at her with genuine admiration. "Madeline is absolutely right, ma'am. You look charming."

Aunt Ruth merely snorted.

"Oh, and before I forget, if you will both pardon me." Drew dashed out of the room and came back a moment later with the gift-wrapped box from the boot of his car. "I saw this when I was in Winchester and thought you might like to have it."

The older woman took the package from him, eyeing him suspiciously. But as she undid the wrappings and lifted out the doll, the expression on her face turned to one of surprise and then softened into something more like wonder.

"Oh, my."

That was all she said, but seeing the pleasure in her eyes, Drew found it more than enough.

"How very sweet." Madeline touched her fingers to the delicate lace that trimmed the old-fashioned satin dress. "Oh, Drew, that's precious."

He gave her a hopeful, questioning glance, and she nodded in return. Then she turned to her aunt. "Wasn't that thoughtful of him, Aunt Ruth?"

"It was . . . it was . . . . Yes."

Aunt Ruth gave Drew a brisk nod, not quite meeting his eyes, and then quickly busied herself with repacking the box, immediately afterwards handing it off to a maid with firm instructions to put it on her bed in the cottage. Madeline, on the other hand, beamed at Drew, and he counted the whole venture a success.

"Oh, I say. You ladies look the very thing." Nick breezed into the room, smiling his admiration at Madeline and her aunt.

"Drew, old man, tonight we have on our hands an embarrassment of aesthetic riches."

"We'll have to get you into white tie and tails one day, Nick." Madeline adjusted the flower in the lapel of his dinner jacket. "I know Carrie would like it."

"I'd certainly haul out the old glad rags if she were to come back. We'd have to have a proper bash then."

Drew scowled. "She's all right enough, but she'd likely bring that Muriel with her."

"Now, now." Madeline came and straightened Drew's already straight tie. "I'll make sure she stops calling you Adorable Drew, even though we all know you love it."

Drew gave her a pretend glare, and Nick grinned.

"At any rate, I hope Farthering Place will have more formal occasions in time. It's rather a delicate thing, though, isn't it, knowing when to ease a home out of mourning and back into the social whirl?"

Madeline glanced at Drew and then smiled into Nick's eyes. "This'll be a fine way to start."

"If you don't have much respect for the dead, of course." Aunt Ruth folded her hands. "Certainly, a fine way."

Already the sound of guests arriving was coming from the entry hall, probably Mr. and Mrs. Allison.

Madeline took her aunt's arm. "It's just dinner, Aunt Ruth. We're not having bareback riders and sword swallowers."

"Of course, you young people know best. Still, I'd feel much better if you were seeing some nice American boy. If I've said it once, I've said it a hundred times . . ."

Her voice faded as she and Madeline left the parlor, and Drew turned to follow them out. "Coming, old man?"

"Always the life of the party, eh?" Nick said under his breath as he came up beside him, but there was humor in his voice, and Drew shook his head, laughing low.

"I tell you, Nick, she's been a challenge, but I'm determined to win her over."

"You may have met your match in this one, you know."

"No, I refuse to give in. I just can't let her get me off course. But I see where Madeline gets her contrary streak. I suppose if I can win over the old pepper pot, Madeline won't be able to hold out much longer, either." Drew straightened his tie one final time. "Come along. We can't have Auntie telling Madeline tales about us."

The two of them strolled into the entry hall and found Madeline introducing herself and her aunt to the Allisons. The older couple were the picture of respectability, and even Aunt Ruth could have no objection to them, especially as Mrs. Allison had been gracious enough to hostess Drew's dinner party.

"Ah, Mrs. Allison." Drew hurried to her and bowed over her hand. "I see you've met Miss Parker and Miss Jansen. Thank you again for coming. You know, it's deuced awkward for us bachelors in these situations, especially those of us with no family to speak of."

"It's the least I can do for your dear grandmother's sake." Mrs. Allison's eyes sparkled as she glanced over at Madeline. "And I daresay you'll have a proper hostess for your parties before long."

Her husband chuckled and shook Drew's hand. "How are you, young man?"

"Very well, sir. And most grateful for your cooperation in all this."

"Anytime, son. Anytime. Mrs. Allison was born for these little occasions and hasn't had nearly enough opportunity to display her talents."

Mrs. Allison laughed softly. "Go on, Alvin. We'll see to things from here on out."

With a nod and a bow to the ladies, Mr. Allison wandered off toward the drawing room. A moment later, Dennison opened the door to an old gentleman of military bearing and his equally martial middle-aged daughter. The daughter wore an unfortunate sallow green gown and an eyeglass on a cord round her neck.

In her place at Drew's side, Mrs. Allison smiled. "Good evening, Colonel Potterhouse. Miss Potterhouse."

"So pleased to have you, Colonel." Drew shook hands and then turned to the daughter. "Miss Potterhouse, charming as always."

"Pshaw." She gave him a playful shove that nearly set him off his feet. "When are you coming down to Greyfield to ride with us?" She took up her glass and peered at Madeline through it. "Of course, you're all welcome."

"Won't that be lovely, darling?" He took Madeline's arm. "May I introduce Miss Madeline Parker and her aunt, Miss Jansen? Madeline's quite a rider herself, you know."

"Is she?" Miss Potterhouse peered again, obviously unconvinced. "Then you must come."

Her father jiggled her arm. "Hurry along, Agnes. I want to have a word with Mr. Sim and his lady wife. Pleasure to meet you, Miss Parker."

Madeline smiled slyly once they had left the entry hall. "Well, at least she likes *you*."

"Freddie Bell, ma'am. Most pleased to meet you."

Drew and Madeline both turned to see the American, impeccably dressed, bowing to Mrs. Allison, and then he turned to them.

"It's a fine evening, Miss Parker."

"Hello again." Madeline took Mr. Bell's hand. "How nice of you to come."

Drew shook the man's hand, this time with a grudging smile. "Yes, do come in, Bell. Now that you've come, I hope you'll enjoy yourself."

"Thanks. I've heard a lot about your place here, Farthering. I like it. I like it a lot."

"Very kind of you."

"You think I might look around a little before dinner?"

"If you like. I'd show you myself, but I really should see to my guests at the moment."

Aunt Ruth joined them just then, studying the American with evident approval. "You show him, Madeline. I'm sure the two of you have a lot in common."

"Well, I . . ." Madeline glanced at Drew. "If Drew doesn't mind, Aunt Ruth. Oh, this is Mr. Bell. He's the one I met in the village the other day." She turned to Bell. "This is my aunt, Miss Jansen."

"Pleased to meet you, ma'am." Bell seized Aunt Ruth's hand and pumped it up and down. "Always nice to meet someone from the States."

"Yes, how nice to meet *you*, Mr. Bell. Madeline, you go on ahead and show this gentleman around the place."

"Well—"

"Now, don't keep the young man waiting, dear." Aunt Ruth smiled at Drew with only a touch of combative smugness. "We'll be just fine here."

Drew returned the smile, determined to display nothing but gracious good humor, and stood aside. "By all means."

The big American took Madeline's arm and hurried her away.

"They make a nice couple, don't they?"

Obviously subtlety wasn't one of Aunt Ruth's strong suits, and Drew had to keep himself from chuckling.

"Madeline's company improves any man, I'd say, ma'am."

"Drew, how are you, my boy?"

An older gentleman and his wife came into the entryway, and again Drew shook hands.

"So glad you could come, sir. And who's this young girl you've brought along?"

The woman, comfortably sixty or so, simpered and shook her index finger at him.

"Naughty. Your father was just the same. Always threatening to steal me away from my husband if he didn't take care. Oh, it was sweet of him."

Aunt Ruth cleared her throat, and Drew turned to her.

"May I introduce Mr. and Mrs. Paignton? This is Madeline's aunt, Miss Jansen."

Then more guests began to arrive, and Aunt Ruth stood at Drew's side as he and Mrs. Allison welcomed them, commenting on how her niece was about somewhere "with a really fine boy from home."

It was nearly time for dinner when Madeline finally reappeared. She was alone.

"What's happened to your friend Bell?" Drew asked.

"I'm afraid someone stole him from me." She took his arm, her periwinkle eyes twinkling. "That Daphne Pomphrey-Hughes said she was 'just perishing' to talk to an American boy."

"Good. He deserves her."

Madeline gave his arm a sympathetic squeeze. "Has she been after you for a long time?"

Drew made a face. "Since her mother decided I was perfect for her, I believe."

"Three years now, isn't it?" Nick laughed. "But you're losing her, old man. I warned you this would happen if you continued to neglect the poor girl."

"Bell can have her, I say." The words came out with rather more bite to them than he had intended, and he smiled faintly. "Always nice when the guests hit it off, eh?"

Madeline glanced up at him, reading him as always, no doubt. "Are you feeling all right? You're not mad at me for going off with Freddie, are you?"

"No, of course not."

Nick grinned in the most annoying way. "'The count is neither sad, nor sick, nor merry, nor well; but civil count.'" He winked at Madeline. "'Civil as an orange.'"

"*. . . and something of that jealous complexion.*"

That was the rest of the quote. Drew knew it well and knew Nick very likely might be devil enough to say it aloud.

"Then it's all much ado about nothing." Madeline gave Nick a very superior smile. "We studied Shakespeare in the backwoods where I come from, too."

Nick clasped both hands over his heart, a lovesick expression on his face. "Miss Parker, will you marry me?"

Drew shoved him. "Go away, cretin."

"Hmmm, yes, I can see it already. He's getting rather apricot-colored just there in the jowls. Or perhaps cantaloupe better describes it."

Madeline laughed and squeezed Drew's arm. "You really are a terrible tease, Nick. As if he would be jealous of me."

Drew patted her hand. "Of course not, darling. What's this Bell doing in Britain anyway? Run out of his own country by the Ladies' Decency Committee?"

"He's traveling all over Europe, a graduation gift from his parents before he opens his law practice in San Jose."

"So he's from California. I suppose he's got whole vats of Hollywood stars for friends."

She glanced over Drew's shoulder. "You can ask him yourself."

"Ah, there you are, Bell. Having fun? We were just discussing your Hollywood connections."

Bell's laughter was hearty and good-natured. Some people might have found it a likable attribute. Drew merely smiled coolly.

"To be honest, Farthering, San Jose's a little far north for much in the way of Hollywood connections, but it was awful good of you to invite me to your party when I really don't know anyone here in England."

"For that, you must thank Miss Parker," Drew said.

Madeline's delicate eyebrows went up slightly. "Me?"

"For the invitation, darling."

"But I thought you . . ." She faltered, glancing from Drew to Bell and back to Drew.

The American looked grave. "You didn't invite me? Neither of you?"

Drew gave Nick an accusatory glance, but Nick only grinned and said, "It wasn't me, old man. If I was going to invite someone from the States, it would be that Hoover fellow. These days, he looks as though a nice holiday would do him a world of good."

Madeline smirked. "He just might get one, too."

Bell put his hands in his pockets. "Well, now I feel the fool. Believe me, Farthering, I wouldn't have horned in here without an invitation."

"Do you have it with you?"

"Never had one. I just got a message at my hotel that I was invited here tonight at eight if I wanted to come. I assumed it was from you or one of your people. Maybe I'd better make myself scarce."

The poor fellow looked truly chagrined, and Drew couldn't help feeling a bit sorry for him. Only a bit. "No harm done. Can't have a chap feel he's not wanted, can we, darling?"

"Of course not." Madeline took Bell's arm, smiling up at him. "You have to take me in to dinner, like it or not, and then you can tell me what they're saying about the presidential election this fall."

Drew watched as the two of them wandered out of the entry hall, talking and laughing like old friends. "Cheeky devil."

Nick's grin was even more annoying than before. "Hmmm, I'd say you're growing more and more carrot-colored as the night goes on."

"Rot."

"I take it you don't believe his story—about being invited?"

Drew scowled. "I do. I just can't imagine who would have invited him."

"You don't suppose she did but was afraid to fess up?"

"That hardly seems like her. She'd have asked me first. Or if she hadn't, she'd have looked pert when I asked her about it and owned doing it."

"I wonder—"

He broke off when Dennison appeared at Drew's side.

"Pardon me, sir, but Mr. Morris is on the telephone for you."

"Ah, thank you, Denny." Drew glanced over at Madeline and her American, stopped on the other side of the room, admiring a landscape by William Linton. "See to things here for me, will you, Nick?"

He excused himself and went into the study to take the call.

"Roger, old boy, where in the world are you? We're all pretty keen to get better acquainted with this Bohemian of yours. If this Clarice is going to make you late to the best parties, she'd dashed better be worth it." He was answered only by silence. "Roger? You there?"

"Drew."

Roger's voice was scarcely a whisper, and so broken that Drew knew he wouldn't have recognized it if he hadn't known who it was.

"Drew. Oh . . ."

Drew heard a wrenching sob, then silence once more.

"Roger? I say, Roger!"

"You've got to help me. I just . . . I don't . . . Sweet mercy, she's dead. She's dead."

"What?"

"She's dead, I tell you. Clarice is dead. You've got to come, Drew. To her cottage."

"Roger—"

"You've got to come. She's dead. You've got to come."

"All right, all right. Get a grip on yourself. Tell me what's happened."

Again there was silence.

"Roger?"

"She, uh . . ." Roger sniffled and then caught his breath. "She didn't come to the front door when I called for her, so I went round to the back. The door wasn't locked, and I went inside. I found her sitting in that big modern chair she'd just got, the zebra one. I thought she'd fallen asleep, but when I touched her, she was cold. You've got to come, Drew. You see, you've absolutely got to."

"All right, old man. I'll be there directly once I've rung the police."

"No." Roger made a little whimpering sound. "They'll think I've done it. They'll think I've done them all."

"All? All what?"

"Drew, she had one of those horrible notes pinned into her. Like the other two. Dear God, help me."

"Dear God, help *me*," Drew breathed heavenward. What was this about? What could Clarice Deschner possibly have to do with the other victims?

"Drew," Roger pleaded, "you *are* coming, aren't you?"

"Yes, straightaway. Hold on, and whatever else, don't touch anything."

"I pulled out that ghastly pin. I couldn't stand it anymore."

That was the worst thing he could have done. Now the police were certain to suspect him.

"It's all right," Drew soothed. "Just sit down somewhere and don't disturb anything else. Do you understand?"

All that came from the other end of the line was another low whimper.

"Do you understand?"

"Yes, all right, but you've got to hurry. Oh, Clarice . . ."

— Seven —

Drew rang off and then called for Denny. "Will you ask Nick and Miss Parker if they would join me for a moment, please? Mrs. Allison too, if you will."

Mrs. Allison agreed to continue as hostess in Drew's absence and see that everyone was entertained, and Madeline decided she had better stay on as well, to keep an eye on Aunt Ruth. A few minutes later, Drew and Nick were at Long Cottage, not half a mile from Farthering Place.

Drew pulled the Rolls round to the back of the house and turned off the engine. Roger was crouched on the back step, silhouetted in the rectangle of yellow light from the doorway. A trembling pinpoint of glowing red marked the end of his cigarette.

Drew and Nick hurried over to him.

"You didn't call them." Roger's eyes were red-rimmed, fierce, and frightened. "The police, I mean."

"No, not yet." Drew pulled him to his feet. "But we'll have to in time. You know that."

"Best go in and see what's what," Nick suggested, and Drew took Roger by the arm.

"No." Roger tried to pull away. "I can't go back in there. She's . . . I just can't."

"Steady on now. We've got to know what's happened. Let's just go into the kitchen, all right? You don't have to see her again."

Roger screwed his eyes shut but didn't resist when Drew led him past the body in the zebra-striped chair and into the kitchen.

"Just sit here and don't do anything. Here's an ashtray."

Roger nodded and took another drag on his cigarette.

Drew and Nick went into the other room. The girl was in the chair as Roger had said, looking as if she had fallen into a deep sleep. For a dressing gown she had on a man's silk smoking jacket, gaudily red with black Chinese dragons on it, just long enough to reach her knees, even with her bare legs curled up under her as they were. A hint of a black slip peeped out beneath it. A long stylish cigarette holder, also black, had slipped out of her limp fingers. As Roger had said, she was cold.

"No obvious cause of death," Drew said. "No noticeable marks on her except the puncture there over her heart."

He didn't touch the cup on the table next to the chair. Perhaps something in the little bit of tea left in it contained a clue to what had killed her.

Nick scrutinized the small wound. "You said he pulled out the hatpin. I suppose there was a note, as well?"

"He said there was, but I don't see anything."

Nick got down on hands and knees to look under the chair. "Ah, the cretin's probably burnt the deuced thing."

"I don't think the fire's been lit for some time. Perhaps he has it with him." Drew fingered the black-and-white evening gown draped over the back of the sofa. Next to it was a necktie, maroon and navy, not done up. "Looks as if she meant to come to dinner."

"What do you suppose she wanted with that tie?" Nick asked, standing back up. "You don't suppose it's Roger's?"

"Nobody would wear that to an evening affair. It's hard to tell with that sort of girl. Roger said she'd wear most anything and somehow make it look chic. Bohemian type, don't you know."

Drew glanced at the girl again. She was a pixyish little thing with fiercely red, lacquered nails and bobbed hair dyed an impossible shade of black. Roger would fall for a girl like her.

"Come on, Nick. We'd better see to Rog and then ring up the police."

When they returned to the kitchen, Roger had his head down, his face buried in his arms. His cigarette had rolled onto the table and was leaving a tiny charred mark in the wood. Drew put it back into the ashtray.

"Better tell us about it, Roger."

He groaned as he lifted his head. "She *is* dead, isn't she?"

Drew nodded.

Roger closed his eyes. "What'll I do now?"

Drew looked at Nick. "Better see if there's brandy or something in the house."

"You don't think he might have had too much as it is?" Nick whispered. "No, I suppose we'd have smelled it on him."

Nick spotted an unopened bottle of whiskey on a side table. A little more searching brought to light a juice glass that would serve the purpose. He set both in front of Roger.

Drew filled the glass about an inch deep and then pushed it over to Roger. "Drink that down."

Roger obeyed him mechanically. Then he picked up his smoldering cigarette and began puffing away.

"All right, Rog, now tell us what's happened. You said there was a message. Where is it? And the pin, as well."

"Uh, I don't know. I suppose I left them in there." Roger jerked his head toward the other room, but he wouldn't look that way.

"We didn't find anything," Nick said. "Anywhere else you might have put them?"

Drew steeled himself. "You didn't burn the message or anything."

"Of course not." Roger hesitated, then a look of befuddlement came into his eyes. "I . . . I don't think I did. It's all a bit of a blur."

Drew tried his best not to scowl. Roger had never had any spine to him. "Think, man. What exactly did you do when you found her?"

Roger tapped the ash from the end of his cigarette and looked up at the ceiling, his eyes filling with tears. "I touched her arm. To see if she was dead. Then I pulled out the pin and read the note."

"What did it say? Do you remember?"

"Something about being hot-tempered and humbled and a queen or something. Odd stuff. I don't know what it meant."

Drew glanced at Nick and then back at Roger. "All right. Then what?"

"I suppose I rang up Farthering Place." Roger wiped his upper lip with the back of his trembling hand. "I tell you, I don't remember."

He'd go off his head in a minute if they weren't careful. Drew poured him another drink.

"All right. Take that and think again. You must've put the note and the pin down somewhere so you could use the telephone. What would you have done?"

Roger held the glass in both hands but didn't drink. "Put it on the end table, I guess."

"It's not there," Nick said.

For another moment, Roger stared into the whiskey, as if the answer lay somewhere in its amber depths. "Wait." He patted down his dinner jacket. "Wait."

He pulled from his pocket a crumpled ball of paper and a hatpin adorned with a jeweled dragonfly. Drew took both from him, touching them as delicately as possible.

"There weren't any fingerprints on any of the other messages and things. I don't suppose there are any on these either, besides yours, Rog, but one can't be too careful."

Holding only the corners, Drew tugged until the paper was relatively flat and legible.

Mismatched, hot-tempered, simply waiting for greatness to be humbled, she, but for the scandal, might have been queen of them all.

The three of them merely stared at it. No wonder Roger had made nothing of the message. Mismatched and hot-tempered. That could certainly describe the girl herself, but what greatness was to be humbled? Whose greatness was to be humbled? And what had that to do with poor Clarice with her Bohemian ways and her zebra-striped armchair?

Drew glanced over at Roger. "Was there a scandal of some kind? Involving Clarice, I mean."

Roger shrugged and twisted his neck slightly, chafing against his collar. "I never heard of one. I mean, not anything more than the way she did her hair or wore her clothes. Some of the beaux she had. Nothing anyone would murder her for."

"Tell me what the two of you did today."

"There's not all that much to tell. We were to come to Farthering Place for dinner, as you know, so we didn't want to motor up to London or anything like that. Turned out we spent the afternoon in the village."

Drew nodded. "Doing what?"

"Not much of anything really. She liked to look in the shops, but she never did buy much of anything here. Said it was all too bourgeois for her taste. You've seen the kind of thing she liked."

"And that was all?"

"Till I came back and found her. Like that." Again he took a puff of his cigarette, and afterward he became oddly calm. "They're going to think I did it, aren't they?"

Drew glanced at Nick, then turned back to Roger. "Why do you say that?"

"I found her. No one else was about. I pulled that . . . that pin out of her, so it's got my fingerprints on it, as you say. And the note."

"You've explained that," Drew assured him.

Roger ground out the stub that was left of his smoke and then patted his pockets for his cigarette case. He fumbled with the thing before he finally got it open and removed another cigarette. Then he slid it across the table toward the two others.

"Have one if you'd like. Either of you."

"No, thanks." Drew reached for the silver case, meaning to return it, but then he got a better look at it. "I say, Rog? Where did you get this?"

"What?" Roger managed to strike a match, but Nick had to steady his hand before he could light his cigarette.

Drew pushed the case closer to him but didn't relinquish his hold on it. "This."

Giving it a glance, Nick's eyebrows shot up, but Roger only looked at Drew as if he'd lost his mind.

"What possible difference could that make? It's a cigarette case. It's—"

"Just tell me."

"My father gave it to me, ages ago. Birthday or Christmas or something."

"Your father thinks your initials are JLC?"

Roger's heavy brows came together in puzzlement. "That's not mine."

"I gathered as much." Drew took it back, examining it. The engraving JLC was unmistakable, but there were no other marks on it. "How do you expect it ended up in your pocket?"

"I don't know. Picked it up by mistake somewhere, I suppose. It's about the same as mine." He took another puff of the cigarette, but this time the movement was jerky. "Put an ad in the *Times*, if you like, saying it's been found. I'll return it to any reasonable claimant. What the devil does it matter? Clarice is dead and you have to go on about a cigarette case?"

"This isn't just any case, Rog. Remember the doctor who was stabbed on the golf course?"

"What about him?"

"The police didn't find his cigarette case when they searched his body. His name was Corneau, if you recall. Joseph Latimer Corneau."

"I don't—" There was terror in Roger's eyes. "No, no, no . . ."

"I'd better telephone the police now, don't you think, old man?"

Roger blinked three or four times, then wilted in his chair. "I suppose. I'm for it now, no matter what you do." His voice was a low monotone, and there wasn't a flicker of feeling in his expression.

Drew wanted to shake him. "You can't just chuck it all in

114

now. It's likely you'll be arrested, I won't deny that much, but they'll sort everything out."

"Everyone saw us together in the village. I haven't any alibi for when I left her here."

"What did you do during the time you were apart?"

"I changed into my eveningwear."

"That whole three hours?"

"I don't know what I did exactly." Roger tugged at his bow tie, tightening the knot. "Read a bit, I suppose. Walked."

"You didn't see anyone? Or telephone anyone?"

"No."

"But see here," Nick said. "It might be that the police will charge you about Clarice, but surely they can't think you've done the other murders."

Roger shook his head. "This one had the note and the pin just the same as the others. They're sure to think I'm guilty of the whole lot."

Drew thought for a moment. "But you must have an alibi for at least one of the other murders, don't you?"

"I don't know when the others happened. How can I possibly remember what I was doing?"

"Montford was killed on the nineteenth. Where were you that afternoon?"

"What day was it?"

"Wednesday before last."

"I don't . . . No, wait. Yes, I do. I remember it because I was going to have to go to Blenheim the next day, Thursday, for Mother's birthday."

"But where were you on Wednesday?"

"Drove down to Land's End. Just for a lark, you know." A little color came back into his face, along with a weak smile.

"They'll have to see I couldn't have killed Montford because I was driving to Land's End."

"Alone?"

"No, I was with Clarice."

"That'll hardly be verifiable at this point. Did anyone see you there?"

"I don't think so. No one who'd remember."

"What about for the doctor's murder? I suppose that cigarette case will do you in there."

"I tell you, I don't know how that came to be in my pocket. I never even heard of the man until he was in all the papers. After he'd been killed."

"That was the following Monday. Do you have any alibi for then?"

Roger thought for a bit, and then, with a groan, covered his face with both hands. "I was here. With Clarice."

Inspector Birdsong's hound-dog eyes remained neutral. "Rather convenient, isn't it, sir? I mean, having the one person who could vouch for your whereabouts turn up dead?"

Roger gave the chief inspector no answer. He just sat there at the kitchen table, rocking slightly, forward and back. His last cigarette had smoldered into ash long since, and Birdsong had taken away Corneau's silver case and put it on a side table.

"So you say you and Miss Deschner were in the village this afternoon?" Birdsong consulted his notes. "Shopping?"

"Yes." Roger stared at the floor with his chin tucked well down.

"Did she buy anything?"

Roger shook his head. "We stopped to look at Bunny's new motor car. He was at Price's."

"Bunny?" Birdsong turned to Drew, eyebrows raised.

"Clive Marsden-Brathwaite," Drew told him. "Son of the Right Honorable Gervaise."

"Oh, yes. I have met Mr. Marsden-Brathwaite. I'll be speaking to him, as well."

That overbred twit, Birdsong's expression added for him. Ah, well, Bunny did rather notoriously fit the type, Drew couldn't deny it, but he was a good sort all the same and unfailingly sunny. Too bad he wouldn't be able to help out poor Roger.

"What else did you do, Mr. Morris?" Birdsong asked.

"I don't know. Just chatted and walked mostly. We had tea at the Rose Garden, there across from the church. That was last of all because, after that, I brought her here and told her I'd be back at a quarter till eight. It gave us both time to dress for dinner. Oh, and she wanted a newspaper, so I bought her one."

"At the post office or at the bookshop?"

"Bookshop. I remember because she wanted a book on avant-garde painters, and the lady at the shop said they never had much call for such things in Farthering St. John, but she could have one sent from London if Clarice liked."

Birdsong duly noted all this. "Anything else you'd like to tell me?"

"No."

"Do you happen to know a Thomas Hodges? Goes by Tommy?"

"Who's he?"

"Never you mind that for now. Do you know him?"

Roger merely shook his head, his chin on his chest now.

"Very well. Roger Earl Morris, I arrest you for the murder of Clarice Deschner. Now, if you'll be good enough to go with the constable, sir . . ."

Roger turned to Drew, eyes pleading.

"Steady on." Drew put his hand on his friend's shoulder, then turned to the chief inspector. "You don't really think he could have killed her, do you? Why would he?"

"We'll just have to find that out, now, won't we, Detective Farthering?"

Birdsong motioned to one of the constables, who escorted Roger out of the room.

Drew crossed his arms over his chest. "You know you haven't any sort of a case here. A jury would acquit him in five minutes for lack of evidence and lack of motive."

"There's the cigarette case for a start."

"Oscar Wilde says it's a very ungentlemanly thing to read a private cigarette case." Nick took the elegant item off the table, admiring its craftsmanship. "This is a very fine one, to be sure, but hardly motive for murder."

Drew took it from him, studying it, too. "Any man would be a fool to murder someone and then carry something as easily identifiable as this about with him."

Birdsong snatched it back and shoved it into the pocket of his overcoat, scowling at both of them. "That's not my problem just yet, is it? For the moment, all I have to do is not give a suspicious character a chance to scarper before we've got a chance to see what's what."

"Really, Inspector—"

"Look here, this is the first real break we've had in these hatpin murders. Perhaps your friend here did just what he said and has nothing to do with this killing or the others, but I don't know that. And until I do, Mr. Morris will be holidaying at the expense of His Majesty's government."

Poor Rog was for it. At least for the time being.

"Is it all right if we get the name of Roger's solicitor before you cart him off? I'll get hold of him and let him know what's happened." Drew gave the chief inspector a hopeful smile. "You wouldn't mind if Nick and I stayed behind a bit and had another look round, would you? I promise we'll lock up tight."

Birdsong narrowed his eyes. "You wouldn't have a bit of evidence you'd like to see to, would you? Keep your mate out of dutch?"

"Nothing of the sort, I assure you. Your men have already photographed and dusted everything in sight. And anyway, if there was something to hide, we had plenty of time to see to it before we called you."

The chief inspector slowly nodded. "I suppose you did at that. All right, but don't stay long. And P. C. Patterson will be just outside all night, so mind your manners."

"Oh, I say, Inspector."

"Well?"

"Who's this Tommy Hodges you were asking about?"

There was a touch of sly satisfaction in the chief inspector's grudging smile. "One behind me for a change, eh?"

Drew put his hand over his heart. "Ever and only your humble pupil, sir."

Birdsong looked unimpressed. "Our Mr. Hodges is a caddy at your golf course. He carried Dr. Corneau's clubs every Wednesday afternoon from May of 1927 until his death."

"I see. You don't suspect him, do you?"

"No, but you remember he was called away that day the doctor was murdered. He had a telegram saying his grandmother was dying up in Inverness and asking him to come at once."

"A fraud, I suppose."

"The old lady was on a cycling tour in the Lake District

with several other old-age pensioners from her street. Took this Hodges some time to trace her whereabouts and satisfy himself she was all right. Meanwhile it took our men a while to track him down and make certain he wasn't involved in Corneau's murder."

"You're satisfied with that?"

Birdsong nodded. "He has solid alibis for the other killings, and we know he was on his way to Scotland when Corneau was killed."

"And no trace of who may have sent the telegram?"

"No such luck. It was phoned in. With all the messages they take, the operator couldn't even remember if it was a man or a woman on the other end of the line. But it was most certainly not phoned in from Inverness."

"No surprise there. Did your men find out where the call was made from?"

"Local call. Winchester. We couldn't get any nearer than that, I'm afraid."

"I'm sorry neither of us has made any headway, Inspector, but there has to be some connection here."

"That may be, Mr. Farthering, and then again it may not. It's been my experience that what seems a sound line of reasoning to one man might be pure madness to another." Birdsong settled his hat on his head and pulled his battered overcoat more snugly around himself. "Good night, sir. Oh, and mind what I said about P. C. Patterson."

Soon Drew and Nick were alone in the cottage. Clarice De-schner's body had been taken away and so had Roger Morris, and Drew had placed a call to a Mr. Barlow, Roger's solicitor.

"I don't suppose there's much else to be done here, Nick, old man. Still, it couldn't hurt to have another look round, maybe figure out what she did during the afternoon." Drew ran his hand over the back of the zebra chair. "Obviously she changed her clothes from what she was wearing earlier in the day."

"The outfit Roger described is in a hamper in the bathroom."

"Right, she put on her dressing gown and had a cup of tea, but what else did she do?" He scanned the room. "Listen to the wireless? Read? There had to be something. No one takes that long just to dress."

Nick turned over a book that lay on the end table next to the chair where the body had been found. "*Art and the Avant-Garde: A Survey* by Professor A. C. Esterbrooke." He made a face. "Perhaps she died from boredom."

"A bit more to the purpose, if you please."

"Why do you suppose she asked Mrs. Harkness for a book on this modern stuff if she already had this?"

"Smells and looks new, too." Drew shrugged. "I don't know. Perhaps she wanted something a bit livelier. Or maybe she asked just to impress Roger. From what I heard, she did rather enjoy making people uncomfortable with her modern ideas. See what else you can find."

"There's a fashion magazine under it." Nick flipped through a few pages and then snorted. "Seems she liked to add a bit of drama to the photos."

He handed Drew the magazine, open to an advert showing a young couple drinking with straws from the same frothy glass, their eyes dreamily on each other. In a bubble over the man's head, Clarice had written, *Won't she make the sweetest little wife?* Over the head of the girl, the caption said, *Drink up, mate. I've got another date at—*

Drew studied it for a moment. "I wonder what interrupted her?"

"Could have been anything." Nick glanced at the picture again. "Might have done that a month ago as much as today."

"I don't know. The magazine looks new, latest issue and all. And if I don't mistake myself—" Drew picked up a fountain pen from the end table where the book and magazine had been and made a small mark at the bottom of the page Clarice had embellished—"that's the pen she used. Besides, if she didn't do this today, then why didn't she finish it? She would've had plenty of time."

"Perhaps she couldn't think of what to end with," Nick said. "Or maybe she simply got bored with the idea."

"Well, even without an ending, it says what she meant it to. Not a romantic, our Miss Deschner."

— Eight —

t was well past midnight by the time Drew arrived home to Farthering Place.

"Hullo, darling."

"Oh, Drew."

Madeline tossed down her book and hurried to him with open arms. She then glanced back at Aunt Ruth, who was sleeping soundly in the armchair by the library fire with Mr. Chambers curled up in her lap. Madeline put one finger to her lips, and Drew took her hand and led her into the hall.

She pulled the library door silently closed and then kissed him. "I'm so glad you're finally home."

"So am I."

She stroked the hair back from his forehead. "You look exhausted. Don't you want some coffee or something?"

"I am a bit done up, I confess it, but I hate to roust out any of the staff at this time of night. Nick's already headed up to bed. This business with Roger's an awful mess."

"Poor thing. Would it be improper if we sneaked out to the kitchen and got some coffee ourselves?"

He smiled. "You are the most perceptive creature."

"Someone has to take care of you," she said, taking his arm as they walked. "And Denny can't always be around."

"We've got to be quiet," he warned as he turned on one light in the kitchen. "If Mrs. Devon finds us here, she'll insist on making cake or biscuits to go along with the coffee. Or sandwiches or an eight-course meal."

Madeline looked around, unsure of which of the myriad cabinets to open first. "I don't suppose you know where the coffeepot is kept."

"Not really, but Mrs. D is a logical woman, so I expect it would be in a logical place."

They found it in a cupboard above the sink, next to the tea things, just where it ought to be. The coffee grinder was next to it, along with freshly roasted coffee beans.

"Maybe tea would be easier," Madeline said.

"Nonsense, darling. You like coffee, so we'll have coffee. We don't need any help. Besides, I don't want anyone here but you right now."

He ground the beans while she poured water into the pot, and somehow they ended up with two decent cups of coffee. A few hot sips seemed to take some of the weariness out of him.

"This is lovely," Drew said. "Thank you." He reached across the kitchen table to take her hand.

Madeline smiled. "You're very welcome. Now, don't you think you'd better catch me up on what's going on?"

The light in his eyes faded, making him look tired again and a little bewildered. "I suppose so." He took another drink of his coffee, lingering over it, reluctant to go on. "I rather hate pulling you back into this sort of thing, though. I mean it hasn't been very long since your uncle—"

"You're terribly sweet, Drew. I miss Uncle Mason. It still hurts to remember him dead there in the study with that knife . . ." She bit her lip and hated the tears that welled up in her eyes. "It still hurts. But if we can spare someone else that pain, then it's a good thing, isn't it? A right thing?"

"Yes, darling, it is. I don't know how I keep getting pulled into these situations, but maybe it's what I'm meant to do. I don't know that for certain, but I want to find out. And more than anything, as long as you're out of danger, I want you in it with me."

She swallowed hard and then nodded. Those tears would never go away if he kept talking to her like that.

"So then, down to business, as they say." He winked at her. "Tell me what happened here after Nick and I left."

"The party didn't last long after dinner. Bunny and some of the others decided to drive up to London, to some of the night-clubs there. Freddie went, too. Then Mr. and Mrs. Allison went home. I wish I could have come with you and Nick."

"It was a grim scene. The woman was poisoned or something. It's all so terribly sad."

"And how is your friend Roger?"

"He's always been a bit high-strung. You can imagine him finding her dead there with that ghastly note pinned into her. I thought he'd lose his wits when he realized he had Dr. Corneau's cigarette case on him."

"How do you suppose he came by that? Did he know the doctor?"

"No. At least he says not. I can't imagine why he'd lie about it unless he's behind all the murders."

"You don't think . . . ?"

"Old Roger? Hardly. He couldn't bear even being in the same room with the poor woman's body. I could never see him actually committing a murder."

"What about the note?"

He sighed. "I wrote it down."

He gave her the slip of paper he'd used to copy down the cryptic message.

She puzzled over it for a moment and then shook her head. "You don't think the murderer's just writing these to confuse things, do you? I mean, maybe they don't mean anything at all."

"No, there's some method in it, I'd lay odds on that. We just have to figure out the key. Nothing for it but to let the little gray cells do their work." He squeezed her hand. "Sorry to have left you and Mrs. Allison to see to the guests here, darling. Must have been deuced awkward for you."

"Well, I knew you were in a jam, and Freddie kindly agreed to be my escort. He even spent a while chatting with Aunt Ruth."

He was silent until she looked up at him. He was staring off into the darkness outside the windows.

"That was good of him."

He didn't say anything more.

"What are you thinking?" she asked after a few moments.

This time he turned to her, a wistful smile on his face. "Lots of things. I don't know if Roger actually loved Clarice. More than likely just a pash. But it had to be a great shock to him for her to be suddenly gone forever like that, someone he'd been with just a few hours before."

He squeezed her hand and was silent again, but she knew what he was thinking.

"I'm still not ready to make a decision," she said.

He pulled back from her, the melancholy in his expression replaced with puzzlement and a touch of irritation. "I didn't ask you to."

"Not in so many words, no, but I could tell where you were headed when you were talking about Roger and about losing someone suddenly."

"All right, I was thinking of you. I was thinking how rotten it would be to lose you like that. Is that a crime?"

"No, of course not." She stroked his cheek. "I love that you feel that way about me. I love that you want me to marry you. I want that, too. You don't understand how very much I do and how very much that scares me."

His expression softened. "Is being married to me such a terrifying prospect?"

She smiled, ignoring the lump that forced its way into her throat. "No, it's wonderful, more wonderful than I can believe. But we've known each other such a short time."

He sighed. "I see you've been listening to your aunt Ruth again."

"I haven't talked to her about you all day, and she never said a word about us getting married."

"I don't mean just now. I mean all your life. Certainly, much of what she says is very wise. One shouldn't just leap into something without counting the cost. But one oughtn't be afraid of life, either. Anything worth doing involves risk, marriage most especially. We could spend the next decade getting better acquainted, and that still wouldn't guarantee a happy marriage."

"I realize that. It's just that I've had such a sheltered life really. I want to make sure . . ." But she let the words trail off, not knowing what else to say.

"You want to look about a bit before tying yourself down.

I suppose spending the evening with Bell has made you think more along those lines."

"I hardly know him."

"But you'd like to find out more."

"Don't be silly. He's a nice boy, but I'm not interested in him. I mean, it *is* good to talk to someone from home, but that's all it is."

He studied her face for a long moment. Then his eyes warmed, and he brought her hand to his lips, pressing it with a gentle kiss. "I understand. Really, I do. And I wasn't trying to press you into a decision before you're ready to make one. I love you, and I want the honor of having you for my wife, but only if that's what you want, too. And if it takes a while for you to be sure that's what you want, it's well worth the waiting. In the meantime, we have a puzzle to keep us occupied, as well as the winning of your aunt."

Madeline laughed softly. "It's a toss-up which one is going to be more difficult."

"Nonsense. Your dear auntie won't be able to resist the Farthering charm much longer."

"Don't bet on it," she teased. "But that was awfully sweet of you, Drew, bringing her that doll."

"Do you think she liked it?"

"Very much so. She doesn't quite know what to make of you yet, and you keep refusing to be what she expects."

Laughing, he stood and extended a hand to her. "Come along, darling. It's late, and your aunt will be cross."

She put both dirty cups in the sink. "Why should she be cross?"

"Well, either she's awake and wondering what mischief I've drawn you into, or she's still asleep in the chair and will have a stiff neck when we wake her up."

"I don't wish her a stiff neck, but I hope she's still asleep. I suppose I'd better go get her and head back to the cottage."

Sure enough, Aunt Ruth was still sleeping when they returned to the library. They helped her to her feet, found her more groggy than cross, and escorted her back to the cottage. Drew stole a quick kiss from Madeline as the older woman tottered inside, and then he went up the moonlit path back to the house.

Breakfast the next morning was serene and pleasant. The August day was warm and windy, and the smell of rhododendrons wafted from the garden below the terrace, competing with the equally delicious aroma of rashers and eggs and Mrs. Devon's homemade marmalade on toast.

"I thought Nick would be down by now," Madeline said when the meal was almost over. "What's he up to today?"

"Sleeping all hours, no doubt," her aunt observed.

Drew offered her another slice of bacon. "Actually, ma'am, I understand that he and Mr. Padgett, the manager here at Farthering Place, went off quite early this morning to see to some business matters. Nick will be taking over here when the old gentleman decides to retire. He's really quite industrious."

"Well, you could learn from his example, young man." Aunt Ruth speared two slices of bacon with her fork and slid them onto her plate, and he smiled in answer.

"No doubt. And I do have quite a lot to keep me occupied today."

Madeline's eyes met his, and he saw worry in them.

"Have you thought more about who could have killed that woman?" she asked.

Drew added another spoonful of honey to his tea. "I've

thought of little else. Poor Rog, sitting there in the jail in Winchester. I've got to drive over and see him this morning. I promised him cigarettes, and I'd like to talk to Birdsong if I can."

"Pardon me, miss, but I believe this is yours." With a curtsy, Anna set Madeline's little beaded handbag on the corner of the table. "Tessa found it when she was cleaning this morning."

"Oh, thank you." Madeline smiled at the girl and then at Drew. "I didn't even realize I didn't have it. Come to think of it, I don't remember taking it back to the cottage with me last night."

"You'd better see if anything's missing," Aunt Ruth said.

Madeline laughed. "There's nothing in it worth much of anything. Besides, Anna wouldn't take anything, I'm sure."

"Maybe not, but who knows about this Tessa she was talking about, or any of the other staff here."

"I'm not worried, Aunt Ruth. They're all good people." Madeline turned to Drew once again. "Maybe Roger will have remembered something today that will help out. Do you think I could come with you?"

"I'd rather you didn't, if you don't mind, darling. The jail's not at all a nice place, and I promise I'll fill you in on every detail the moment I come back."

Aunt Ruth pursed her lips. "I'm sure that nice Mr. Bell would think of something much more pleasant to talk to a young lady about, at breakfast or any other time."

A gust of wind whipped a strand of hair into the older woman's face. She swept it back with one hand, feeling with the other through the rest of her iron-gray locks.

"Oh, I'm losing hairpins left and right out here in the open air. I doubt I have three left. Run over to the cottage and get some for me, will you, Madeline?"

"Take some of mine." Madeline slid her handbag over to her

aunt, then looked back at Drew. "They don't really think Roger could have killed her, do they?"

"He's their prime suspect at the moment. They just don't have anyone else, and even he doesn't seem very likely to have committed all three murders."

Aunt Ruth rummaged in the bag and made a little huff of exasperation.

Madeline turned to her. "What's wrong?"

The older woman glanced at Drew, a smirk curling her lip. "Are you sure you'd like me to say, Madeline? In company, I mean."

"What are you talking about?"

Aunt Ruth reached into the bag and took out a large, heavy key. It was attached to a little wooden oval with a number four carved into it.

"Were you planning to visit someone, missy?"

"Where did you get that?"

"Straight out of your bag. I'm not so worried about where it was as how it got there."

"I've never seen it before. Drew, do you recognize it?"

"Could you have taken it with you by mistake from your ship when you came over, or perhaps one of the places you stayed before you came to Farthering?"

"I'd have noticed long before now if that were the case. Besides, I bought this purse here. Well, not in Farthering St. John, but in Winchester. It was after Carrie and Muriel and I came to stay."

Drew studied the key. "Could be from the Queen Bess, I suppose. When was the last time you were there?"

"When we had lunch, you and Freddie and I."

"Could you have accidentally picked it up? Off the table or something?"

"I don't think so. I suppose it's possible, though."

"Oh, well. Don't let it trouble you, darling. I'll take it back after I go see Rog. Or maybe we'll walk down there later on and return it. How'd that be?"

She smiled and then sobered at the piercing look coming from her aunt.

"Really, Aunt Ruth, I don't know how that got in my bag. You're making some kind of scandal out of nothing. It's just a key. I don't even know what it unlocks."

"Mischief, if you ask me. That's what it unlocks."

Drew slipped the key into his coat pocket. "Well, we'll send it right back to where it belongs, mischief and all, and no harm done."

"Humph."

And for the rest of the meal, Aunt Ruth said no more.

The trip to the jail in Winchester proved singularly unproductive. Drew wasn't allowed to see Roger Morris, who was "in interrogation," and he had no choice but to leave the cigarettes for him. He was also not allowed to talk to Chief Inspector Birdsong. Though the desk sergeant did not say, Drew suspected Birdsong was also "in interrogation."

He was back home before eleven, and he and Madeline walked down to Farthering St. John just in time for lunch. Drew couldn't help smiling when he saw Mr. Llewellyn's shiny red two-wheeler leaning against the wall at the side of the inn.

"Looks as if we'll be safe for the time being. He's likely in there having a pint with his shepherd's pie."

Madeline shook her head. "He's a nice old man, even if he can never remember my name. He's told me all sorts of interesting things he remembers hearing about our civil war from when he was a little boy."

"You should ask him what he remembers about *our* civil war."

She laughed. "When was that? Two hundred years before ours?"

"More or less, but I don't know how much he'll remember. He may have still been in his cradle then." Drew winked and then shook an index finger at her. "Just you remember to keep out of his way when he's on his bicycle. Now, let's go see to this key business, and then maybe we can find Bunny and ask him about Roger and Clarice."

"Why don't you just call Bunny on the telephone?"

"Well, I could, darling, but then I wouldn't get to see his new motor car. It's a Lagonda."

She rolled her eyes. "You boys and your motor cars."

They went into the Queen Bess and straight to the front desk where a frazzled Mrs. Burrell greeted him with a reasonable amount of cordiality.

"Have you and the young lady come to lunch again?"

"No, actually." Drew took the questionable key from his pocket and showed it to her. "I think this may belong to you. Has one of yours gone missing?"

The woman drew her heavy brows together as she studied it. "It's certainly one of ours, but no, I didn't know we were missing of it. Of course, with Sarah and Maggie both out sick and me left to do their work and my own, I might not take notice if the kitchen went missing."

Drew leaned on the desk conspiratorially. "I wonder who's in room four right now."

"None of your honeyed words this time, Mr. Drew. Don't think I've forgotten the mischief you made in my inn the last time I let you talk me into something."

He put a touch of roguishness into his smile. "Now, admit it. There was no harm done in the least. In fact, I imagine there will be a lot of people wanting to come here, not in spite of that little scandal but because of it. How many of them have the chance to stay where a famous cinema star has stayed?"

"That's as may be, Mr. Drew, but I have a duty to my guests to keep their business private. So if you'll kindly return hotel property, I'll be getting back to my work."

Sighing, Drew surrendered the key into her outstretched hand.

"Thank you. Now, if there's nothing more—"

"I wonder if that's my cousin in room four." Madeline appealed to her with a smile. "I can't think of how else I might have picked up this key without noticing it."

"Cousin, miss?"

"Yes, Mr. Frederick Bell. The gentleman we had lunch with here a couple of days ago."

"The American gentleman. Oh, yes. I should have known he would know you, being American and all, but I didn't know you were cousins."

Drew gave Madeline a suspicious look, but the expression of innocence on her face did not change.

"Well, we're not really cousins, you know. Not technically. But we say 'cousin,' even though it's not so close a family relationship."

The older woman displayed a reluctant grin. "Well, I know how that is, dearie. My mother had an aunt her same age, couldn't abide when Mum called her Aunt Tilda. Always made her say cousin, too." She jangled the key playfully. "And no harm done with this. I'll see Mr. Bell has it back, though how he's gotten in and out since he lost it, I'll have him explain."

"Is he in at the moment?" Drew asked.

"Mr. Bell? Haven't I got enough to keep me hopping here without minding the whereabouts of all my guests day and night?" Just then the telephone rang, and she threw up her hands. "It just doesn't stop, I tell you."

Drew took Madeline's arm. "Come along, darling. If we're going to track down your Mr. Bell, I suppose we'll have to—"

"You two looking for me?"

They turned to see Bell standing not two feet behind them, grinning as usual.

"Oh, hullo, Bell." Drew shook the man's hand. "In point of fact, we were."

"Really? What for?"

"Have you been missing your room key?"

"Why, yes. Yes, I have. Did you find it?"

"Madeline came across it this morning. We've just turned it in."

"Well, that's a relief. I looked all over for the stupid thing. Where'd you find it?"

Madeline's cheeks turned a little pink, but she smiled. "In my handbag, as a matter of fact. Do you know how it could have gotten in there?"

Bell glanced at Drew. "That's kind of awkward, isn't it?"

"Rather." There was no humor in Drew's expression. "But the question remains. Do you know how it got there?"

He shrugged, shaking his head. "You've got me."

"When was the last time you had it?"

"Last time I know for sure was when I left the room yesterday morning to go buy some things here in the village. I went to the drugstore and the post office, a couple of other places. I don't remember. I bought a few things here and there and then came back. That was when I had the message that I was invited to your party last night. After that broke up, I went up to London with your friend Bunny and his gang, got in at a reasonably prodigal hour this morning, and darned if I couldn't find my key."

"Why didn't you tell Mrs. Burrell you'd lost it?"

"Heck, I didn't want to get on her bad side. I was afraid I'd have to tell her if I was going to get into my room, but then I saw one of those passkeys hung up behind the desk. I didn't think it'd hurt anything if I borrowed it until I found my own."

"And you didn't put yours into Miss Parker's purse?"

"No. Why would I?"

"An invitation perhaps?"

Bell's affable expression turned decidedly cool. "In my country, we consider those kinds of remarks an insult to a lady."

"I'm glad to hear it."

Drew fixed him with a hard glare, but blast it if the American didn't give him as good in return. Madeline finally came between them.

"Grow up, both of you. Maybe I picked it up by accident somewhere when Aunt Ruth and I were in the village yesterday. All that matters now is that it's back where it belongs, right?"

Drew still stared at Bell, his jaw clenched. Bell narrowed his eyes. Madeline shook Drew's arm. "Right?"

"Oh, yes, right. Right."

She smiled sweetly and turned to Bell. "And I can't imagine you'd be so ungentlemanly as to make that kind of assumption about me, Freddie."

"I hold you in the utmost respect, Miss Parker." He made a slight bow. "I apologize for any embarrassment I may unwittingly have caused."

She smiled again and took his arm, too. "Now that's settled, where are you both taking me for lunch?"

"My treat this time," Bell said. "I insist."

"Now, hold on here a moment, Madeline." Drew extricated himself from her grasp. "I have another question or two before you make us swear brothers and all."

She laughed. "Well, ask them then. I'm hungry."

Drew glared at Bell once more. "If you *misplaced* your key somewhere in one of the shops, how did you get back into your room to dress for the party?"

The American's ubiquitous grin reappeared. "I never lock up during the day. I didn't bring anything on the trip worth stealing except what I've got on me."

"So you couldn't say if you did or did not have the key at that time? Or if you lost it later? At the party, for example?"

"Afraid not."

Madeline took Drew's arm again. "You're making an awful fuss over nothing, aren't you?"

He gave her a reluctant nod. "Perhaps I am. All right then, I believe Mr. Bell was about to treat us to some sort of ostentatious feast, wasn't he?"

"You just see if I don't."

Bell led them into the dining room, and just as they were about to sit down, someone called from the far corner of the room.

"Young Farthering!"

Drew grinned, gave Madeline a sly wink, then turned to the older gentleman raising a pint to them.

"Good afternoon." Drew escorted Madeline to him, Bell in tow. "How are you, Mr. Llewellyn? You remember Miss Parker?"

"Oh, certainly, certainly." Llewellyn stood, shaking Drew's hand and then bowing over Madeline's. "Charming to see you again, ma'am."

"It's good to see you too, Mr. Llewellyn. Have you and Mr. Bell met?"

Bell gave the gentleman's hand a hearty shake. "We have."

"Did you find your guidebook, young fellow?" Llewellyn asked Bell.

"A suitcase full, sir, but none as thorough as these two." He grinned at Drew and Madeline. "And none as good with current events."

Llewellyn laughed and gestured to his otherwise empty table. "You'll all join me, I hope. Miss Parker?"

"Oh, no, Mr. Llewellyn. We wouldn't dream of disturbing your lunch." Drew could see his plate of bangers and mash was more than half gone. "You wouldn't want to be bothered with our nonsense."

Llewellyn grinned and pulled out a chair for Madeline. "Your nonsense wouldn't happen to be about these recent, um, incidents, would it?" He glanced at Madeline, but when he looked again at Drew there was a conspiratorial glint in his rheumy eyes. Madeline was already sitting by then, so the two young men sat at the table with her. "Any break in the case, Farthering?" Llewellyn asked.

Drew frowned. "Not really, sir. No."

"Pity about the Deschner girl, eh?" Llewellyn shook his head. "Shocking stuff."

Drew nodded, remembering the poor girl sitting there, still and cold, in that zebra-striped chair. "Certainly that."

"Still, a girl like that was bound to have a wrong end. Nearly unavoidable." Llewellyn leaned forward a bit. "Fast, you know. I heard they're holding Roger Morris for it."

"For now."

Llewellyn made a sour face. "Extremely unlikely. Not at all the type, young Morris. I knew his father. Bit of a weed when he was a boy, but right enough."

"Little enough to go on for the son, isn't it?" Drew observed.

Llewellyn shrugged. "Might be, I suppose. You'll see, though. Study this sort of thing, and you'll see. There's always method in the madness, mark you that."

"And have you studied 'this sort of thing'?" Bell asked with his usual smile. "I'd've thought, out here away from the city, you'd have very little to work with. Until recently, I mean."

"True enough, young man, true enough. Sometimes the quarry is close to hand. Sometimes it is to be chased after. And sometimes it is to be driven from the brush by oneself." His bushy white brows lifted. "Ah, there's Mrs. Burrell to take your orders."

After lunch, and after declining Bell's invitation to take in the marvels of Eastleigh, Bishopstoke, and Fisher's Pond, not to mention Lower Upham and even Upham itself, leisure and weather allowing, Drew and Madeline took their time walking back up to Farthering Place.

"Funny old man, Mr. Llewellyn," she said. "He knows a lot about a lot of things."

"Does know a bit about the Civil War, doesn't he?" He squeezed her hand. "Yours and mine."

"And bicycles."

"And murders too, it seems."

Madeline shuddered. "I realize he wants to know everything about everything, but I wish he hadn't always wanted to talk about that in particular. Especially the last one."

Drew put his arm around her. "Sorry, darling. It's like any small place, in America as well, I suspect. People have little else to amuse themselves other than local gossip, even something as lurid as murder."

"Even?" She laughed. "Especially."

"Yes, well, there is that." He handed her across the little stream that ran behind Rose Cottage. "What I'd like to know, though, is what made you come to the conclusion that the key to room four belonged to your 'cousin.'"

Again she laughed. "I didn't come to any conclusion. I just figured that since he's the only one I know who's staying at the Queen Bess, he was as good a guess as any."

"And just what is this cousin business? Not only are you not cousins, you're not related in the slightest."

"I told the woman at the inn that it wasn't a close relationship. We're all related to Noah, aren't we?"

Drew chuckled. "I see I'm going to have to keep a close watch on you, my girl."

Chief Inspector Birdsong was good enough to arrange for Drew to meet with Roger Morris the next afternoon. The interview room at the jail was small and grim, just four gray walls with a table and two chairs.

The guard was friendly and exhibited no more than routine suspicion. "You don't have anything on your person you shouldn't, do you, sir?"

"I assure you, officer, all the cakes with files and saw blades baked into them are securely locked up at home."

The officer grinned, showing a gap between his front teeth, and left Drew alone with the prisoner, locking the door firmly behind him.

Roger sat in the chair, his body twisted up, as if he wanted to curl up into an oblivious little ball but was only just managing to refrain.

Drew sat in the chair opposite him. "How are things, old man?"

Roger merely rocked himself in the chair, the motion hardly detectable, his eyes large and dark and staring at nothing.

"Rog?"

Finally he looked at Drew. "It's good of you to come, but I don't expect you'll want to waste your time coming here to see me. It's all over."

"Nonsense." Drew tried to sound encouraging. "We'll get it all sorted out and you'll be fine."

"I didn't tell you everything last night."

Drew raised one eyebrow. "You didn't?"

"They'll hang me."

"What didn't you tell me, Rog?"

Roger again stared at nothing.

"Rog." Drew snapped his fingers in front of his friend's face. "What didn't you tell me?"

Roger flinched. "It's not . . . it's not all that much. Not really. But it looks bad. It looks dreadful."

"I didn't come to play parlor games. Just tell me."

Roger hesitated a moment more and then pulled down his shirt collar on the left side, revealing three still-fresh scratches, angrily red.

"Clarice?"

Eyes closed, Roger nodded.

He was right. It was dreadful.

"Why in the world didn't you say something straightaway? You had to have known they'd find out."

"I don't know." He seized Drew's sleeve with both hands, clinging to him. "You've got to help me. I swear, I didn't kill her."

Drew could either pity the man or help him. But pity wasn't going to keep his neck out of a noose.

Drew shook free of him. "Get hold of yourself."

Roger swallowed hard and then sat up in his chair.

"Now, I want you to start at the beginning, when you came to Long Cottage to call for Clarice. Did you or didn't you go into the village?"

"Yes, we did, just as I said. We looked at Bunny's new car and bought a paper and had tea, and afterwards I took her back home."

"And then what?"

Roger put one elbow on the table and leaned his head on his hand. "Give me a smoke, will you?"

"Then what?" Drew repeated.

Roger sighed. "She told me she was going to wear that dress she had over the back of the sofa, that black-and-white thing. I said it was jolly nice and she'd look topping in it."

"So?"

He bit his lip. "It seems rather petty now."

"What happened?"

"She showed me a necktie. I'm sure you saw it there by the dress. She told me she was going to wear that, too. It was blue and red and not at all what a lady wears to a party, you know."

"You knew she was a bit of a Bohemian. All right, more than a bit. Good heavens, man, I knew that much about her, and I'd hardly met the girl."

"I know. I know. I just told her I would be very glad, as a favor to me, if she would leave the tie off that night. You know, wear something a bit more conventional. A necklace or a brooch or some such."

"I take it she didn't appreciate the suggestion."

"Not half. You'd've thought I'd asked her to go without the dress entirely."

Drew glanced at the scratches on his neck and then again at his face. "It must have been more than that, Rog."

Roger twisted his fingers together. "Give me a smoke, for pity's sake." The chair squeaked with his fidgeting.

"I haven't any. Tell me what happened."

Roger slid down into the chair, his legs sprawled out in front of him and his arms crossed over his head. "I don't know what happened. She'd been acting peculiar since the morning, as if she'd been looking for something to quarrel about. I had tried humoring her all day, but by then I was out of sorts myself. I told her if she couldn't dress properly, she could bally well stay home and I'd go to Farthering Place without her. She told me that would suit her, but I shouldn't think she'd be spending the evening alone if I did."

"And this was in the sitting room, where you found her later on?"

Roger looked pleadingly at the ceiling. "I suppose I lost my temper properly then. I grabbed her arm and asked her if she was seeing someone else. She only laughed at me, so I shook her. It wasn't more than that, but it was a good shaking. Then she turned all teeth and claws on me, spitting out words ships' cooks wouldn't use. She was going for my eyes with her nails, I expect, but I pulled away, and all she got was my neck." He tugged at his shirt, pulling it out of the waistband of his trousers, displaying a roundish purple bruise on the left side of his abdomen. "She landed a pretty good one with her fist, too."

"And then what?"

"I flung her back into the chair." He was crying now, just a silent trickle of tears out of the corners of his eyes. "That hideous zebra-striped thing she loved so much."

Drew offered him a handkerchief, but Roger wiped his face on his shirtsleeve. "Then what happened?"

"Then nothing. I left swearing I'd never be back. I drove about a bit, and then I went home. I rang her up, oh, I don't know, five or six times. She didn't answer, so I decided that, whatever else, I was going to your dinner party. I got dressed and tried to telephone her again. Still no answer, so I went round to the cottage. You know the rest."

"And she never said if she was seeing another man?"

Roger shook his head.

"Do you know where she got that tie?"

Again Roger shook his head. "Probably the church jumble. It's certainly not new."

"It wasn't one of yours?"

"No."

"Very well. Have you told this to anyone? Inspector Birdsong?"

"No."

"Not your solicitor?"

"No."

"You've got to tell him straightaway. The longer you wait, the worse it gets. Shall I tell him?"

"He won't . . . You don't think he'll refuse the case if he knows? I mean, if he thinks I did it?"

Drew clasped his shoulder. "You've money enough. Trust me, old Barlow will stick by you."

It was cold comfort, they both knew it, but Roger managed a bit of a smile nonetheless. "I'd be awfully grateful, Drew, if you'd let him know for me, if you could make him understand what happened. I swear, it's all true."

"I believe you, Rog." Drew jostled his shoulder and then released it. "Chin up, man. We'll get you through this somehow." He then rapped on the door to let the policeman outside know he was ready to leave.

"I say, Drew?"

Drew turned back and nodded. "Yes, Rog, I'll bring you some cigarettes."

— Nine —

With the *clank* of the lock still in his ears, Drew walked away from Roger's jail cell and turned the corner at the end of the corridor.

"Following up a clue, Detective Farthering?"

Chief Inspector Birdsong looked at him with that smug blandness that said he felt himself ahead in the game. Drew made his own expression equally bland.

"Merely visiting those in prison, Chief Inspector, as the Scriptures direct."

"I take it you've seen your mate Morris."

"I have. He's innocent, of course."

"Oh, of course. I don't suppose you'd care to have a wager on that?"

"You'll lose that one, Inspector. I wouldn't advise you make it."

"Do you think so?" Birdsong clasped his hands behind his back and rocked back on his heels, coming as close to a smirk as Drew had ever seen. "Would you care to hear a bit of news I've just had from Dr. Saxon, the coroner?"

"What? That the girl had blood and skin under her nails?" Birdsong's eyes narrowed. "So Morris confessed, did he?"

"I'm afraid he did, but only to having a row with the girl. Evidently she had a bit of a temper."

"And neither of you thought to mention this before now?"

"He's only just told me." Drew shrugged and gave the inspector an apologetic smile. "I was just going to tell his solicitor about it and then, unless they objected, discuss the matter with you."

"And you think that proves he's innocent, do you?"

"Not in itself, no, but none of it hangs together properly. Suppose he did kill her. Why all this business with the note and the hatpin?"

Birdsong dismissed the objection with the wave of one hand. "Simplest thing in the world. They quarrel, he kills her, and then he makes it look as if this hatpin murderer is to blame."

"No, no. I tell you, it's all wrong. Roger's a bit of a cretin, you know. I could see where he might lose his head and strike her or shove her, killing her accidentally. This was never an accident or a crime of passion. Poison like that? Do they know what it was yet, Inspector?"

"An overdose of Veronal. Neat as you please."

Both of them were silent for a grim moment.

"I just don't see Roger as the poisoning type," Drew said. "No. And suppose someone did plan a murder and make it look as if it were the hatpin murderer? He couldn't have the same handwriting and the same ink and paper as the others. It just doesn't fit."

"Would if he'd done the first two, as well." There was a stubborn set to the chief inspector's mouth. "He hasn't got an alibi for those, you know."

"Yes, well, we've been through that. He hadn't any motive for killing Montford or Corneau. Didn't know either of them as best anyone can tell."

"He could have done them so as to later put the girl's murder off on some lunatic, you know. He did have Corneau's cigarette case."

"Kill a man and carry his engraved cigarette case about in his pocket?" Drew gave him a sardonic grin. "He'd be the lunatic in that event. You'll have to come up with something a little more convincing, I'm afraid, Inspector. Roger just won't do."

"Then who will, Detective Farthering, since you know ever so much more than the police?"

"Daniel Montford came to see me." Drew's voice was light, nonchalant. "Seems he doesn't appreciate me using my particular talents as concerns his father's death."

"Oh, no?"

"He says you've already cleared him of any involvement. Is that right?"

"He was in his bedroom at home that day. His mother vouches for that much."

Drew frowned. "I don't suppose she'd be asking me to look into things if she was trying to protect him for any reason."

"Wouldn't think so. Do you have any reason to suspect him?"

"None, except that he's obviously angry at his father over this *affaire de coeur* with the Allen girl, and he's absolutely refused to give me any information that might be of help in the case."

Birdsong pursed his lips. "Maybe he just doesn't like you."

"Let's not consider the more fanciful possibilities until we've exhausted the ones that are actually likely."

The chief inspector gazed heavenward.

"At any rate," Drew continued, "he has an alibi only for his father's murder. What about Dr. Corneau's?"

"We haven't spoken to him about that one. There doesn't seem to be any reason for him to have killed the doctor."

"It may be well worth looking into. I don't suppose you've found out where he was yesterday afternoon, either."

"We've been rather occupied since last night." Birdsong paused, narrowing his eyes. "Do you have any reason to connect young Montford to the Deschner case?"

"Not particularly, except the three murders are obviously connected. If he killed his father, it seems almost certain that he killed Corneau and Clarice, as well."

"Perhaps some independent verification would be in order. I'd hate to doubt Mrs. Montford's word, but more than one mother has lied for her son before now. Have you shown young Daniel's photograph around? At the golf course? At the hotel?"

"I suppose it wouldn't be a bad idea. If you don't mind me doing you chaps' job for you." Drew couldn't resist just a hint of a grin. "Again."

Drew found the lobby of the Empire quiet and empty except for the diminutive figure lounging beside the lift.

"Hello, Phipps. How are you this afternoon? Where's Mr. Leonard today?"

A smile lit the young man's freckled face. "Afternoon, sir. Mr. Leonard is seeing to a problem with one of the guests up on five, a Mrs. Richards, but he should be back down in a jiff. Would you like to wait or shall I take you up?"

"Actually, it's you I've come to see, and I wanted to make sure we were in the clear."

Phipps grinned. "More police business, eh? I'm your man. You can rely on me, no questions asked."

"Excellent."

"Did the rozzers have her in for questioning, the girl from the toy shop? Did she kill that bloke in one-twelve?"

"We don't know yet, I'm afraid. You haven't said anything to anyone about her, have you?"

"Lumme, no, sir. Mr. Leonard, he was all smooth and clever, trying to get a hint out of me. But I kept mum." Phipps put up his hand as if to forestall any doubts Drew might have. "First to last, mum. Police business, I says, and that's all I says."

"Good lad. Now, can you tell me if you've seen this fellow around anywhere?"

Phipps studied the photograph of young Montford, his forehead puckered. Reluctantly, he shook his head. "No, can't say as I have. Not to remember anyway. Can't swear for certain he wasn't never here, but can't say as he was neither. Sorry."

He handed the picture back to Drew, who with a disappointed sigh returned it to his coat pocket. "I suppose you see just about everyone who comes in and out of the hotel."

"When I'm on duty, of course. If I don't take 'em up in the lift, I generally see 'em go up the stairs."

"I'm certain the police have already asked you this, but was there anything unusual about that day? Apart from the actual murder, was there anything you remember as being odd or out of place? Perhaps a stranger you may have noticed?"

"Mr. Farthering, this is a hotel. We deal in strangers."

"That's what makes it so difficult. Well, if you happen to think of anything, here's my card. You ring me up anytime."

Phipps nodded as he took the card. "You can count on me, sir. Service and discretion are our stock in trade."

Drew handed him a pound note. "Buy your Doris some flowers."

"Very kind, sir. Very kind. I could buy her a field of 'em with this. She wouldn't even see me, there'd be that many." He frowned, considering. "Hang on a tick. It's not so much of a thing, but it was on that day the gentleman was murdered."

"What was?"

"I took a delivery boy up to the first floor. He had a great boo-kay of lilies to leave for one of the guests. I said it was a grand lot of flowers for some lucky lady, and all he said was 'First floor' and wouldn't say nothin' else. I minded my own job after that."

"What did this delivery boy look like?"

"Couldn't say, really. He was behind the flowers the whole time. He was tall, I suppose. Not much meat on him. I remember thinking it odd that he wore his gloves, as warm as it was, but I suppose the flower shop makes their boys wear 'em, winter or summer."

"Do you recall who the flowers were for?"

"Come to think of it, that was a bit strange, as well. They was left outside the door of a Mrs. Maplethorpe, but she had checked out earlier that day. There wasn't a card, and nobody ever called for them. We used them for some posh do we had on the day after."

"You didn't see the delivery boy when he came back down?"

"I never thought of it again, but no, I didn't. Might have slipped by on the stairs when I had the lift up on one of the top floors."

Drew removed the picture from his coat pocket once again. "Any chance it could have been him?"

"A chance, I suppose. Couldn't swear it was or wasn't. You reckon he done it?"

"Your guess is as good as mine, I'm afraid. Well, you keep

my card. If you think of anything else, you ring me up. You won't forget?"

"Sooner forget my own name, sir, and that's a fact."

Back home at Farthering Place, Drew managed to get Madeline away from her aunt without undue resistance, and the two of them met with Nick over tea in the library. Drew was eager to let them know what he had most recently found out.

"According to Mr. Phipps, the lift boy at the Empire Hotel, around the time of Mr. Montford's murder there was a delivery of a large bouquet of lilies to a tenant on Montford's floor. The lilies were never claimed by anyone, and the hotel finally used them as a centerpiece for a banquet they were catering the next day. The purveyor of said floral extravaganza was a tallish, slender young man who kept his face carefully out of view and spoke very little."

"Do we know he was young?" Nick asked, lounging against the mantel of the great fireplace.

Madeline, seated next to Drew on the sofa, arched one eyebrow. "Do we know he was a man?"

"Hmmm." Drew frowned, thinking. "I expect we have quite a few possibilities at this point. Daniel Montford, of course. Old Russ from our solicitors. Even Miss Allen, if one wasn't to look too closely. But which one?"

Nick shrugged. "Why not all three?"

"What, together?" Madeline said. "All of them?"

"None of them has an alibi or a motive for all the murders," Drew said, "but they each have an alibi and a motive for at least one of them."

"A sort of murder cooperative." Nick moved from where he'd

been leaning against the mantel to pace near the window that faced the garden. "I'll kill your embarrassing father for you on Monday if you'll dispatch my faithless lover on the Friday next? Why not indeed?"

Drew scowled. "That's a possibility, I suppose, but it still won't do, old man. Murder, even by proxy, demands a motive. And certainly we have supposed a number of those, but we haven't exactly nailed any one of them down."

Madeline sighed. "So we're back to square one. Who would want to kill Montford?"

"There are a number of people who'd do away with him just based on his profession." Nick grinned. "The first thing, kill all the lawyers, eh?"

Drew started to laugh, then caught his breath. "That's it. By George, that's it. Dick the Butcher's advice to the rebel Jack Cade in Shakespeare's *Henry the Sixth*. 'The first thing we do, let's kill all the lawyers'!"

Nick halted stock-still. "Good heavens. Advice to Jack."

"But what about the others?" Madeline asked. "You don't suppose they're something to do with Shakespeare, too?"

"Could be, but I still don't know how." Drew tapped his fingers on his knee. "'Kentish wisdom would have him paid so'? 'But for the scandal, she might have been queen of them all'? Whose greatness was to be humbled, and why the waiting?"

"One at a time, if you please. Start with 'Kentish wisdom.'" Nick perched on the arm of the sofa. "Cade was from Kent, wasn't he?"

"And so was Alexander Iden who killed him. But what wisdom would pay in murder?" The words of the three messages whirred through Drew's mind. Advice and wisdom ending in death. Queens and humility and scandals. What did it all mean?

"If Montford was killed because he was a lawyer, perhaps Corneau was chosen because he was a doctor. But what has that to do with being from Kent? I believe, besides Cade and Iden, Kent is mentioned several times in Shakespeare's histories, but I don't recall any of it to do with doctors."

"Perhaps we ought to read through some of the plays again," Nick suggested. "Might jar the old memory, eh?"

"Maybe so." Drew considered for a moment. "What about Clarice? She hadn't any profession at all."

"Unless it was a terribly old one." Nick raised his eyebrows, and Drew laughed grimly.

"Perhaps she wasn't the most circumspect of ladies, Nick, old man, but I should hardly put her in that category. Though our murderer's standards may have been rather more strict." Drew sighed and squeezed Madeline's hand. "It's rather like your auntie's lacework after Mr. Chambers has gotten hold of it. Lots of tangled threads and no pattern."

Drew was just tucking into a nice plate of eggs, bacon, and mushrooms the next morning when Nick strode onto the terrace.

"Morning, old man." Drew pulled out a chair next to himself. "You're about rather early, aren't you? I mean, for you, you know."

"Have you seen this?"

Nick slapped the early edition of the newspaper down on the table, and Drew picked it up. He didn't have to ask which article Nick meant him to see. Margaret Allen looked out at him from under a headline that blared *SOLICITOR'S MISTRESS DENIES INVOLVEMENT IN HATPIN MURDERS.*

"Blast that Phipps. He told me he hadn't mentioned her to

anyone." Drew slung the paper into the empty chair. "I ought to go up to the Empire this minute and give him the thrashing of his life."

"Phipps the lift boy?"

"Well, who else could it have been? The police? I couldn't see Birdsong standing for such a breach of protocol. The girl wouldn't have said anything herself, would she?"

"Maybe she wanted the notoriety." Nick put the paper on the table and sat down. "Some do, you know."

Drew considered for a moment. "That's what Mrs. Montford said when I asked why the girl would claim an affair when there was none. She said maybe she wanted to be in the newspapers."

"You don't suppose Mrs. Montford was the one who talked, do you?"

"No. Couldn't be. There hadn't been anything more than the usual suspicion of this sort of thing in the news until now. It's got to be a terrible embarrassment to her. No doubt young Daniel is in a fine state about it, too."

Nick sighed. "Then we're back to Margaret Allen."

"No, look at her." Drew pushed the newspaper back across the table toward Nick. The girl was looking back over her shoulder, her dark eyes wide and frightened, as she tried to escape having her photograph taken. "She's terrified. It had to have been Phipps. He was paid off or some oily reporter weaseled it out of him. Either way, I'll find out."

Denny appeared at the door.

"Pardon the interruption, sir, but there is a young lady to see you—Miss Allen. I told her I would inquire whether or not you were at home."

"Oh, yes. Yes. Send her in. See if she'll have some breakfast."

Drew turned to Nick. "The poor kid, we'll have to try to do something for her, though I don't know what at this point."

"She has had it rough, I daresay. Shall I stand by or would you like me to go speak rather sharply to Phipps at the Empire?"

"No, stay here. It may take the both of us to cheer her up."

"Miss Allen, sir."

Denny showed the girl in. Her face was blotched and tear-streaked.

Drew stood up. "Miss Allen, how lovely of you to come. May I introduce my friend, Nick Dennison?"

Nick nodded, standing. "Good morning. Will you have something? Eggs? Sausage? We have some lovely marmalade."

She shook her head, looking like a fawn backed into the brambles by a pack of hounds. "I couldn't. Not right now."

"At least some tea," Drew insisted.

She agreed to that, and Nick was quick to pour out.

"Milk? Lemon?"

"No. Nothing, thank you."

He handed her the steaming cup, and she took a sip. It seemed to help.

"I'm sorry to come here like this, Mr. Farthering, but you said I might call on you if I needed to."

"Certainly." Drew gave her an understanding smile. "How can I be of help?"

The newspaper with her photograph was lying there on the table. She did no more than glance at it.

"Obviously, you know why I've come."

"Yes." Drew pulled out a chair for her. "Won't you sit down for a moment? I promise you, things will look better after you've finished that tea. And our Mrs. Devon makes strawberry jam that can mend nearly anything, broken hearts included."

She sat heavily, closing her eyes and trembling so much that he thought she would drop her cup. He sat down beside her and pushed the rack of toast and the jam pot within her reach.

"Just take your time, Miss Allen. I'm sure this must be difficult for you."

"I'm ruined. I knew already that I was foolish, but now I'm ruined."

"Surely it's not as bad as all that, is it? I know a scandal is never easy, but they do blow over in time."

"Mrs. Hirsch dismissed me after she saw that headline." The girl gave Drew a trying-to-be-brave smile. "It's hard enough to find a decent position these days and harder to keep one. I'll never find another respectable place."

"Perhaps there's something I can find for you at my company."

"No. I don't want that. There or anywhere, I don't want people staring at me. Talking about me. I couldn't go anywhere in the whole country now and not be known."

"I'm sorry your name came into it." Drew filled the girl's cup again. "I believe I know who might have leaked it to the newspapers, and I mean to have a word with the guilty party."

"You know Mamie?"

"Mamie?"

Miss Allen nodded. "Mamie Blankensop. She has the flat next to mine and we've been rather good friends for a while now. She came over yesterday to borrow my rhinestone brooch when she was going out. I couldn't help it, I told her everything. I had to talk to someone or I knew I'd absolutely die."

"Quite understandable," Drew murmured.

"She knew I was seeing someone already, just not who it was. Anyway, she came back first thing this morning, crying and saying she didn't think this would happen and showing me the headline. She had told her young man what I said, not thinking it would go any further, but he works setting type for the newspaper. He thought if he gave them the story, it would be a way for him to get into reporting as he's wanted to for so long. Reporters have been calling at the flat and ringing up on the telephone ever since. It's been horrid."

"I can imagine." Drew stirred more honey into his tea. "How did you manage to get over here without them following you?"

"Poor Mamie, she wants ever so much to help me now. She was talking to the reporters through the door of my flat, pretending to be me and telling them to go away. That gave me a chance to slip out my back window and into hers and out her door. I took a taxi over. I don't know how I'll ever pay for it."

"Don't you worry about that."

Drew gave Nick a glance, and he was quick to excuse himself.

"Now," Drew continued, "tell me how I can help."

"I don't know. I don't know. I was just thinking about poor Mrs. Montford." The girl looked up at him for the first time since she had sunk into the chair, her expressive eyes swimming in tears. "I wouldn't dare call on her, but she doesn't deserve this. It's hard enough for her to lose her husband, but the scandal . . ."

Drew handed her a napkin, which she crumpled into her hands and pressed to her face. After a moment she calmed herself and sat upright in the chair.

"I'm sorry."

"No need to apologize, Miss Allen."

"I'm not sure how all this even happened. I wasn't brought up this way."

"No, to be sure."

"I suppose it's an old story, and I wasn't clever enough to realize it until it was too late." She managed a wan smile. "I guess every girl likes to think she's different, that a man's talk of love to her must be sincere." Tears again filled her eyes. "Oh, God . . ."

Drew patted her hand. "He wouldn't be a bad place to begin, you know, if it's forgiveness you want."

She pulled away from him. "I didn't come here for a sermon."

"I didn't think I'd offered one."

The anger faded from her eyes. "You meant only to be kind. I know." She swallowed hard. "I merely thought you could speak to Mrs. Montford for me. Tell her that her husband loved her. Tell her that I meant absolutely nothing to him."

"Is that true?"

"I swear it is the truth. No use having her imagine things that aren't true, even if I did."

"It's good of you to be so considerate of her."

The girl shook her head. "If I had been considerate, none of this would ever have happened. I wouldn't have had to . . ." She glanced at him and then looked away. "I wouldn't have been so foolish."

"So you knew he was married from the very start?"

She sighed. "I wasn't sure. I knew he had a son and at first assumed he was a widower. Every time I mentioned the loss of his wife, he said he didn't care to talk about her. After a while I realized she was alive. By then I had convinced myself that we were in love and deserved our happiness. When I finally told him I knew he was still married, he told me he was going to leave her and marry me. He said it, even if he didn't mean it."

"How do you know he didn't mean it? You told us earlier that he had come to the Empire that day to tell you he had told his wife he was divorcing her."

"Yes, well." She laughed softly, bitterly. "I've had my eyes opened since then. I was the one who was deceived, not Mrs. Montford. I want you to tell her that. Tell her I'm sorry that all this has come out in the papers. She didn't deserve that."

He nodded. "Now, what can I do for you?"

"Nothing but that."

"What are you going to do? Are you sure I can't help you find a new position somewhere?"

"No. I have family in America. They have a farm out away from anywhere, and their family name isn't Allen. I won't know anyone and they won't know me."

"Times are rather bad in America these days too, you know. Are you sure you will be all right there?"

"I telephoned my aunt this morning. She said as long as they have a garden and a cow and some chickens, they'll be all right, and that I should come. She didn't even ask why I wanted to come, which is so like her."

She laughed again, but now most of the bitterness had lifted. He smiled, too.

"That's grand. And perhaps it is best. Can you manage the passage money?"

"I pawned what I could. Actually, Mamie did it for me so I didn't have to try to get past the reporters. I have enough for steerage. I'm going to ask if I can't do some sort of work on the way over so I'll have something left for getting out to the farm."

She told him the name of the ship on which she had booked passage, and he nodded.

"That's a good line. They'll have you across the pond in a jiffy. But I say, have you discussed this with the police? You don't think they'll mind if you leave the country?"

She bit her lip, her dark eyes uncertain. "The chief inspector knows I haven't killed anyone and that I don't know who did. I'm just no help in the investigation. I don't know why it shouldn't be all right for me to go now."

Drew lifted one eyebrow. "Perhaps we ought to ring him up just to be sure. I know you've been through rather a rough time of it, but if you try to go before he's ready for you to, it won't get any easier."

"Would you . . . ?"

"I'd be happy to speak to him for you. Why don't we go through to the telephone."

They went into the study, and a moment later a constable connected Drew to the chief inspector's office.

"Birdsong here."

"Good morning, sir."

Drew made sure to put a sufficient amount of good cheer into his voice to provoke the grumbling reply he received.

"Isn't it a bit early for you to already be meddling in police business, Detective Farthering?"

"I'm afraid the morning newspapers have left me little choice in the matter."

"Ah. So you saw that bit about the Allen girl, did you?"

"If I hadn't, Inspector, I imagine I'd be one of perhaps three people in the entire country."

Miss Allen's brows were drawn together as she listened, and Drew gave her a reassuring nod.

"Look here, sir," he continued, "I've got the young lady at Farthering Place right now. These reporters have given her rather a bad time, and she'd like to know if it's all right if she goes to stay with her aunt. At least until this has all blown over a bit."

"Aunt, eh?" Drew could almost see Birdsong purse his lips as he mulled over the idea. "Not a bad idea, I suppose. Where is this aunt of hers?"

"Ah, well, that may just be the most infinitesimal fly in the ointment."

"Where?"

"In America."

Drew held the telephone away from his ear until most of the shouting had died down, and then he brought it close once again.

"I'll take that as a no, shall I?"

For a long moment there was a fierce silence at the other end of the line. When the chief inspector finally spoke, it was with infinite and exquisite patience.

"As Miss Allen is a person of interest in at least one and possibly all of the hatpin murders, we at the county constabulary would prefer that she remain nearby until our investigation has been completed. If of course that does not inconvenience the young lady to any marked degree."

"I was afraid that might be your answer."

"Do apologize to Miss Allen on our behalf for any difficulties this may cause her."

"All right, no need to be snide, Inspector. I did call you up voluntarily, you know."

"Well, there is that, Mr. Farthering, and wise thinking it was, too. Now you see the young lady stays close at hand. And if she does decide to change her place of residence, within reason, of course, you see she lets us know. Understood?"

"Perfectly, Inspector. Good morning."

Drew hung up the telephone, smiling reassurance into the worried eyes of the girl.

"As you might have guessed, the inspector isn't too sanguine about your departing for the New World just at present. Do you have anyone nearby you might stay with? Anyone?"

She shook her head. "I suppose it's back to the flat for me, though I don't know how I'll be able to keep even that now that Hirsch's have dismissed me."

"Does anyone know you here in Farthering St. John?"

"No, though they're all likely to know *of* me after this morning's papers."

"True enough. Hmmm. There must be someplace you can go until all this has been sorted out."

Just then Nick popped his head into the room. "Anything else you need me to do?"

"Come in, old man, and put on your thinking cap."

"What? Before breakfast?"

Drew seized him by the arm and pulled him back to the table. "You can think while you're eating."

"Oh, all right." Nick made himself comfortable and began dishing out a plate of food. "Now, what am I meant to think of?"

"Where would you go, hereabouts, I mean, if you didn't want anyone knowing you were here?"

Nick contemplated the question while salting his eggs. "Have I any money?"

"Enough so it's no difference."

Nick ate a piece of bacon and then another in silence. Then he nodded. "I'd go to Mrs. Chapman's."

Drew laughed, earning a startled look from the girl. "Nick, old man, you're an absolute genius. Nobody ever pays any attention to the fishing cottage or knows if anyone's staying there. Mrs. Chapman will be discreet if we ask it of her. It's perfect."

Miss Allen shook her head. "Wait. What are you talking about? I can't possibly—"

"You can possibly." Drew held up a hand to silence her protests. "It's only temporary, until you are allowed to go to your aunt's, but it really is the best solution. You'll stay there, tucked nicely out of the way, and we'll let our dear chief inspector know where you are. Mrs. Chapman is a lovely old lady who'll take excellent care of you and keep the reporters and other undesirables at bay. All you have to do is have a nice rest and not tell anyone where you are for a bit. What do you think?"

"But I could never pay for—"

"Just you let me see to that. Besides, I doubt if Mrs. Chapman asks much in rent. The cottage is sound and clean, but it's small and rather spartan. It's not likely you'll be bothered with the Duke of Kent popping by at odd hours to borrow ha'p'orth of sugar for when the king comes to tea."

She looked at him, wary, bewildered, as if she might cry again, and then a softness came over her face along with a hint of a smile. "You're very kind. I'll repay you in time."

"Not at all. Not at all." Drew took her arm and brought her to her feet. "Now I'll ring up Mrs. Chapman, and you go along with Mr. Dennison here. He'll see you're properly settled. And if you need anything at all, don't hesitate to let us know."

"You'll speak to Mrs. Montford for me? Promise?"

He took the hand she offered. "Most certainly."

"You're really too kind, Mr. Farthering." She looked down then, a shy smile on her face. "And I'll remember what you said. In your sermon. I'll wait for you in the cab, Mr. Dennison."

She gave Drew one final grateful glance and scurried out the door.

"Do you think it wise?" Nick asked. "Keeping her close like this? After all, she's still a suspect."

"I haven't forgotten that. I still can't imagine she'd kill anyone, but if she has, at least she'll be where we can keep watch on her. When I said Mrs. Chapman would be discreet, I didn't mean she would be discreet with us."

"Well thought out, as always." Nick bowed briefly. "I salute you."

"Yes, yes, all right, now don't keep the young lady waiting. I'll ring up Mrs. Chapman and see to that end of things. And on the drive over, if you happen to find out a bit more about our Miss Allen, her family, past history, if she has someone who calls on her regularly or who used to before Montford, that would be all to the good."

Nick grinned. "Leave it to me."

— Ten —

G iven the generosity of his proposed financial terms, Mrs. Chapman was more than happy to agree to Drew's plan to rent her cottage. He was still at the breakfast table, rereading the salacious article beneath the girl's picture, when Nick returned from the cottage.

"Our charge has been safely delivered and warmly received. What next?"

"Any revelations along the way?" Drew asked.

Nick shrugged. "Nothing all that helpful. She comes from a little place in Derbyshire called Ault Hucknall. Moved to Winchester along with her mother three or four years ago when her father died and her mother took a position as nurse to an elderly relation of theirs. About two years ago, both mother and elderly relation were taken by the influenza, leaving our Miss Allen alone to make her way in the world as she was not provided for from elderly relation's modest fortune. Has an aunt in America as she's already told you. No one else in the world."

"No young man?"

"She describes a rather tepid series of evenings out with a farrier some fifteen years her senior when she was still in Ault Hucknall. He did not approve of her staying in Winchester on her own when her mother died and wanted her to come back to be his wife."

"I don't suppose she'd care to go to him?"

"Apparently that would be a bit sticky at this point in time. It seems she rather firmly refused the man the last time they spoke and invited him to never call upon her again. Heated words were exchanged, ties severed. All in all, it wasn't a conversation meant to engender future amicable relations."

"But would she like to go to him now? Sometimes a bit of stability, even dullness, is quite welcome in uncertain times."

Again Nick shrugged. "I had the distinct impression that making a fresh start in America was far more appealing to her. You don't suppose he . . . ?"

"Made away with the man who had soiled his innocent darling? I shouldn't think so. Yes, all right, perhaps he'd have a motive in the Montford murder, but what about the good doctor? What about Clarice?"

"Well, what would be the harm in letting the police know about him? They could take it from there, and we'll have done our duty."

Drew thought for a moment. "Did she mention the man's name?"

"Called him Alfred. I didn't like to press for a surname."

"It's a start, though. How many approximately thirty-seven-year-old farriers named Alfred could Ault Hucknall have?"

"Shall we go find out?"

"No, Nick, old man, I think you were right in the first place. No need to tear clear across the country. We'll let the police investigate our would-be bridegroom." Drew put down the newspaper and got to his feet. "I'll ring up our beloved chief inspector once more."

"Very good. Mr. Padgett and I have some estate affairs to see to anyway, so I don't expect I'll see you until this evening. No fair doing any sleuthing without me."

Drew laughed. "Madeline said the same thing when she told me she's taking Auntie up to London for some shopping. Ah, well, I suppose I shall try to confine my efforts to discussing my theories with the chief inspector and, when he tires of me, with Mr. Chambers. He's the best listener of the lot of you, at any rate. No promises, though."

At the mention of his name, the little white kitten came trotting into the room, head held high, dwarfed by the feather duster he had stolen from parts unknown and was dragging alongside. He stopped to furiously shake his prey, rolling over with it and kicking it. Then he carried it off to his secret lair under the sideboard.

Drew merely shook his head. "I suppose I'll go telephone Birdsong now, seeing Chambers is occupied."

"Good idea. I expect Mr. Padgett is waiting for me as it is. Shall I let Mrs. D know about the feather duster? I expect one of the girls will be wondering where it's gotten to by now."

"Yes, do that, Nick, and give old Padgett my best."

"Righto. Let me know what the chief inspector tells you, as well."

As soon as Nick had gone, Drew rang up Birdsong's office.

"You again, eh?" Birdsong grumbled when the desk sergeant put him through. "What is it now?"

"A bit of information you might well thank me for, I daresay."

"Oh, yes?"

"May well be nothing of course, but we had discussed the possibility of Miss Allen having a young man she was seeing before Montford."

"You mean Alfred Begbie from Ault Hucknall in Derbyshire?"

"Ah. You know about him already, do you?"

"We have our little ways, Detective Farthering." Birdsong's tone was smug. It always was when he knew something Drew didn't. "We've been at this a bit longer than you have, you know."

"Naturally, naturally. At any rate, Mr. Dennison and I—Nick Dennison, I mean—were discussing our little problem and wondering if this Alfred chappie might not have taken offense at seeing his girl taking up with someone else."

"You can forget that idea, sir. This Begbie was born in Ault Hucknall and, to hear him tell it, will die there. And in between, he'll stay there. He's a bit of a local character, my man found out. They claim he's not been more than five miles from the village green in all his life. His family has been farriers in Ault Hucknall since Cromwell's time and before, and he sees no reason to be anything or anywhere else. No doubt the whole village would come out for the spectacle were he ever to leave."

"Little wonder he wasn't pleased to have the object of his affection move to Hampshire."

"Indeed. According to the people there in the village, he had made some sort of agreement with her father and was quite put out when the old gentleman died and the girl refused to stay on with him."

"I suppose he could have hired the murder done if he felt strongly enough about it, couldn't he?" Drew asked.

"Might do," the chief inspector agreed, "but for one thing.

The constable who interviewed him says that, finding the young lady's personal conduct a bit lacking even before the recent publicity, he's washed his hands of her."

"The story's got as far as Ault Hucknall already?"

"I'm afraid so. Evidently he'd had rather a fixed idea about her since she left the village, determined yet that she'd come back to him, but this last has been the death of it."

"Ah, well, at least we know. Oh, one thing you don't know, Chief Inspector. The girl's staying at Mrs. Chapman's cottage for the time being. You remember the one."

"I'd hardly forget."

"We thought it was the ideal place, since you didn't seem too keen on her going to stay with her aunt."

"Why couldn't she just stay where she was?" Birdsong complained.

"For one thing, the reporters and gossipmongers wouldn't let her alone where she was. For another, she's been dismissed from her job and hasn't money enough to stay there now."

"I see. And so it's Detective Farthering to the rescue once again."

"It's little enough. And yes, I do know she's still a possible suspect."

"She is. But thank you for keeping us informed of her whereabouts. You might prove useful yet."

"We live in hope, Chief Inspector. We live in hope."

Once he had rung off, Drew wandered out of the study and back into the dining room, prepared for an in-depth review of the case with Mr. Chambers. Unfortunately he found the little beggar sprawled on his round belly, his head buried under the feather duster, obviously fast asleep.

"I suppose I'm on my own then, eh, Chambers old man?"

After a brief walk in the garden to clear his head, Drew returned to the study and sat down at the desk. He found a freshly sharpened pencil and a note pad and wrote SUSPECTS at the top in bold letters. Then he began listing names:

> *"Jack"*
> *Thos. Hodges (caddy)*
> *Margaret Allen*
> *Alfred Begbie*
> *Mrs. Montford*
> *Daniel Montford*
> *Roger Morris*
> *Delivery Boy (florist)*

He paused before adding one more:

> *Person/Persons Unknown*

He tapped his chin with the pencil and then, leaning back in his chair, caught sight of Mr. Chambers's mother, Minerva, sunning herself in the study window.

"Hullo, my lovely."

"Hello."

He smiled when he saw Madeline standing in the doorway. Holding a wide-brimmed hat, she looked fresh and breezy in her mint-green dress and crisp white gloves.

"Hullo, darling, and yes, you are quite lovely. I thought you and your aunt were off to London."

She came over to him and kissed his cheek. "Not quite yet. She has a letter she wants to put in the mail this morning, and she's not done with it."

"That important, eh? Telling the home folks what a monstrous place it is, this England?"

She giggled and sat on the edge of the desk, reading his list over his shoulder. "That last one is helpful."

He gave her a grin. "We can't ignore the possibility that the actual killer is someone we haven't yet thought of. Unhelpful as the designation is, it wouldn't do to confine our theories only to the people I've already listed."

"I suppose not. But what have you come up with so far?"

"Well, we have the mysterious 'Jack.' Is he actually a suspect or just a motive?"

She frowned. "Does he even exist?"

Drew shrugged. "Hodges seems a rather unlikely choice at this point, though it is possible that he carried off an elaborate scheme where he pretended to be called away, disguised himself, and returned to the club to kill Dr. Corneau."

"That seems a little farfetched even for an Agatha Christie novel."

"I'm afraid so." He smiled when she slipped her hand into his. "Besides, in addition to having been seen in Inverness and on the train there and back, he had no motive for Corneau's murder, much less Montford's or Clarice's."

Once again, she peered at his list. "Margaret Allen doesn't seem like the type to kill anyone."

"That's neither here nor there at this stage of the game. The question is, might she have. She certainly had motive."

There was pity in Madeline's eyes. "I feel so bad for her."

He squeezed the hand he still held. "So do I, darling. It's not a pretty story, is it?"

She only sighed, and he went on.

"Begbie seems out of the running, mostly because of the distance between Hampshire and Derbyshire."

She nodded. "He might have a motive for making away with Mr. Montford, but I don't see any connection between him and Dr. Corneau or Clarice. Same with Mrs. Montford or her son."

"Right," Drew said. "She's a bit like Miss Allen, I think. Not the murdering type."

Madeline gave him a sly little smile.

"And not just because she's a woman." He shook his index finger at her. "And don't be smug."

"All right, but I think I agree with you anyway about her. I'm not as sure about Daniel." There was sympathy in her expression as she looked at the list once again. "What about Roger Morris?"

Drew sighed. "Poor Rog. I can't imagine him having the nerve to kill anyone. And it seems that, along with everyone else on the list, he might have motive for one murder, but not all three. Yet clearly the three murders are connected."

She frowned, thinking. "The delivery boy for the florist?"

"The boy who delivered the flowers," Drew corrected. "We don't know he was actually connected to any florist at all."

Drew wrote a note on the pad: *Find out if the Empire knows which shop sent the flowers.*

"Anything else come to mind, Madeline?"

"I'm afraid not. Sorry."

"Very well, we'll try a different route."

He slashed his pencil across the middle of the page, dividing top from bottom. At the top of the lower half, he wrote *Messages.*

"What do we have so far?"

"The first one," she said. "Mr. Montford. 'Advice to Jack.'"

He wrote it down.

MONTFORD: Advice to Jack. "First thing, kill all the lawyers."

"Montford was a lawyer," Drew observed. "Were the others killed because of their professions?"

She could only shrug. "What about the second one? The doctor?"

He added to his list.

CORNEAU: *Kentish wisdom would have him paid so.*

"I'm a bit stumped on this one." He wrinkled his forehead. "Jack Cade who wanted to kill all the lawyers was from Kent."

"What about other references to Kent in Shakespeare?" she asked. "Or to doctors?"

"Do the other notes necessarily refer to Shakespeare? Perhaps 'Kentish wisdom' is a reference to something completely different. Kentish folkways or something."

She shook her head. "You'd know much more about that than I would."

He tapped his pencil against his chin once more and then added the third murder to his list.

DESCHNER: *Mismatched, hot-tempered, simply waiting for greatness to be humbled, she, but for the scandal, might have been queen of them all.*

"What is or was mismatched?" Madeline asked, picking up the note pad. "That necktie?"

"It certainly didn't go with that dress she was planning to wear." He chuckled and then considered the words of the note. "What greatness is or was to be humbled? And why wait? For what?"

"And what was the scandal?" Madeline added. "Are you sure Roger couldn't tell you anything about that?"

Drew could only shake his head. "And of whom might she have been queen?"

"Drew, if this has something to do with people being murdered over their careers, what was Clarice's?"

"Still haven't a clue on that one, darling."

Drew frowned at the page and then added something to the list of suspects: *Clarice's lover(?)* And under his note about the florist, he added: *Ask Rog who Clarice might have been seeing. Have police interviewed her family, if any?*

Madeline tilted her head to one side, thinking. "Didn't Roger know any of her—"

"Madeline! Come on, the morning's wasting!"

Madeline grinned sheepishly, hearing her aunt's voice. "—family?"

"Not that I heard of." Drew stood and gave her a quick kiss. "Now hurry along. We don't want any international incidents."

"But Drew—"

"I promise I'll tell you all of my brilliant deductions once you come back. Now chop-chop."

She gave him a pout and then another kiss. "Behave yourself while I'm gone."

"I always behave." He gave her a cheeky grin. "In one fashion or another."

She giggled and hurried off. He took a moment to jot down notes about what he and Madeline had discussed, and then he considered how he might best spend the rest of the morning. He could pop up to Winchester, talk to Birdsong and visit Roger to see who his mystery rival may have been. Or he could pull out his volume of Shakespeare's plays and see what references to Kent he might find. Or references, perhaps, to humbled greatness and scandals.

Smiling to see Mr. Chambers still sprawled out under his pilfered feather duster, he went over to Minerva again. She favored him with a slow blink of her green eyes.

"You must speak to your little boy," he told her as he stroked her velvet ears. "He's taken to petty theft, and it will be the ruin of him if he's not taught to mend his ways."

She merely closed her eyes and stretched out her tabby-striped legs, purring.

"Yes, I know," he soothed. "He hasn't any father about to set him straight."

The thought of fathers brought Daniel Montford to Drew's mind, and he went back to the desk. Inheritances were often motive for murder, but was Daniel the sort to carry out something like that? He certainly seemed overly upset by the idea of anyone looking into his father's death. Surely there was more to that than a desire to protect his mother.

What about his mother? She certainly seemed the epitome of gentle womanliness, but her husband had betrayed her trust and his vows to her. Was there a murderess beneath that soft exterior?

Drew shook his head, not liking that possibility. Still, he rummaged in his pocket for the telephone number to the Montford home. It wasn't long before he was being shown into Mrs. Montford's dainty sitting room.

"Mr. Farthering, how nice of you to come. Do sit down. May I ring for tea?"

"Thank you, Mrs. Montford, but I really must come straight to the point. I want you to tell me about Daniel."

"Daniel?"

"The day your husband was murdered, where was Daniel?"

"I told the police already. He was in his bedroom. He had some sort of paper he had to write for his literature class. Why do you ask?"

Drew took the chair she had offered and sat for a moment studying her face. She'd already lost her husband. He couldn't blame her for wanting to protect her son. Even so, there was nothing for it now but the absolute truth.

"Is there any possibility, any possibility at all, that he may have left his room sometime during that day?"

"Left it? No. Why would he have left it? He was there all day. He told me he was."

"But do you know for certain?"

"I wasn't in there with him, no, but I never saw him leave. Why? What's happened?"

"Nothing's happened, not for certain. It's just that Daniel is roughly the sort of fellow we think might have killed your husband and the others."

Mrs. Montford's dark eyes filled with tears, and she sat shaking her head, her full lips trembling. "No," she whispered. "No, no."

"I know this must be very difficult for you, but I must ask. What were relations like between him and your husband? Did they, as a rule, get along well?"

"Have you told the police your suspicions?"

"Not actually suspicions at this point. I wanted to talk to you first."

She blinked away her tears. "You can't think he's responsible. Not Daniel."

"Were relations between him and his father . . . difficult?"

She looked down at her soft, white hands. "He would never kill anyone. He couldn't."

"Did he and Mr. Montford quarrel?"

"Oh, Mr. Farthering." She looked up, smiling pitifully. "Don't all fathers and sons have their differences? Daniel loved his father, and Quint doted on him. Of course, a young man learning to make his way in the world doesn't always agree with what's laid out for him. Surely, it was no different with you and your own father."

Drew smiled a little. "My father died when I was twelve. I never really had the chance to get past the hero-worship stage."

"Daniel . . ." She closed her eyes, and a tear slipped down her cheek. "Daniel wanted part of the money his grandmother left for him in trust. Quint wouldn't allow it. He was to have been trustee until Daniel reached twenty-five. They had been rowing over it for weeks."

"What did he want the money for?"

"I don't know. He'd only say the money was his and he should have at least some of it."

"Tell me what you did when the police told you Mr. Montford had been killed."

"I . . . I couldn't believe it. I suppose I just sat here, where I am now, for a long time. Then I thought I'd better tell Daniel."

"Where was he then?"

"I went up to his room, but when I didn't find him there, I rang for Meadows, our butler. He said he'd just seen Daniel in the kitchen and sent him up to me."

"Does Daniel usually spend his time with the staff?"

She pressed her lips together and shook her head.

"Did he say why he was there that day?"

She dabbed her eyes with her handkerchief. "I didn't even think about it. How could I when I'd just been told my husband had been murdered?"

"Did you ever ask about it later?"

"No. I still don't think it means anything. So he was in the kitchen. What harm could that be?"

"Who else was there when he was?"

"I don't know. Cook, I suppose. The scullery maid. Whoever else is usually there."

He stood up. "May I have your permission to ask Meadows and Cook myself?"

"I suppose," she said after a moment's hesitation. "If you like. I'll ring for Meadows."

"Actually, if you don't think it too irregular of me, I'd much rather go down to the kitchen. Alone, if you don't mind."

She lifted her chin, and her eyes were firmly on his. "What is it you don't want me to know?"

"Mrs. Montford, I assure you—"

"Mr. Farthering, my husband has been murdered. There's scarcely anything I could hear that would be worse, unless it's that my only child is the one who killed him."

"We don't by any means know that."

"But you think it. Why else would you be asking?"

What a wretched little mess in which to be mired. "To be perfectly honest, I hope I can rule him out. Wouldn't you want to know positively?"

She closed her eyes and seemed to sink into herself a little bit. Then she nodded. "If you go out this door and turn to your left and then, at the end of the hallway, go through the door and down the stairs, you'll find the kitchen on your right. If Meadows isn't down there, have Cook send for him."

"Thank you."

When he saw that she was not going to speak or even look at him again, he made a slight bow and turned to go.

"Before I forget, ma'am, I have a message for you."

She lifted her eyes. "A message?"

"From the, uh, young woman in question. She very much wants you to know that your husband had no feelings for her whatsoever. It's quite important to her that you understand that."

Mrs. Montford gave him a triumphant little smile and said no more.

— Eleven —

adge, sir. Madge Wheaton."

Drew smiled at the sturdy little woman, glad to know she had an actual name. Something besides Cook. She could have been anywhere from fifty to seventy, judging by her round, shiny red face and the single strand of iron-gray hair that had escaped her cap and the severe knot at the back of her head. Her beefy arms and gnarled hands told of years of toil, but her jet-black eyes were merry for all that.

"And you've been here with the Montfords how long?"

"More than fifteen years, sir. Mr. Daniel hadn't even begun school, as I remember, and now look at the lamb. Oh, will you sit down, sir, beg pardon for not asking sooner? And will you have some tea?"

"Thank you. That would be very nice."

She began bustling about with the kettle and cups while he sat down at a table dominated by a huge bowl of well-scrubbed carrots and another of peeled potatoes ready for the pot. Like everything else in the kitchen, they were immaculate and appetizing, and he couldn't help just a touch of covetousness for whatever she would be serving at supper that night. The simmering smells were already making him salivate.

"Lemon or cream, sir?"

"Honey, if you have it."

That made her grin, a great showing of near-toothless gums. "Oh, lumme, sir, that's how my own father always took it. And Mum claimed it made him the sweetest man in all Christendom."

He gave her a smile in return. "I'll have to tell that to my young lady. Perhaps it will convince her there's hope for me after all."

"Oh, do, sir." She brought him a porcelain cup painted with violets and filled with strong tea. "She might well do worse in this bad world."

He nodded. "You don't know how many times I've told her just that."

She brought some shortbread on a plate that was of a set with the cup. "I made this for Mr. Daniel, but I don't reckon he'll mind if you have a bit. Fresh today."

"Oh, lovely. I suppose he must be a great favorite of yours, Mr. Daniel."

She grinned again. "I've cooked for a few houses in my time, and I can tell you plain, sir, I can't say as all of them was pleasant places, but this was never anything but. And, God love him, Mr. Daniel was always a joy to have round, laughing and playing in the kitchen garden and then coming in begging sweets and all."

Drew took a bite of the shortbread. "Very good."

"Thank you, sir."

"So, does he still? Beg sweets?"

"No, not so much these days. I suppose he feels as he must be a grown-up gentleman now and put the childish things back of himself. Of course, I send something up to his room now and again. He likes that, I know."

"But he doesn't usually come down?"

"Not often. Not anymore. Just now and again." She picked up a bowl that contained some sort of batter and started stirring. "You don't mind if I carry on, sir? I do have the supper to prepare."

"By all means."

He pulled out a chair for her, and she dropped down into it with a grateful sigh. "My feet do sometimes give me trouble. It's the standing that does it, day in and day out."

"I can see how it would. So Mr. Daniel doesn't come to the kitchen much? Do you remember when the last time was that he did?"

She leaned her spoon against the edge of the bowl, and the twinkle left her eyes. "I do. It was the day Mr. Montford was killed. I was making currant buns for tea, sitting just here and stirring, like I am now, and Mr. Daniel came in behind me."

"And you had your back to the door, as you do now."

"I did. He near scared me to death."

"Which door did he come in by?"

"The same one you did, I reckon, but I didn't see him come in."

"So he might have come in from the garden, and you wouldn't have known the difference."

"No, sir, I suppose I wouldn't have. Though I don't see how that signifies." She looked into her bowl, considering. "He could have been in the garden. I have to say he doesn't much go out there anymore, either. Not since he was a little fellow and kept rabbits."

"What did he want that day?"

"Bless him, he'd been up in his room doing his studies and wanted something to tide him over until tea. I told him tea wasn't that far off, but he wheedled some cake from me before time. You were a boy once, sir, and not too very long ago, I'd wager. You know how hard it is keeping the young ones filled up. Then Mr. Meadows came in to fetch him about his father."

"What did Meadows say to him? Did he tell him his father was dead?"

"Oh, no, sir. Just said the missus wanted him to come up to her sitting room. That was all he said, and that's what Mr. Daniel did. Us belowstairs didn't hear what had happened to Mr. Montford until after."

"I see. And where can I find Meadows now? Mrs. Montford is a bit upset at the moment, but she said you'd know where to find him."

"I'll just go and fetch him for you, sir." She set the bowl on the table and began to struggle to her feet, but Drew stopped her and stood up himself.

"Don't trouble yourself. If you'll just direct me to where he is, I'll see to things from there."

"I believe he's up in the master's bedroom with Mr. Carstairs, he was the master's valet. They're packing up his clothes. The missus, she didn't want him to at first, but now she's resigned to it, poor lady." She took up the bowl and then set it down again. "There's not something wrong, is there, sir?"

"Nothing to worry over. Just sorting a few things out."

"You did say you weren't with the police?"

"That's right. I'm just making some inquiries. You must have heard that Mr. Montford was not the only one killed as he was. We'll all sleep better for finding out who's been doing these murders and why, don't you think?"

She gave him a nod and a weak smile.

"Now, if you'll just direct me to Mr. Montford's bedroom . . ."

"Madam said you wished to speak to me, sir."

Drew smiled at the portly man standing in the doorway.

"Ah, you must be Mr. Meadows."

"Yes, sir. May I help in any way?"

Drew sat down again and gestured toward the chair on the opposite side of the table. After a brief hesitation, the butler also sat.

"Mrs. Wheaton and I were just talking about when Mr. Montford was killed. Do you remember much about that day?"

"Certainly, sir. It's not a day that we in this house are likely to forget."

"Tell me what happened when Mrs. Montford found out about her husband."

"Two gentlemen from the police came to tell her and then left. She rang for me from Mr. Daniel's room all in a state. I called for Lily, her maid, and got her to go lie down for a bit until I could find him."

"And did you find him?"

"He was down here, sir, eating cake and talking to Cook. I sent him straight up to his mother."

"Do you know where he'd been before that?"

"No, sir. His own man, Pole, looks after Mr. Daniel as a rule, so I don't generally know what his schedule is unless it affects the household. Mrs. Montford had given me to understand that he was in his room studying that day."

"I see. And did you happen to see him or speak to him at all? Before you came to fetch him, I mean."

"No, sir. As I said, I didn't generally—"

"I thought I told you to stay out of things."

Drew turned to see Daniel Montford in the doorway that led out to the garden, eyes blazing and hands balled into fists. It wasn't a pleasant way to begin a conversation.

Drew stood up once again. "Your mother was gracious enough to allow me to speak to the staff for a moment. I hope it hasn't caused you any inconvenience."

"Inconvenience?" Daniel cursed at him. "I told you if you didn't leave us alone, I'd kill you."

Mrs. Wheaton leaped to her feet, quivering and wadding her apron in her hands. "Mr. Daniel, Mr. Daniel . . ."

"No cause for alarm. I've finished." Drew winked at her and picked up his hat. "If you'll excuse me, Mr. Montford, I'll see myself out."

Daniel stepped back, ostensibly to let him pass through to the garden, but just as Drew stepped onto the narrow brick path, the young man stopped him. Drew turned, glanced at the hand on his arm, and gave Montford a cool smile. "This is such a pleasant garden. We wouldn't want to have it mussed up, now, would we?"

"For the last time, Farthering, leave us alone and keep your nose out of our business."

Still smiling, Drew shrugged free of his grasp and put on his hat. "Please say farewell for me to your mother."

Montford raised his fist and then found the motion of his arm abruptly halted.

"That would be ill-advised, young man."

"Ah, Chief Inspector Birdsong, and you've brought along a London officer." Drew's smile broadened. "Who says the police are never available when needed?"

"We came to have a chat with young Mr. Montford here."

Montford jerked his wrist out of Birdsong's hand with another curse, and the chief inspector shook his head in reproof.

"Temper, temper."

"This man is trespassing." Montford's voice was petulant, and Drew wouldn't have been surprised to see him stamp his foot. "I want him removed immediately."

"Oh, dear. Is that right, Mr. Farthering? Have you entered private property without invitation?"

"Merely a misunderstanding, Chief Inspector." Drew removed his hat once again. "I'm sure Mr. Montford here was unaware that I was asked in by the charming lady of the house."

Montford's face grew red. "He's been annoying my mother ever since my father was killed, and I want you lot to do something about it. I'll file a complaint if need be."

"Daniel!" Mrs. Montford squeezed through past a distraught Mrs. Wheaton and took her son's arm. "Daniel, this has got to stop this instant."

"Good afternoon, madam." Birdsong removed his rumpled hat, then nudged the plainclothesman with him who then removed his own.

Mrs. Montford managed a gracious nod. "I'm so sorry, Inspector. As you can imagine, things have been quite difficult since my husband passed away."

"Yes, madam, I can understand that."

Daniel Montford drew himself up stiffly. "Mother, I want you to go into the house. I'll see to this."

"No, Daniel, I want *you* to go into the house."

"Mother, I—"

"I'm afraid I can't allow that just at the moment, madam." Birdsong cleared his throat. "Mr. Montford, I'll have to ask you to come along with us now."

Daniel made a squawk of protest, and his mother clung more tightly to his arm.

"Why?" she demanded. "Are you arresting him?"

"Don't upset yourself, madam. We only want to ask him a few questions. Making sure we have all our facts in proper order."

"Couldn't you do that here?"

"This way is best. We'll be able to sort everything out without any distractions."

Mrs. Montford lifted her chin. "Do you have some new development about my husband's murder?"

"Your son was seen in Winchester that day. He was seen at lunchtime at a restaurant round the corner from the Empire Hotel, just before Mr. Montford was killed. And a cabman remembers later picking him up at the corner of Jewry and St. George's, driving him about and then taking him back to the train station."

Birdsong drew the young man away from his mother.

Daniel could only shake his head, his eyes wide and frantic. "It's not what you think. Mother, you can't let them do this. I haven't done anything wrong."

"You told me you were in your room. You said you were there all day." Mrs. Montford started trembling, and Drew caught her elbow to steady her.

"Please, come inside, ma'am," Drew murmured. "The chief inspector will see to things."

She drew herself up straighter and patted her face with the lace handkerchief from her sleeve. "No, I'm all right. Daniel, you go with them and tell them everything. Whatever it is, you tell them." She caught his hand, pulled him close and kissed his cheek, then stepped back. "Go along now."

"If you have a family solicitor, madam, you may wish to send him round to the station."

She gave the chief inspector an almost imperceptible nod. "Thank you, I will."

By then the sergeant had the boy halfway down the walk, and with one more pleading look at his mother, Daniel disappeared around the side of the house.

Birdsong cleared his throat. "Very sorry to have upset you, madam. We hope to have an explanation for everything and your son back to you as quickly as is possible."

Staring into the empty air where her son had been, she again nodded.

Birdsong put his hat back on and then touched the brim of it. "Good afternoon, madam. Mr. Farthering."

"Come inside, madam," Mrs. Wheaton blubbered once the chief inspector had gone. "Come inside and sit down."

"That's a fine idea," Drew said, taking the lady's elbow again and guiding her toward the kitchen door. But before they reached it, she stopped and looked up at him, her brown eyes welling with tears.

"Mrs. Montford, if there's anything I can—"

Her palm cracked across his mouth, surprising in its force, and then she wilted against him.

"I'm sorry. I'm sorry. I'm sorry."

The words tumbled out of her unchecked, barely audible. Then she pushed away from him and groped blindly toward the door and Mrs. Wheaton.

"Oh, madam . . ."

Supporting each other, the two women went inside.

"Will there be anything else, sir?" Meadows asked Drew, maintaining a professional air.

Drew smiled faintly as he wiped the back of his hand across his stinging lips. "Just tell Mrs. Montford that I'm going to go see Mr. Russ and, hopefully, take him to the chief inspector's office. I doubt they'll let me in on the questioning, but I'll do what I can to find out what's happening with Daniel. As soon as I know something, I'll ring up or come by."

Meadows bowed. "Thank you, sir. I'm sure Mrs. Montford would want to know."

Drew put on his hat. "I surely hope so."

— Twelve —

Charles Russ stopped at the door to the interrogation room and turned to Drew. "Would you like to come in with me? When Mrs. Montford rang me up to ask me to represent her son, she said you were acting on her behalf and were to have whatever cooperation I could give."

"I don't suppose she mentioned that Daniel and I haven't exactly hit it off."

"She did, as a matter of fact." Russ smiled, and his thin, mustached face lost a bit of its hawkishness. "Never you mind that. I was in partnership with his father long enough to know young Daniel can be a bit of a hothead, but I can handle him. His father spoke highly of you, you know, and I wouldn't mind having an extra set of eyes and ears in on our side."

"I was thinking I'd just wait for you and see what you found out, but I'd much rather hear it firsthand. But you're the solicitor. I'll just do my best not to antagonize anyone."

"Very good. Now we'll see what's what."

At Russ's knock, a man in a dark suit opened the door and

showed them inside. Birdsong and Daniel Montford were seated at a large table, which was the only furniture in the small, grim room.

"Ah, Detective Farthering, come in." Birdsong indicated the man in the dark suit. "This is Sergeant McRae. I presume this is the solicitor we've been hearing so much about."

Russ shook Birdsong's hand. "I'm Charles Russ of Whyland, Montford, Clifton and Russ. I'll be representing Mr. Montford."

Daniel's eyes flashed. "I told them I didn't have to say anything unless you were present. And what's *he* doing here?"

Despite his glare, Drew merely nodded and sat down.

Russ sat down, as well. "Your mother wants him here, Daniel, and so do I. Do try and behave yourself. Now, Inspector, what are the exact charges against my client?"

"It's a bit premature for charges, Mr. Russ. As I told Mrs. Montford earlier this afternoon, we merely want to sort things out. No need for any unpleasantness, provided of course our questions are answered to our satisfaction."

"I see. And just what questions do you have in hand?"

Birdsong consulted his notes. "When we spoke to her after her husband was murdered, Mrs. Montford said her son hadn't left home the day of his father's death, and Daniel here confirmed that. Now we have evidence that he was just round the corner from the scene of the murder, and that's before *and* after the established time of death, and we'd like to know why he didn't mention that to us in the first place."

Daniel shook his head. "I told you—"

But Russ quickly lifted his hand to silence him. "How reliable is your evidence, Inspector? Perhaps your witness saw someone who only looked like Mr. Montford here."

"He was identified by a waiter at Le Jardin d'Idylle Restaurant at half past twelve that day, and by a cab driver at the corner of Jewry and St. George's Street at a little after two. The driver claims he seemed agitated at the time. It's rather unlikely that both would be mistaken. So, Mr. Montford, I would like to ask you again. Where were you on the afternoon of your father's murder?"

Sneering at the inspector, Daniel remained silent.

"Young man," Birdsong said, raising his voice a little, "if you don't give us a reasonable explanation for why you were seen near the Empire Hotel that day, we'll have no alternative but to assume you don't have one."

"All right, Inspector. You want to know why I was seen there that day? I was seen there because that's where I was."

"And what were you doing there?"

"I was eating lunch, and then I was riding in a taxicab, neither of which is against the law."

"Were you alone?"

"I presume your network of spies has already answered that one for you."

"I'd rather you told me yourself."

"Very well, I wasn't alone. There was an entire restaurant full of people and later there was the cabman."

The sergeant huffed his impatience, while Birdsong let out a sigh.

"How about we save the clever talk for your university friends, shall we, Mr. Montford? Were you in the company of someone in particular that afternoon?"

Daniel folded his arms across his chest and said nothing.

"Do you know a tall, slender young lady with dark hair?" Birdsong persisted. "Perhaps wearing a navy-colored jacket?"

Drew struggled to keep his face blank. A tall, slender young lady with dark hair? Surely not. Not the father *and* the son. He kept his eyes on Daniel, searching for clues in the younger man's haughty face, but Daniel merely stared at the peeling gray paint on the wall. Russ fixed his attention on the papers he'd brought with him, though there was a keenness now in his expression.

Birdsong glanced over at the notes the sergeant had taken so far, stroked his mustache contemplatively, and then looked at the solicitor. "You may wish to advise your client to reconsider, Mr. Russ. If he refuses to cooperate, I will have no choice but to charge him with the murder of his father and place him under arrest."

"I would like to speak to Mr. Montford in private, if I may, Inspector. I can hardly be of use to anyone until I've gotten sufficient information."

"Very well. We don't seem to be making much progress as we are." Birdsong stood. "Come along, McRae."

The two members of the constabulary made their departure, and then Drew nodded toward the door.

"Shall I . . . ?"

Daniel's eyes flashed. "Yes."

"No. Do stay here, Mr. Farthering." Russ laid his hand on his client's arm. "Daniel, I want you to tell me about that afternoon. I don't care if you were stealing the crown jewels or setting fire to St. Paul's, I want the truth, every bit of it, and I shall absolutely know if you're lying to me."

Daniel ducked his head, pouting. "I didn't kill my father. I didn't kill anyone. Isn't that enough?"

"Then tell us why you were near the hotel that day."

Daniel hesitated and then leaned closer and lowered his voice. "You want to know why I was there? I'll tell you. Why I was there is none of your business."

Drew held back an incredulous smile. The little blighter was working himself into the hangman's noose, yet he couldn't see it.

Russ looked the prisoner up and down, an air of almost disdain in his expression. He took out a cigarette, lit it, and leaned back in his chair. "Your mother will want to know how you are. What shall I tell her?"

Daniel's lower lip quivered, but he only shrugged.

"I mean, what shall I tell her apart from the fact that you've been charged with your father's murder and won't cooperate with the police or with me. Of course, we could get you another solicitor, if you like, though if you're determined not to answer questions with honesty, I don't see the use of that."

Again Daniel shrugged. "Do as you please. I tell you I didn't kill my father, and that's all anyone need know."

"Very well." Russ took another drag of his cigarette and then smiled at Drew. "Sorry, Mr. Farthering. I suppose you'll have to tell Mrs. Montford you couldn't be of much help, either. The chief inspector will be pleased to know he can close this case without much trouble."

Drew nodded. "I daresay he will be. It's rather amazing how quickly they can push these things through with the right suspect. Of course, there are the guilty ones, but they always have some ready excuse, don't they? On those, it seems to take forever to get a conviction. But the others, the ones where a fellow was put in a tough spot because whatever would alibi him for the murder he's charged with would ruin someone else? Can't but feel bad for a chap like that." He looked at the prisoner, who was staring at the floor with a tautness in his body that belied his show of disinterest.

"Quite right." Russ tapped the ash from the end of his

cigarette. "A gentleman never mentions his peccadillos in public, especially if there's a lady involved. But it's a bit extreme, isn't it, to go to the noose for a woman's reputation?"

"Rather, but I expect, at least in some of these cases, the woman's name need never come out." Drew glanced at Daniel once again. "Tell me, Mr. Russ, if the inspector were satisfied with the alibi, he needn't bring charges at all, isn't that right?"

"Oh, yes, certainly."

"And, I expect, if such a chap were to tell his solicitor, in absolute confidence, of course—"

"Oh, of course."

"Then that solicitor could advise him on whether it might not be worth his while to make a clean breast of it with the chief inspector." Drew smiled. "If there were such a case."

"Ah, well." Russ stood and picked up his hat. "No use talking hypotheticals at this point, Mr. Farthering. I suppose we ought to be going along to Mrs. Montford's."

Drew nodded and stood, as well. "I hate to tell her we've come a cropper on this whole thing already, but there it is." He put on his hat. "Anything you'd like us to have your mother send on to you, Mr. Montford?"

"All right. All right." Daniel glared at him, his eyes red-rimmed and his chin trembling. "You two don't have to go on being so terribly clever. I'll tell you, Mr. Russ. But I swear, if a word of this gets out, I'll kill you both."

Drew sat back down, removed his hat, and refrained from mentioning that one's claim to be innocent of murder was not likely to be supported by repeated threats against the lives of those hoping to prove that innocence. Daniel Montford had enough to worry over at present.

Russ took his seat again and faced his client. "Just tell me,

Daniel, what you did that day. Whatever it was, at least then we'll know how to proceed."

"It was rum luck, that's all. I didn't know my father would be there at the hotel, especially not that one in particular. I expected he'd be in London, as he always was on weekdays, if not in court then at the office working."

"Rather a coincidence," Drew observed.

"I didn't kill him!" Daniel slammed his fist against the worn, laminated tabletop. He then drew himself up straight in his chair and wiped his face on his sleeve, abruptly calm. "He was my father. I didn't kill him."

"All right then." Russ's voice was low and soothing. "Tell us what happened."

"I went to have lunch with my . . . with someone. We went to the French place there on the street just the other side of the Empire Hotel, and afterwards I took a cab ride in the countryside and then back to the train station. It's nothing more than that."

Russ nodded. "And who were you with?"

"What difference does it make? It's the truth."

"Then you won't mind if we contact this person to see if the story can be corroborated."

Daniel shook his head. "You can't do that."

Russ waited for him to continue, and finally Daniel smiled, a bitter smile.

"Very well. It was a woman. A married woman. I suppose it's nothing different from what you see every day in your practice."

Russ sighed. "Did you usually meet this woman in the afternoon?"

"While her husband was at his office generally. When I was supposed to be in class."

"Did you generally meet in public?"

"Sometimes. Not in London, of course, because we might be seen. But we did sometimes meet in Winchester or Canterbury or anyplace where she wouldn't be known. It was all a lark, taking the trains down and all, pretending to be strangers again and again."

"Any particular reason you wanted to meet at a restaurant this time?"

"I didn't want her to make a scene." Daniel fidgeted in his chair. "I suppose I thought she'd control herself in public."

"Did you have reason to believe she wouldn't otherwise?"

Drew could see Daniel struggling with the question, how best to respond to it. He could see too that Russ, competent solicitor that he was, already knew the answer.

"Daniel?" Russ prompted.

"I had decided to break off with her. I reckoned she would be upset, and I knew she couldn't afford to make a scene. Not with me there and her husband elsewhere."

"I see. And why had you decided to break off with her?"

"My father." Daniel started to laugh. "My father had found out about her. He told me it wasn't right, that marriage was a sacred bond that should never be broken. And I believed him." He laughed again, laughed until the laughter turned into deep, painful sobs. "I believed him, and he was the greatest liar and hypocrite ever born."

Drew waited until he'd calmed himself a bit and then said, "Your mother doesn't think there's anything to what this Allen girl says."

"Mother." Daniel laughed again, low and half hysterically. "Dear mother."

Russ blew twin streams of cigarette smoke from his nose. "Let's keep on the subject at hand, shall we? The Allen girl is of no importance at the moment. How did your father find out about this woman you were seeing?"

"I had been asking him for money, some of the money my gran left me. I'm not supposed to have it for another four years, but I knew he could have approved some withdrawals if he'd wanted to."

Russ nodded. "But he didn't want to."

"No. He said he'd have to know what it was for and it would have to be a pretty good cause, as well. I told him I couldn't tell him, and he asked me straight out if it was for a girl. He wanted to know if I'd gotten someone in trouble, but I told him it was nothing like that. Still, he kept at me until I told him. That's when he went on about marriage and honor. And to be honest, I thought he was grand about it at the time. He didn't scold me or try to shame me. He just told me to consider what I knew of right and wrong and said he hoped I would think it best to ask God's forgiveness and end things with the woman." Daniel's eyes filled with tears, but he ignored them. "And that's what I did. I suppose I'd known it was wrong from the beginning. But I guess he knew about that well enough himself."

For a moment, there was only silence in the little gray room, and then Russ cleared his throat. "What else did you do that day?"

"That was all. I told her I couldn't see her again, I wished her well, and I went home."

"How did she take the news?" Drew asked.

"She shrugged. She said it'd been fun and all, but she'd already realized that the thing had run its course. She said I hadn't been her first and I wouldn't be her last." Daniel shook his head. "And I'd been afraid I'd break her heart."

"And the ride in the country?" Drew asked.

Daniel shrugged. "I wanted to clear my head before I went home. Mother would have known I was upset. It doesn't matter what happened with me and the girl. I have my mother to think of now. It's bad enough that she's had to carry the shame of what my father did. I won't have her hearing that I'm no better, do you understand? If you tell her this, I'll deny everything." Daniel managed to look smug again. "She'll believe me, too. She always has."

Russ lit another cigarette. "The problem is, can we get the police to believe you?"

Drew leaned forward in his chair. "Tell me, Mr. Montford, what did you do after the cab took you to the station?"

"Took the train back to London, of course, and another cab after that."

"And what did you do after it let you off at home?"

"It didn't. I mean, not right at home. I didn't want my mother to know I'd been out, so I had the driver let me out at the corner. Then I came round through the garden and into the kitchen. Cook hadn't seen me come in, and I acted as though I'd just come downstairs for something to eat."

At least that much tallied with what Cook and Meadows had said. More and more, it was looking as if Daniel's presence at that particular time and in that particular place was no more than a hideous coincidence.

"How did you get out in the first place?"

"Oh, that." Daniel smirked. "That's never been much of a problem. I simply waited for my chance, went down the hall to the bathroom and out the window. The roof is nearly flat under that window, and it's easy to walk from there round to the trellis at the back of the house. Once I was down that, it was simple to go through the garden to the next street over and get a taxi to the train station. I've done it a hundred times before."

"And when did you first hear that your father was dead?"

The smirk left Daniel's face, replaced by anger and bitterness laced with grief. "Just a few minutes after I'd gotten back. I couldn't believe it. I thought it had to be a joke. A mistake. Something besides what it was. Then we found out about the . . . the girl he was seeing. He'd just gotten through telling me I should do the right thing, be a man of honor, not lower myself to a tawdry affair, and here he was carrying on with some vulgar working-class chit who wouldn't know a Shakespeare couplet from a Guinness advert." He closed his eyes, his mouth working helplessly. "It made me sick. Just sick."

"Did you talk to your mother about it?"

Russ's voice was professional, detached, and he didn't look at his client.

"Not really, no. I don't think she was even going to tell me, but I made her. I knew there was something she was keeping back. I suppose she didn't want me disillusioned about him. About what he claimed to believe. About God. I mean, what sort of God lets himself be claimed by so many failures and hypocrites?"

"A merciful one." Drew looked steadily into Daniel's scornful eyes. "If He judged us, any of us, as we deserve, who would He have left? You?"

There was a touch of gentle humor in that last question, though this time Daniel looked far too weary to reply.

Russ cleared his throat. "Well, theological questions aside, I'm afraid we have more practical matters to deal with at present."

Drew smiled. "Right you are, Mr. Russ. To the business at hand."

"Thank you. Now, Daniel, as your solicitor, here's my advice to you. Tell all this to the chief inspector immediately. He'll want the woman's name and address and any other information you have about her. I'm certain he'll agree to keep all of that confidential, unless, for some reason, your story cannot be corroborated. If you're telling the whole truth, I don't see why it need come out in court or why you should have any sort of charges brought against you at all. To my knowledge, there's no statute against foolishness on the books, so you should be safe from prosecution."

Daniel took hold of Russ's sleeve, leaning toward him. "You've got to swear to me that my mother won't ever hear about this. Not ever."

"I can't make any guarantees, young man, but I see no reason it should ever have to be told, either in public or to Mrs. Montford. However, if you don't tell the police about this, you'll very likely be tried, convicted, and executed for your father's murder. Which do you think your mother would rather have? A son disgraced and repentant or one hanged?"

Daniel's grip tightened, and then, letting his breath out in a rush, he released Russ's sleeve and sprawled back in his chair. "Get the inspector. I'll tell him everything."

"Excellent."

Russ knocked on the door, and the officer outside opened it.

"Go and get Chief Inspector Birdsong, please. My client would like to speak to him."

"I'm sorry, sir, but I can't leave my post. If you like, you can go down to my chief's office and speak to him there. It's all the way to the end of this hallway, then left and left again and just at the very back. The name Edgerton is on the door."

Russ frowned, glanced back at Drew and Daniel, thanked the

officer, and disappeared down the corridor. The officer shut the door once more and locked it.

Drew studied the prisoner for a moment longer. "So, tell me, Daniel, who do you think is doing these killings?"

"I tell you, I don't know. I still think that girl killed my father."

"The one who doesn't know Shakespeare from Guinness?"

"Yes, that Allen girl."

"Why do you say that about her? I mean, why Shakespeare in particular?"

Daniel scowled. "Why not Shakespeare? It's not something a shopgirl is likely to know very well, that's all. I could have said Byron or Ovid for all the difference it would make."

"Yes, I suppose. But would she have killed the others?"

Daniel's scowl turned into a sulky shrug. "Could have. Perhaps she's one of those who can't stop after the first murder."

"Interesting theory. How do you suppose the Shakespeare comes into it?"

"How should I know how the blasted Shakespeare comes into it? Perhaps she has some sort of monomania."

Drew smiled faintly, watching the prisoner's eyes. "Could be. Could be. Funny about the killer using Shakespeare, though. Not everybody has a taste for it, do they?"

Daniel snorted. "I never did. I couldn't wait to get through that in school, all that nancy talk. If he wanted to say it was morning, he should have just said it was morning. Not that rot about day standing jocund on the misty mountaintops."

Drew chuckled. "'Jocund day stands tiptoe on the misty mountaintops,' I believe is the line."

"That's even worse. Though I imagine the ladies like it. I know my mother gets all weepy over *Romeo and Juliet* and the rest of that mush."

"A lot of women are that way. I suppose she pushes it on you all the time."

"Not really. When I was younger, she tried to get me interested, and of course they do drown one in it at school. I guess it's all right and that, but not something I'd sit about reading as she does."

"Does she have a favorite?" Drew asked.

"Oh, the ones you'd expect," Daniel said. "*Romeo and Juliet, As You Like It*, the romantic ones. She doesn't like the historical ones so much, but I always thought some of those were rather keen."

"Even with the nancy talk?"

"Some of it." A flicker of a smile passed over Daniel's face, and then it vanished and he glared at the locked door. "Where's Mr. Russ got to? I want out of this foul place."

"These things take time, I expect. You might have saved yourself all this trouble if you'd told the police everything from the start."

Drew waited for a sharp retort, but it didn't come. Evidently it took a great deal of energy and concentration to keep up the level of ill-temper that Daniel had so far displayed, and at this point he could only sigh.

"I don't know what's what anymore."

"It may not be so grim as it seems, old man. Let's see what Mr. Russ can manage for you, eh?"

Daniel ducked his head. "I'm sorry, you know."

"Sorry?"

"Sorry I've been such a wretch about all this. About you."

Drew shrugged. "Don't let it worry you. I know you've had a rather rotten time of it lately." He paused until Daniel was forced to look up at him. "I understand more than you realize about what's happened to you, and I *am* on your side here."

Daniel dropped his head into his hands. "I just didn't want Mother to be hurt. I mean more than she is already, you know?"

"I know. And it's admirable of you, no doubt."

He looked up again, his dark eyes pleading. "If they . . . if they don't let me out of here, she'll need someone to look after her. There really is no one else, no one to speak of on her side of the family, and she trusts you. If they—"

"I'll see she's all right, Daniel, but first we've got to see to you here."

As he'd agreed, Daniel told the chief inspector everything. He gave a detailed account of his movements on the day his father was murdered, provided the name and address of the woman he'd been seeing, and even gave credible-sounding alibis for the other hatpin murders. After cautioning the young man to stay close to home until further notice, Birdsong told them all to clear off.

Afterward, Russ was good enough to drive them back to the Montford home. Daniel returned to his mother's grateful, waiting arms while Drew and the solicitor parted friends.

— Thirteen —

Once he'd returned to Farthering Place, Drew hardly had time to dress for dinner. As much as he would've liked to have foregone formal dress and instead taken something cold at Mrs. D's kitchen table with only Madeline for company, he knew Aunt Ruth would take that as scandalous proof of his barbarism.

Once the meal was over, he waited until Aunt Ruth had left the dining room, and then he grinned at Nick and Madeline. "I thought the three of us would never have a moment to talk privately." He caught Madeline's hand under the tablecloth and linked his fingers in hers. "Did you and Auntie have a good time today?"

"Yes. I really thought she'd be tired after we spent all day shopping, but she doesn't seem to be. I'm sure she's gone to read or crochet or something now." Madeline squeezed his hand. "Miss me?"

"Horribly. And I've been desperate to tell you and Nick what

I found out today, but I couldn't say in front of your aunt. She thinks I'm rather morbid already."

Madeline frowned, though there was a twinkle in her eyes. "You said you wouldn't do any sleuthing without me."

"You promised me, too." Nick leaned back in his chair, tipping it on two legs. "Bad form, if you ask me."

Drew took a sip of his coffee. "I didn't promise either of you. Not really. Now, do you or do you not want to hear what I found out?" He then proceeded to tell them about the interview with Daniel Montford.

"What did you think about Mr. Russ?" Nick asked afterward.

Drew shrugged. "Didn't think much about him at all, I suppose. Why?"

"I don't know," Nick said. "I suppose they worked together for a long time."

"Has anybody asked him about Mr. Montford and whether or not he might be seeing someone outside his marriage?" Madeline gave them both a knowing look. "You men always say women gossip, and we all know you're the worst."

Drew laughed. "It's a scandalous lie, I'm sure it must be."

Madeline only smirked at him. "And what else have you accomplished today? Have you figured out any of those messages yet?"

"If indeed the first one was a reference to Shakespeare's Jack Cade and killing all the lawyers," Nick observed, "it seems as though the others ought to be related."

Madeline nodded. "It does."

Drew looked into his almost empty coffee cup, considering. "First I thought that, being a Kentish man, the next note, the one about Kentish wisdom, might well refer to Cade, as well. But bless me if I didn't read *Henry the Sixth, Part Two*, right through last night and found nothing that seemed to fit. I checked the other histories too and found only brief mentions of Kent and men of Kent, still nothing to suit the message and the victim. Not as the first one did Montford."

"Maybe it doesn't mean Kent the place," Madeline said.

"But what else . . . ?" Nick began.

Drew stood and hurried into the library. Nick and Madeline were immediately after him.

"Drew," Madeline said, clutching his arm.

"Wait just a minute. I think I am divinely inspired." He gave her a kiss on the cheek. "By you, my angel."

He flipped through the large volume of Shakespeare's works he'd left on the desk the night before, searching for a particular play and a list of *dramatis personae*.

"There. *King Lear*." He paused, waiting for her and Nick to make the connection, but Madeline shook her head.

"I don't—"

"Kent, my darling. Not Kent the county, but Kent the earl."

Madeline digested that for a moment and again shook her head. "But what wisdom?"

Nick only looked at her and then Drew. "He never ordered anyone's death in the play, did he?"

"Not ordered, per se." Drew smiled. "But remember what he said when Lear would have killed him for giving him good counsel? For his *Kentish wisdom*?" He turned to the appropriate page. "If Lear was determined to send away those who would do him good and reward those who meant him ill, Kent told him to go ahead. 'Kill thy physician and the fee bestow upon the foul disease.'"

"Physician." Now the understanding came into Madeline's eyes. "Dr. Corneau. Just like first killing all the lawyers for Mr. Montford."

"But what about Clarice?" Nick asked.

"I haven't quite worked that one out yet," Drew admitted.

"Besides, what does it really mean?" Madeline looked up at him with an intensity in her eyes. "If these men were killed because they happened to have certain professions, it still doesn't explain why. What does the murderer expect to gain from it?"

"That we shall have to find out." Drew took both of her hands and stepped back, drawing her with him. "Until then, it's far too fine a night and we've been far too long apart for us to talk nothing but murder and mayhem."

Nick made a slight bow. "I believe that is my cue to claim fatigue and excuse myself."

Drew beamed at him. "Definitely a brilliant deduction on your part. You don't mind, do you, Nick?"

"Not in the least. I'll try to keep the little gray cells humming, though. I'll let you know if I think of anything." Nick nodded at Madeline. "Good night."

"Good night, Nick."

"Good night, old man," Drew called after him.

Once Nick had left, Drew led Madeline out onto the terrace. It was a warm night, and the moon was only a sliver above them. He could hardly see her face in the darkness, but what he couldn't see, he could imagine. He could picture that touch of mischief and the hint of a dare that was no doubt in her eyes.

"Isn't it pretty out here?" She released his hand and leaned on the stone railing. "All the tiny lights from the village look almost the same as the stars, twinkling in the distance."

"Too bad the stars aren't so short a walk away. I'd take you to one and shower you with stardust." He slipped his arms around her, and she leaned back, relaxing against him.

Closing his eyes, he pressed his cheek to her hair. "You're very wicked, you know."

He nuzzled the back of her ear, and she laughed softly.

"Am I?"

"Being so beautiful." Her dress was satin, soft and smooth, tantalizing his fingers as they stroked the curve of her waist. "Making me want to forget I'm a gentleman."

She tilted her head to one side, and he traced his lips down the side of her neck. "When are you going to marry me, darling?" he murmured, his voice low and urgent, and he could feel a shiver go through her.

"Now," she breathed, and then she laughed and pulled away from him. "Or never. I'm not sure."

The air shuddered out of his lungs, and he shook his head, laughing softly. "You do devil a man past all patience."

She leaned back against the wall, a mischievous, provocative gleam in her eye.

"Madeline Felicity Parker!"

Madeline straightened immediately, and even in the near darkness, Drew could see the color that had flamed into her face.

"Aunt Ruth. I . . . we . . ."

"Don't try to explain. I've got eyes, you know." Aunt Ruth got up from the chair in the opposite corner of the terrace. "And ears."

"But we were just—"

"I won't say a thing, young lady, except that with this behavior you're choosing yourself a steep and thorny path."

"I didn't—"

The older woman held up her hand. "No. I have nothing else to say." With the aid of her cane she thumped back into the house.

"Poor darling." Drew put his arm around Madeline. "Well, it could have been worse."

He couldn't tell if the shaking in her shoulders was from laughter or crying. Perhaps both.

"It could?"

"She could have overheard us on the way back from Bunny's party last month."

Her eyes flashed. "She didn't overhear us. She was eavesdropping. Why does she have to always make me feel as though I'm still fourteen years old?"

"Now, be fair. She was out here first."

"Well, she could have said something so we'd know."

"I'll grant you that, but she's only trying to look after you, to protect you from the cad who's had dark designs upon you since the moment he met you."

He was glad to hear a faint giggle coming from her. "You've been a perfect gentleman."

"Yes, dash it all."

She laughed again and put her arms around him, smiling up into his eyes. "It's one of the things I love best about you. I never have to worry about you taking advantage."

"Because I love you even more than I want you, and that, my darling, is a prodigious amount."

She buried her face against his chest. "Oh, Drew, I know you do. And I love how patient you're being with me." She looked up once more, smiling again despite the glimmer of a tear in her eye. "And with Aunt Ruth, too."

He cupped her face in both hands and touched his forehead to hers. "You know, we ought to be grateful for the old pepper pot. Despite one's best intentions, it's easy to get a bit, uh, carried away from time to time. And nothing cools the ardor like a word or two from your dear auntie."

There was a decorous cough from the doorway, and they both laughed.

"Or Denny." Drew released Madeline and turned around. "Yes?"

"Pardon me, sir, but you have a telephone call. Shall I say you are engaged?"

Drew winked at Madeline. "I hope to soon be."

The butler's impassive expression did not change.

"Oh, all right, Denny, yes, I'll take the call. Perhaps you'd best go make up with Auntie, darling. I'll join you both in a moment."

Drew went into the study and picked up the telephone. "Hullo?"

"Is this Mr. Farthering?"

It was a woman's voice, brisk and businesslike, vaguely familiar but not one he recognized right away. "Yes, it is. Who's speaking, please?"

"I don't know if you'll remember me, Mr. Farthering. Oh, dear, I don't know if I should be calling at all, but I just had to say something to someone."

"Mrs. . . . ?"

"Forgive me. This is Amelia Burroughs. I was Dr. Corneau's nurse. At his surgery. You were with the police when they interviewed me and our receptionist the day the doctor was murdered. You said I might call you anytime."

"Of course. Mrs. Burroughs. How can I help?"

"Well, to be perfectly honest, I'm not sure you can. I most likely should have rung up that Inspector Birdsong about this, but I feel so foolish, not being certain and all. I thought perhaps you could tell me if you thought it was important."

"Certainly, if I can. What is it?"

"That . . . that girl, the one in the newspaper today. They

said she was the mistress of the first man who was murdered. Mr. Montford."

"Yes?"

"Well, I'm not absolutely sure, but she may have been one of our patients."

"Oh, yes?"

"I just don't know. She looks quite like a young woman who came to us in June. It's so difficult to tell just from the photograph they printed, but I think she must be the one."

"Could you look her up in your records?"

"That's just the problem. If it was this girl, she didn't use the name Allen, I know that much."

"I see. Do you know the name she did use?"

"Johnson. Mrs. Mary Johnson."

"Not exactly original. If I might ask, why did she come to see the doctor?"

"I'm really not supposed to divulge any information about our patients, you understand, but if she's in some way connected to the doctor's murder . . . Oh, dear. What should I do?"

"I can understand the delicacy of the situation, to be sure, but you may trust in my discretion absolutely. And if you don't feel you can confide in me, I most certainly think you should discuss this with the chief inspector. There may be nothing in it, but then again, it may be just the link we've been searching for."

He could hear her quavering intake of breath over the telephone.

"You'll give me your word as a gentleman not to mention this except as it pertains to the investigation?"

"By all means and upon my honor."

"This girl, Mrs. Johnson, she said she had been feeling ill. Nauseated and tired. She thought she had a virus of some kind.

The doctor examined her, of course, and found that she had fallen pregnant."

"Hardly a surprise in your experience, I suppose."

"No. We saw girls like that more than I'd like to admit. And most all of them with men who wouldn't do the decent thing by them, leaving them nowhere else to turn. This girl wasn't any different. The doctor was always kind to them, you know, and asked if the baby's father was going to be pleased with the news. I know he was trying to make sure she and the baby would be cared for."

"What did she say?"

"She about took his head off, I can tell you. She said, and quite emphatically, that her *husband* would be delighted with the news, and she made an appointment to come back in a month."

"And did she?"

"No. I knew she wouldn't. They never do. Probably went to some back-street butcher to take care of things, if you know what I mean."

He knew, and the thought sickened him. "That wasn't the sort of thing Dr. Corneau did, then? Not on the side?"

"No! No, I'm sure it wasn't. It was only me and a girl at reception in the office, as it was. I'm sure I would have known."

"Yes, I understand."

"The doctor, well, he just wasn't that way. He always told the girls there were couples who wanted desperately to have children and couldn't, couples who would take their babies and give them a good life."

"And was the good doctor paid rather nicely by these desperate couples?"

"They paid him, yes." Her voice was taut. "They paid him for the care the girls received."

"Did he go through the usual channels with these adoptions?"

She hesitated. "I don't know what you mean."

"They were legal, weren't they? All the paper work done? Carried out through the proper agencies and all that?"

She didn't reply.

"Mrs. Burroughs? Shall I take that as a no?"

"You don't understand. He'd been helping people long before the government decided to get involved. And some of these people couldn't go through the agencies. They were too old or they hadn't money enough or there was some other petty reason they'd been turned down for adopting a baby. Dr. Corneau wanted to help them as well as the girls. But I don't think he would have ever grown rich on the money. He was only doing what he felt was right, helping those who didn't think they had a way out."

"Please forgive me. No doubt you're right, Mrs. Burroughs. I'm just trying to think of who might have a motive to murder him."

He could hear her weary sigh through the telephone. "I don't know. He'd helped so many people, I can't think that anyone would bear him any ill will. But I tell you, I'm almost sure it's the same girl, that Allen girl and our Mrs. Johnson. We do see a great many patients, of course. I suppose it could be no more than coincidence."

"Possibly, but I appreciate the information nonetheless. We'll certainly look into it."

"Thank you." Again she hesitated. "Please don't think harshly of Dr. Corneau. I suppose what he was doing wasn't legal in the strictest sense, but he was trying to help as many people as he could with as little fuss as possible. I don't see how that could be so very wrong."

"Perhaps not."

"I won't be . . ."

Drew waited, but there was only silence from the other end of the line.

"You won't be what, Mrs. Burroughs?"

"I didn't have anything to do with those adoptions, but I did know about them. I'm not going to be in any trouble, am I? With the police, I mean."

"I really don't know."

Drew wished he could have been of more comfort to the woman, but the law could be a capricious mistress, and there was precious little knowing whether it would look with a tolerant eye upon such a tangled issue. Adoptions had only recently become so official and complicated.

"Oh, dear, I shouldn't have said anything. Please, Mr. Farthering—"

"You needn't worry on my account. Unless it turns out to be connected to the murders, I shan't mention this to the authorities. But now the doctor is gone, I shouldn't keep in that particular line of work if I were you."

"No. Certainly. Thank you."

"Thank *you*, Mrs. Burroughs. And try not to worry yourself too much. No doubt the doctor meant well."

— Fourteen —

Drew rung off and stood there for a moment staring at the telephone, his head swimming with the possible implications of what Mrs. Burroughs had just told him.

"Drew?"

He turned to see Madeline standing in the study's doorway, and he went swiftly to her.

"That was the nurse from Dr. Corneau's surgery. Seems there was more to the doctor than we knew."

He told her what Mrs. Burroughs had said.

"Suppose this is the connection. Montford's mistress went to Dr. Corneau because she was expecting a child. Clarice Deschner had implied she was seeing someone besides Roger Morris. Could she have been, too?"

The color came into Madeline's cheeks. "You don't suppose Roger, um . . . ?"

"I have no idea just how intimate she and Roger might have been, though poor Rog was obviously smitten with her. But whether such a child was his or someone else's, if there was such a child, Clarice hardly seemed the type to settle happily into marriage and motherhood."

"No, it doesn't seem that she was. Oh, Drew, what a tangled mess it all is."

"I know, darling. But it will all be sorted out in time, never you fear."

There was a telltale thumping in the hallway, and then Aunt Ruth appeared in the door. "Speaking of time, it's time I retired for the night. I've had enough for one evening. Madeline, I suppose I can expect you back at the cottage no later than ten. That's a quarter of an hour from now."

"All right, Aunt Ruth."

"And you, young man, see that she's not a minute later. No funny business."

"I will do my very best, Miss Jansen, I assure you. Shall I escort you there now?"

"No, no. It's not far, and I don't need any fuss." She fixed Madeline with a piercing gaze. "Ten."

"Yes, ma'am."

Aunt Ruth went out through the French doors and vanished into the darkness. Madeline merely stood there as if there were yet something to see.

Drew took her hand. "What's the matter?"

"I don't know. I'm just jumpy tonight. I wish you had this all solved and we could just enjoy our time together. As it is, I always feel as if something else is going to happen." She peered out into the night again. "I don't like her going down to the cottage alone."

He smiled and pulled her into his arms. "Do you want me to go after her? I don't mind in the slightest."

"Would you? I'd really feel better if you would."

He released her with a kiss. "Won't be a moment."

It was a fine night outside, even if there was very little moon. Auntie ought to have taken a torch with her. No use having her stumble in the darkness and no doubt blaming the entire English race for it.

As he approached the curve in the path, he could hear muffled noises from the other side of the bushes, and he broke into a quick canter. As he rounded the corner, he saw Aunt Ruth's low bulk entangled with another dark shadow at the cottage steps.

"Good heavens!"

He sprinted toward the struggling figures, but the taller of the two broke away.

Aunt Ruth swung her cane. "You come back, you scoundrel!"

There was a solid thump as the stick made contact with the intruder's backside, knocking him to all fours on the gravel path, but he was quick and scrambled up again. Aunt Ruth swung again, catching him a glancing blow on the arm that didn't slow his escape. Before she could strike a third time, he wrenched the cane from her hands and tossed it into the bushes. Then he wriggled into the thicket of trees alongside the cottage and disappeared into the dense wood.

Pursuit was clearly futile, and poor Aunt Ruth was still on the ground, huffing and wheezing, unable to gain her footing and her dignity without the aid of her cane.

Drew knelt beside her. "Are you hurt, ma'am?"

"Just get me up. Where's my cane? Why don't you go after him?"

"He's taken to his heels, I'm afraid. I think it's much more urgent to get you inside."

With a sufficient amount of decorum and no small amount of embarrassment on both sides, Drew managed to haul Aunt Ruth to her feet.

"Just lean on me, ma'am, and we'll have you put right before you know it."

She did lean on him, rather heavily in point of fact, and clung tightly to his arm, but she did not let anything like fear show in her face.

"Where's my cane?"

"Let's just get you inside and then I'll come back and find it for you. The main thing is to have you safe and settled. Afterwards I'll ring up the police."

Aunt Ruth snorted. "The police? Your little bunch of Keystone Cops? You call up Scotland Yard and do it now. The audacity of the man, knocking me down like that."

"Yes, to be sure. You can tell me all about it once you're inside."

"And for goodness' sake, find out what happened to my cane."

He wanted to go inside and make sure there were no other surprises awaiting them, but the woman was so insistent, he settled for switching on a light and sitting her down in the straight-backed chair by the door.

The light from the house made it easier for him to locate the cane. Avoiding the prickly holly leaves as he went on hands and knees to retrieve it was a different matter entirely. Still, anything to placate dear Auntie.

A few minor scratches later, he had the cane in hand. "Found it!"

He scrambled to his feet and turned toward the cottage and saw Aunt Ruth clinging to the doorframe, sagging almost to her knees, her face gray as ash.

"Please," she breathed. "Young man."

"Miss Jansen!"

He rushed to her side.

"What's wrong?" He took her arm, helping her up again. "Come back inside and sit down."

"No, no." The old woman pulled away from him. "You've got to do something. There's someone in the kitchen."

"An intruder?"

"No. He's dead. Oh, he's dead."

"Who's dead? Do you know who it is?"

"I'm just not sure. I . . ." She looked up at him, her eyes pleading. "I think it's that boy from California. Mr. Bell. He's lying on the floor in there. His face . . . he's . . ." Her voice choked down in her throat, and she swayed on her feet. "Oh, where's my cane?"

Drew didn't know how he dared it, but he pressed the cane into her hands and then put his arms around her, letting her sob against his chest.

"Don't think about it just now," he soothed. "I'll take you up to Madeline, and she'll see you're all right."

She made some sort of grumbling protest into the thickness of his coat, but he didn't heed it. Instead he held her there for a few moments and then finally coaxed her into turning toward the house.

Abruptly she pulled away from him and started rummaging in the pocket of her dress for her handkerchief.

"I can walk." She blotted her face and set her mouth into a determined line. "You'd better figure out what's going on here, and do it quickly before we're all murdered."

"I mean to do just that," Drew said, taking her arm. "*After* we get you safely into the house."

Madeline was standing at the French doors when they came up the walk.

"What happened? Are you all right?"

Between the two of them, Drew and Madeline got Aunt Ruth to the sofa.

219

The old woman waved one hand. "Don't mind me. I've lived my life. If I were murdered, it would be no great loss."

"Murdered?" Madeline sat on the sofa and put her arm around her aunt's shoulders. "Drew, what's going on?"

"It looks as if someone's dead down at the cottage." Drew rang for Dennison. "I've got to get the police over here."

"At our cottage?"

"I'm afraid so, darling. Your aunt thinks it may be your friend Bell."

"Freddie? Oh, Drew, no. It can't be. He was just—"

"I haven't looked yet. Evidently it just happened. Your aunt surprised someone coming from the cottage and nearly caught him, too."

"Oh, Aunt Ruth, you didn't. Are you all right?"

"What kind of a country is this with people being killed all the time? She blotted her forehead again with her handkerchief. "I won't stay in that place another night."

Denny appeared in the doorway. "You rang for me, sir?"

"Oh, Denny. Good. Look here, ring up the police in the village, please, and tell them there's a dead body down at Rose Cottage. Then you'd better give old Birdsong a shout, as well. I'm going down there to see what's what."

Denny inclined his head slightly, just as he would have done if Drew had asked him to arrange for tea. "Very good, sir."

"And you'd best have Dr. Wallace out. To see to Miss Jansen and take a look at the body and all that."

Aunt Ruth snorted. "I do not need a doctor."

"Very good, sir," Denny said.

"Oh, and please see if Nick would care to call round at the cottage with me."

"At once, sir."

Madeline's eyes were wide. "Drew, you can't go down there alone."

"I'm not. I'm taking Nick."

"I mean the two of you can't go down there alone. You don't know who might be waiting for you."

"I think this is a perfect occasion for airing that little Webley revolver from your uncle's desk."

"No, Drew." Madeline stood and took his hands. "I don't want you to go out there. Let the inspector take care of it this time."

"Now, don't you worry, darling. The police will be here in no time, and I'll have the gun. Besides, we saw the killer leave. He'll be miles gone by the time we get there."

She clasped his hands more tightly. "I don't like it. I don't like it at all. All these killings. When it was just in Winchester, it wasn't so terrible. I mean, things like that happen from time to time. But this one is close. It's too close. It's like it was when Uncle Mason was killed. Poor Freddie . . ."

Drew held her close to him. "We're just going to take a look to see what happened, and then we'll nip right back up to the house. You'll hardly know we're gone. Besides, your aunt needs you to look after her, so you'll scarcely have time for Nick and me."

Aunt Ruth rolled her eyes. "Humph."

"Be right back."

Drew went into the study, unlocked the bottom drawer on the right side of the desk, and took out the gun his stepfather had brought back from the Great War. It would be good to have this little bit of reassurance within easy reach.

He hurried back to the library just as Nick came into the room, electric torch and golf club in hand.

"The Webley, eh? I guess I won't be needing this then."

Drew nodded. "Best leave it behind, old man."

"I suppose so." Nick looked fondly at the club before leaning it against the fireplace. "Anyway, I'd hate to spoil my Double K mashie having to bash someone over the head with it. What's this Dad says about there being some unpleasantness at the cottage?"

"Miss Jansen had a bit of a run-in with an intruder, an intruder who's left a body behind."

"Not one of the hatpin killings, is it?"

"I don't know. I haven't seen yet. She thinks it may be Freddie Bell."

"Really? That's too bad. I rather liked him."

Aunt Ruth thumped her cane on the floor. "Are you two going to stand around talking all night or are you going to find out what's happened?"

"At once, ma'am," Drew assured her, and then he turned to Madeline. "Now I absolutely forbid you to worry, darling." He touched his lips to her temple. "We'll be just fine."

She nodded and managed a small smile. "Do be careful."

"Don't do anything stupid, young man." Aunt Ruth thumped her cane on the floor once more. "Do you hear me?"

"Wouldn't dream of it, ma'am. All set, Nick?"

— Fifteen —

Drew and Nick were soon at the cottage. Light still flooded from the open front door, so Nick switched off the torch.

"This blighter you saw struggling with Miss Jansen, you say he took to his heels?"

"Yes. I shouldn't think he's back inside, but one can't be too careful."

They made a quick search of the cottage, but it was deserted. The only thing out of place was the body of Freddie Bell sprawled on the stone floor of the kitchen, his face black and distorted, hardly recognizable.

"Strangled."

Drew didn't touch anything but leaned down to read the message that was pinned into the man's flesh.

He was bound to molder before he was all grown up, the first fruit of his kind.

Nick got down on his haunches beside him. "Any ideas on this one?"

"None. Clearly the same killer. Same handwriting, same sort of hatpin, same maddeningly vague message."

The pin was brass with a large dragonfly on the end of it. Bits of colored glass sparkled in the wings. Drew leaned closer to peer at the pin, refraining from touching it. Then he studied the victim's neck.

"Garroted, it looks like. Whatever was used was flat, about an inch wide judging by the marks on the throat. No other marks on the body it seems."

Nick frowned. "Bell seemed a rather robust chap, didn't he?"

"Exactly. Even if someone surprised him from behind, I would think he'd about tear the room apart fighting him off." Drew looked at the cold, curled fingers of the corpse. "He ought to have skin and blood under his nails, bruises on his hands, marks where whatever was used to strangle him shifted in the struggle."

"Perhaps he was hit over the head first. Or drugged."

"Something like that would certainly do it. Then the murderer could strangle him with no complications, neat as you please."

They both stood again, and Drew scanned the kitchen for anything out of the ordinary. Everything was in its place except for two dirty teacups sitting in the sink.

"That's not like Miss Jansen, do you think?" Nick asked. "Leaving a mess when she was going out for the evening?"

"*Is* it like her, Detective Farthering?"

Both young men turned, and Nick immediately put his hands behind his back. "We haven't touched anything."

"Good evening, Chief Inspector," Drew said. "You're here quickly."

"I was at the Queen Bess actually, after spending the day at the Deschner girl's cottage," Birdsong explained. "Nothing like a pint and a game of draughts at the end of a long day."

"And here I was prepared to apologize for disturbing you at such a late hour."

"You should apologize. I was winning." Birdsong turned to the door. "All right, men, in here."

A pair of police constables came into the kitchen. One began photographing the crime scene while the other dusted for fingerprints. Birdsong squatted down beside the body.

"Now, Mr. Farthering, suppose you two tell me what's happened here. What's this about a mess?"

"We were just wondering why Mr. Bell didn't put up a struggle." Drew pointed out the clean mark on the victim's neck. "Looks like a strap of some kind, about an inch wide, strangled him, but it appears as though he just sat still and let it happen. Why?"

Birdsong nodded. "And your conclusion?"

"Knocked out with something. Coshed on the head, or perhaps drugged. And then we noticed the teacups there in the sink. Miss Jansen is an extremely tidy woman. I don't think she would have left the cottage or allowed Madeline to unless everything had been shipshape and Bristol fashion."

"So you think this bloke and the killer had a nice little tea party before he was made away with, is that it?"

"Seems logical. Anyone can slip someone a Mickey Finn under the guise of a friendly cup of tea. Just keep up the cheerful banter until the deed is done, eh?"

Birdsong pursed his lips. "Might be. Might be. Do you know the man?"

"I think so. He's awfully, um, changed at the moment, but it's this American chap Madeline's gotten to be friends with, Freddie Bell."

"American, eh? And how's he mixed into all this?"

Drew glanced at the note. "Sounds as if he meddled where he wasn't wanted."

Sourness came into the chief inspector's tone. "He wasn't helping you lot with your investigation, was he?"

"Certainly not."

"He seemed more interested in Miss Parker than the investigation," Nick put in, and Drew scowled at him.

"That right?" Birdsong's face took on that arch blandness it often showed when interrogating suspects. "And did that cause Mr. Farthering to become upset?"

Drew glared at Nick. "I didn't kill him, Inspector. Don't be ridiculous."

The inspector merely nodded. "So what was he meddling in?"

"It's the oddest thing. I had a bit of a do at Farthering Place last week, and Bell showed up at it. He claimed he'd been left a message at his hotel asking him to come. He seemed terribly embarrassed to find that I hadn't invited him."

"It wasn't the young lady who left the message?"

"No."

Birdsong considered for a moment. "Perhaps he just invited himself."

"I don't think so. He seemed a decent chap. For an American. He just didn't seem the sort. I mean, he was brash enough, to be sure. He once told me he'd jumped into some Hollywood actress's swimming pool. Uninvited, of course. But I think if that had been the case last week, he'd've laughed and owned up to it. Instead he looked genuinely shamefaced. Offered to remove himself at once."

"At which point you asked him to stay, no doubt."

Drew grinned. "*Noblesse oblige*, Inspector."

"What's that to do with him meddling?"

"There was also his hotel key. Madeline found it in her bag a couple of days ago. She hasn't a clue how it got there. Bell utterly denied knowing anything about it and said he was going to find out who put it there and who left him that message inviting him to Farthering Place. Maybe he turned up something someone wanted left alone."

"A bit strange, isn't it? I don't see how this fellow fits into the whole picture with the hatpin murderer."

"Neither do I."

Birdsong stroked his heavy mustache, thinking. "What you reckon this one means? The note."

Drew read the message over again. "'First fruit of his kind.' What kind?"

"American?" Nick offered.

Drew smirked. "Not if the killer holds true to form and this is another Shakespeare reference. The Declaration of Independence was a little after his time, don't you think?"

"Well, foreigner then. Or stranger."

"Possibly. What about 'He was bound to molder before he was all grown up'? Granted, he's not old by any means, but he's not a child either. Grown up into what?"

"Molder into what?" Nick added. "Of course, his body will molder once it's put into the ground, but that happens to everyone, not just foreigners. We'll all be rotten in time, grown up or not."

"Wait . . ." Drew squeezed his eyes shut. "I know this one. Rotten's the word. Rotten before he's half ripe."

He glanced at Birdsong and then at Nick, and Nick's eyes widened. "*As You Like It*."

"Exactly."

"What's this now?" the chief inspector demanded.

"It makes perfect sense," Drew said. "If I can remember it just right, it says, 'It will be the earliest fruit i' th' country; for you'll be rotten ere you be half ripe.'"

"'And that's the right virtue of the medlar.'" Nick finished the quote for him. "Medlar or meddler, there's little difference between the two."

"That's 'his kind,' a meddler, and the first fruit would be the earliest of course." Drew studied the body once more. "Bell said he fancied himself something of a sleuth. Now, if we just knew what he'd been meddling in."

The three of them turned at a tapping sound coming from the kitchen door. Dr. Wallace was there, bag in hand.

"They told me up at the house what's happened. May I come in?"

"We'd be most grateful, Doctor." Birdsong turned to the two constables who'd been working nearby. "You lads finished now?"

The one taking photographs nodded. "Yes, sir."

"All right then. Take a torch and see if there's anything outside that will help."

Drew looked at Nick. "I say, Inspector. I hadn't gotten to this part yet, but Miss Parker's aunt, Miss Jansen, had a row with someone coming out of the cottage. I've no doubt it was the murderer. She gave him a good thrashing with her cane, I daresay, but he made off into the wood there."

"You saw this?"

"I came up just as they were struggling. The blighter was off before I could get to him, and I didn't think I should leave the poor woman on her own in the dark like that."

"I suppose not. What did the man look like?"

"Neither of us got much of a look at him. He wore black all over, I know that much. Tallish."

"And when was this?"

"Right before I had Denny ring up. A bit before ten, I'd say."

The chief inspector made note of the time. "All right. I'll have the men make sure there's nothing disturbed until it's light enough to see. Doctor, if you'd like to examine the body . . ."

"Pretty obvious from what I can see without an autopsy." Dr. Wallace knelt down and turned the dead man's head to one side, examining the inch-wide red weal that ran around the neck. "Strangulation via ligature." He touched the face and hands and briefly pulled back one eyelid to look into the unresponsive eye. "Death no more than an hour ago. Probably less."

Birdsong nodded his agreement. "Any sign he was bludgeoned with anything?"

The doctor lifted the head of the corpse and made another brief examination. "Not that I can see. Obviously, he didn't struggle during the strangling." He checked the wrists. "He wasn't tied down."

"No. Could he have been drugged?"

"Certainly a possibility. I'll look into it when I get him on the table." Dr. Wallace got to his feet. "I'll have my assistants take him out now, Inspector, unless there's something else."

"No, no. You go ahead."

Drew stopped the doctor as he headed toward the door. "I say, when you were at the house, were you able to give Miss Jansen something? To calm her, I mean."

Wallace chuckled. "She'd have none of me, I'm afraid. Said she'd never been sick a day in her life and wasn't about to be letting foreigners tamper with her. I left some sleeping pills with the young lady in case she changes her mind, but she seemed right enough as she was."

"Sounds like the old girl, eh, Nick?"

Nick grinned. "It's a wonder she didn't take after you with that cane of hers, Doctor. From what Drew says, she was about one blow shy of catching our murderer."

"Too bad she didn't." The doctor's expression turned grim. "The killings are getting closer and closer together. We may well have one every day before long if this fellow's not caught."

No one said anything more. A moment later, Wallace's white-coated assistants came in with a stretcher.

Birdsong stood watching, arms crossed, as they lifted the body. "You'll let us know something as soon as possible, will you, Doctor?"

"Oh, to be sure."

"You may want to have your cameraman back in, Inspector." Drew pointed to the belt that had been coiled up under the body. A black-and-white harlequin leather belt just an inch wide. "I'd lay odds that's what finished him."

The doctor knelt down again, peering at the belt without touching it. "Most likely. Most likely."

"Go ahead and take the body out, Doctor." Birdsong hurried to the door ahead of the stretcher. "Here! Tompkins!"

Soon the constable with the camera came back into the cottage and photographed the belt where it lay. The other one checked it for fingerprints.

"Clean as Monday wash, Inspector."

Birdsong scowled. "All right. You and Tompkins get up to the house, see that things are secure there. I'll be along soon."

"Right, sir."

Once the constables were gone, Drew nodded toward the belt. "Might I have a look at it?"

Birdsong nodded. "By all means, whatever good it'll do."

Drew picked up the black-and-white strip of leather. "It's a woman's."

"Recognize it?"

"Can't say I do, Inspector, though it does put me in mind of that dress Miss Deschner was planning to wear the day she was killed. Roger Morris may well remember whether it was with the dress when they quarreled earlier that day."

"Could be."

Drew smiled a little. "Of course, you realize this lets old Roger out, don't you?"

"Could be, Mr. Farthering, but he still has some questions to answer to our satisfaction."

"Don't be a poor sport, Inspector. You never really thought he was guilty in the first place."

Birdsong shrugged. "We're duty-bound to question any suspicious characters. Now, if it's convenient, I should like to go with you up to the house and speak to your young lady's aunt. Miss Jansen, is it?"

"That's right," Drew said.

"I'd like to find out what she remembers about the man she saw."

"By all means."

Birdsong followed Drew and Nick back to Farthering Place, where they found the whole house ablaze with lights. Madeline and her aunt had stationed themselves in the library with Bobby and Mack, the gardener's men, posted outside the library window.

"I'm going to have the maid move our things into the house," Aunt Ruth announced. "I won't stay another night in that terrible cottage."

Madeline looked at Drew. "I told her you wouldn't mind. I hope it's all right . . ."

"Of course I don't mind. In fact, I'm glad you're both here. The chief inspector would like to have a word. You remember Miss Parker, Inspector."

"Certainly. Good evening, miss."

Madeline smiled thinly. "Good evening, Inspector. Thank you for coming. Drew . . ." She bit her lip. "Was it . . . was it Freddie?"

"I'm afraid so, darling."

"How did they . . . I mean, was he . . . ?"

"He was strangled with a belt. Perhaps the belt from Clarice Deschner's dress. I'm sorry, love."

She pressed her fingers to her lips, covering an almost inaudible cry, and he put his arm around her.

"The chief inspector and his men are going to find the man. It's going to be all right."

Drew gave her shoulders a squeeze and then showed Birdsong over to Aunt Ruth.

"Miss Jansen, this is Chief Inspector Birdsong. Inspector, Madeline's aunt from America."

"Good evening, madam." The chief inspector belatedly removed his hat. "I should like to question you about the incident this evening at the cottage."

Aunt Ruth did not offer him her hand. "I see. The chief inspector, eh? I assume you're the highest ranking policeman they could get this time of night."

"I'll try to inconvenience you as little as possible, madam."

"Well, sit down. Sit down." Aunt Ruth fluttered one hand over a nearby chair. "You won't find any of your class snobbery with us Americans."

With a glance at Drew, Birdsong complied. "Now, I can appreciate that this matter has upset you, madam, but if I may—"

"Pshaw. He wasn't but a weedy little fellow. Arms and legs like sticks."

"So he was thin?" Again Birdsong glanced at Drew. "Fits with the caddy at the golf course well enough, and the chap with the flowers. Anything else you remember about him, madam?"

Aunt Ruth continued, "He was all in black. He was tall, I think. Of course I couldn't see much in the darkness."

Birdsong jotted this down. "Did he say anything?"

"No. He came out the front door of the cottage, looking around like he wanted to make sure no one saw him."

"So he didn't see you right away?"

"I don't think so. He had his head down, sort of peeking around the corner, edging toward the trees. Then he saw me and tried to run for it. He stumbled on the steps or I would never have gotten close to him."

"I see, and he said nothing that whole time you were struggling with him? Not a grunt or a groan that might tell you something about his voice?"

Aunt Ruth shook her head. "As I already said, he didn't make a sound. He just got loose and ran off."

"Was that before or after Mr. Farthering arrived?"

"After, but just a few seconds after."

"And once he'd gone?"

"Mr. Farthering helped me up and took me to the cottage door."

"He didn't go inside with you?"

"No. The killer had thrown my cane into the bushes, and this young man went to find it for me. That was when I went into the kitchen and found the body." There was a little tremor in her lips and in her voice. "I . . . I made it back to the front door, and then he took me back to the house."

"Had you invited Mr. Bell to visit you at the cottage?"

"Absolutely not."

"What about you, miss?" Birdsong asked, turning to Madeline.

"No. I hadn't spoken to him since the day we had lunch with Mr. Llewellyn at the Queen Bess, and that was a while ago."

"You didn't go down to the cottage at all since you left to come up to the house for dinner?"

Madeline shook her head. "No, Inspector, I didn't."

The chief inspector paused, then looked back at Aunt Ruth. "I assume you didn't, either?"

"I did not."

"Did either of you tell anyone you'd be coming to dinner here tonight?"

"No," Madeline said, "but we always do. I assume everyone in Farthering St. John knows it by now."

Birdsong made a few more notes. "Miss Jansen, is there anything else you'd like to include in your statement?"

"Just that there is no excuse for your department to let something like this go on. I thought this was a civilized country. May as well have Capone's thugs running things. You write that down."

"I assure you, madam, every effort is being made to—"

"Obviously, it's not enough." Aunt Ruth looked at Drew, her lip curled. "And what kind of police department depends on amateurs to solve their cases for them? Don't you have enough men of your own? Or are they too busy sitting in public houses drinking all night?"

Drew gave the chief inspector a commiserating glance and then turned to Aunt Ruth. "I like to do what I can to help, naturally, ma'am, but as you say, I'm only an amateur. I have no doubt our chief inspector here has things well in hand. He'll have our killer run to ground in good time."

There was a determined pleasantness in Birdsong's mouth. "Anything else I should know, madam? About this evening's incident, I mean."

She shook her head. "Nothing but that I wish I'd given him a few more good whacks with my cane. I'm just sorry I can't tell you anything else."

"We appreciate your cooperation, madam," Birdsong said with a straight face. "If you should remember anything else about the incident, do let us know at once. Anything you'd like to add, Mr. Farthering?"

"I can't think of anything. Unfortunately, I didn't see much."

"Then I'll be on my way. We will keep you informed should there be any developments in the case." Birdsong replaced his hat. "Good evening, ladies. Gentlemen."

Once he had left, Madeline came to Drew's side and put her arm through his. "Thank you for letting us stay here in the house. We'll both feel much safer."

"It's the only sensible thing to do." He slipped his arm around her waist. "And I'll feel much better with you both here, as well."

"Don't think that will make it easier for any shenanigans you may have in mind." Aunt Ruth gave him a cool glare. "Madeline and I are sharing a room."

Drew took the older woman's hand and made a formal bow over it. "A most excellent idea, ma'am. It puts my mind totally at ease."

Evidently she could find no fault in what he said and so had to content herself with a disapproving sniff.

"Besides," he continued, "the police will want to keep everything just as it is down at the cottage until they've finished collecting evidence."

"Oh, poor Freddie. It's too terrible." Madeline shuddered, and he took her into his arms again.

"I know, darling, I know. We'll find the murderer, whoever he is. Don't you worry."

"How can I not worry?" Her periwinkle eyes flashed. "This murderer's getting closer and closer all the time."

"We'll find him. I swear to you, we will. Now, you take your aunt upstairs. She's been knocked about rather badly and ought to get some rest. You too."

Aunt Ruth stood up. "First sensible idea you've had since I've been here. Come, Madeline."

Madeline looked at Drew, uncertainty in her eyes, but he only turned her toward the door.

"Go along, darling. It's late. Everything will look better come morning." He kissed her forehead. "Sleep well, both of you."

"Good night, ladies," Nick called, and soon he and Drew were alone.

They stood for some minutes in thoughtful silence, and then Drew dropped into a wing chair. "It gets more confusing every day."

"Did you hear what she said?" Nick leaned against the mantelpiece. "Think about it. It started in Winchester, that's not five miles from here. Then the golf course, less than two miles away. Clarice's cottage is only down the road in the village, and this tonight was on your own grounds. Good heavens, how can you not see it?"

"You're not saying it's someone here at Farthering Place?"

"Oh, I don't know." Nick blew out his breath and raked his fingers through his sandy hair. "I'm not saying it's not, though I can't imagine anyone on the place being a murderer. But think about it. *Your* solicitor, then someone at *your* golf club, then a girl who's seeing one of *your* friends, then someone at *your* own cottage."

Drew laughed half under his breath. "You're not serious. You think someone is after me?"

"I'm not saying I know for certain, but what else makes sense?"

"But whatever for? And why not come straight for me without all the preliminaries?"

"Sort of a game, I suppose. 'Catch me if you can'?"

"But why me?"

"Perhaps whoever it is didn't like you putting Rushford behind bars."

"Nonsense. For one thing, I didn't do all that much. The police would have sorted him out in time, I expect. Besides, he hasn't any family. He hasn't money anymore to pay to have me seen to."

"What about Clarke? The police don't even know who he really was or much of anything about him. Who knows whom he may have left behind him? A grieving wife? A vengeful father or brother?"

"I didn't kill him or have him put away. I didn't even know he was in on it until he was already dead. If our killer's tied up with Clarke, he should be hounding Rushford, not me. I don't know that they allow that sort of thing at Dartmoor. Besides, the hangman will be ending any idea of revenge against our Mr. Rushford before much longer."

"Regardless, I wish you'd carry the Webley with you until this is all over."

"So do I."

Drew and Nick both turned at the soft voice behind them.

Drew smiled. "Madeline, darling, I didn't know you were there."

Her face was pale with that tinge of pink that meant she'd been crying. Drew went to her.

"What is it? Is your aunt all right?"

Madeline nodded. "She's running her bath."

"Come and sit down."

He led her to the sofa that faced the parlor fire and sat her down beside him. Immediately she curled up against him, her face pressed against his neck with one hand clasped in his lapel.

He nuzzled her sweet-smelling hair and made his voice low and soothing. "Everything will be all right."

At a look from Drew, Nick quietly vanished, closing the door behind him, leaving the couple alone in the quiet.

After a few moments, Madeline sat up. "I'm sorry, Drew." She helped herself to the handkerchief in his breast pocket and then smoothed her hair. "I know I shouldn't let all this get to me."

"Perfectly understandable, although you have nothing to fear. We *are* going to find him. Or them. Whoever is behind this, he can't go on much longer. Not with everyone after him." He paused and looked her in the eyes. "Not with me after him."

Madeline smiled. "I don't know what I was thinking. He doesn't have a chance, does he?"

"Of course not." He cuddled her close again. "And after I catch him, then Aunt Ruth will have to attest to my cleverness, and the chief inspector will have to admit that his department is helpless without me. And *you*, my darling, will have no choice but to fall even more hopelessly in love with me and beg me to marry you."

She laughed softly, and he felt some of the tenseness melt out of her. "Maybe I just will."

"There. You see? And we all live happily ever after."

"Not Freddie." She pressed more tightly against him. "Poor Freddie. Who would want to kill him? He doesn't even know anybody in the whole country."

"Right, and yet we still don't know who invited him to our dinner party the day Clarice Deschner was killed."

"You don't suppose that had anything to do with the murders, do you?"

"I don't know why our killer would have wanted him here that night. Clarice had been dead hours before the party."

"Maybe the invitation had to do with his own death, not hers." Madeline thought for a moment. "And you're sure none of your friends invited him? As a prank?"

"No one's owned up to it, at any rate. I suppose I could ask Bunny if he's heard any tattle about it. And I'll ring up Mrs. Burrish at the Queen Bess and see if she remembers anything about the person who left the message for Bell. Might be a clue there."

"I still don't understand why the killer would have wanted him at the party that night. Was the plan to kill him then and not now?"

Drew nodded. "And then there's the question of his room key. How did that get in your handbag without you knowing it?"

"You don't think I was lying about that, do you?"

"No, not at all. But someone wanted me to. Someone has been trying to put us at odds for some time now. Don't tell me you haven't noticed it, too?"

She bit her lip. "I . . . Oh, Drew, I just don't know. Why would anyone do such a thing?"

"You know why. I'm sorry, darling, and I don't want to be unpleasant, but you do know why. And you know who."

"You think it's Aunt Ruth trying to break us up."

"It's the only thing that makes sense. She wants you to go back to America. She's never liked me, obviously. She thinks I'm a menace to society in general and to you in particular. Perhaps she thought Bell would be enough to lure you away from me. At the very least she could make it look as though you were seeing him and lying to cover it up."

"And now he's dead."

She blinked rapidly, but not before he was aware of the tears in her eyes.

"You liked him, didn't you?"

"Yes. Yes, I did. I wasn't interested in him, you know that, but he was a nice man. He didn't deserve to die like that. None of these people deserved to die the way they did. They hadn't hurt anybody. But Freddie, he was just in the wrong place at the very worst time."

"I don't think he was at the cottage tonight by accident. He had seemed rather keen to know what was going on. With the key and the invitation and all. I wonder what all he found out. And who he talked to. No, tonight was no accidental encounter. Whoever murdered him lured him there. They drank tea together. The murderer knew you and your aunt were going to be out. It was well planned."

"But why?" She gnawed her lip. "Why would anyone want to kill him?"

"Don't forget the note. Clearly his inquiries into some of the recent goings-on were not met with approval."

"But if you think Aunt Ruth was the one who left his key in my bag or who invited him to the party . . ." Her eyes widened. "You can't possibly think she's involved in all this."

Drew couldn't suppress a laugh. "No! Good heavens, no."

"And if she was the one behind things with Freddie, who else would have had a reason to kill him?"

"Well, if she wasn't behind them, who else would be?"

Madeline dredged up a bit of a smile. "That Daphne Pomphrey-Hughes wouldn't mind much if you were available."

"Perhaps not, but actually implementing this sort of campaign is far above little Daphne's abilities. You may trust me absolutely on that. Besides, there may be someone who has his eye on you, you know."

She shrugged that off. "If there is, he's worshiping from afar."

"Perhaps he is. Perhaps he thought Bell was another rival for your affections and made away with him."

"I guess it's possible, however unlikely. Whatever the reason, someone was tampering with Freddie, and Freddie wanted to know who it was."

"Perhaps in trying to find out, he stumbled on to something else. Something the hatpin murderer would kill him over." He hesitated for a moment, weighing his words. "But be honest now. Do you think your aunt's been trying to get between us? Is it something she'd do?"

Madeline sighed. "I don't think so. As you might have noticed, she's more likely to make straightforward demands, and if those don't work she'll try to make you feel guilty."

"I must admit, I had wondered about just such tactics with her. I hadn't told you this, darling, but I asked Tessa where she found your purse that morning. It was in the armchair by the fire in the library, the one your aunt was sleeping in when I got back from seeing to Roger."

"Don't be silly. That doesn't mean anything at all and you know it. Nothing except . . ." She gasped. "Drew, if the key was put in my purse and left in that chair, do you think that means the murderer was here? In the house?"

"Might have been, but you can't take that as absolute proof. Bell said the key went missing the morning of the party."

"No," she corrected. "He said the last time he was sure he had it was that morning. We don't know that it wasn't taken from him while he was here. And we don't know it wasn't put into my purse during the party, either."

"Neither do we know that it was, darling. You and Auntie were in the village that day too, weren't you?"

Dejected, she let her breath out. "And in Winchester, just like Freddie. So it's no help at all."

"Not necessarily. I tell you what. Tomorrow, you and your aunt have a chat about everything you did that day, near as you both can remember, and write it all down for me. Then we can see where you and Freddie may have crossed paths."

"But we don't know everything Freddie did that day. I mean, he wouldn't have left a list or anything."

"No, but we can talk to people at all the places on your list, show round Freddie's picture, and see if they remember seeing him that day." He drew her head down to his shoulder and put both arms around her. "How would that be?"

"Do we have a picture of him?"

"I expect there's one in his passport. Perhaps the chief inspector will let us borrow it for a short while."

Madeline considered this. "Won't he want some of his men doing this kind of investigation?"

"That depends. If he thinks the invitation and the key have anything to do with the murders, he will. If he thinks Bell was merely trying to insinuate himself into an acquaintance with you, he'll likely decide they have better things to look into at the moment. Best to make up your list, and then we'll have a word with him. Fair enough?"

"I'll get Aunt Ruth to help me with it tomorrow. She won't like it, of course, but she'll help." Madeline sighed, and then her expression brightened. "She brought it with her, you know. The doll."

Drew chuckled. "Did she now."

"Most of her things are still at the cottage, but she made sure to bring that."

"Well, well."

Madeline's tone turned sober again. "I wish we could get all this investigating done and over with right now."

Drew cupped her face with one hand. "Right now, my love, you need to get some sleep. You'll remember everything that much better in the morning."

"I suppose you're right." She closed her eyes and leaned into him. "I just wish I could wake up in the morning and find all these terrible things hadn't happened."

He took her to her bedroom door, wishing he didn't have to leave her there, wishing she could stay with him that night and every night thereafter. But wishing wouldn't make it so. Until she was ready to make up her mind about marrying him, their nights would end this way.

"Sleep well." He kissed her soft lips, and she clung to him, saying nothing but clearly not ready to leave him.

As he held her, the memory of their first embrace came back to him, along with the rightness of how she felt in his arms that day as they stood in the meadow overlooking Farthering St. John. He'd known then that he loved her, known in a swift, wonderful, terrifying way, but it meant nothing if she didn't return that feeling. If she wasn't sure.

She murmured something against his shirt, and he lifted her face to him. "What was that, darling?"

She hesitated a moment, and then a hint of a smile passed over her face. "Thank you."

"For what?"

She nestled against him once more. "For loving me."

He pressed his lips to the top of her head. "You can rely on that always, Madeline. Whatever you decide."

He felt a shudder run through her. Whether it was laughter or something else, he couldn't tell. When she looked up at him again, she was smiling, but her lips were trembling.

She caught his face in both hands, bringing it close to hers, and her voice when she spoke was hardly more than a whisper. "I love you more than I know how to say." Then she kissed him with electrifying passion and, just as suddenly, broke from him and disappeared into her room.

He stood there for a moment, stunned and breathless, unable to do anything but stare stupidly at the door she'd just gone through. Then he shook his head and walked to his own room, laughing half under his breath.

She was still maddening.

— Sixteen —

Madeline shut the bedroom door as silently as she could manage and leaned back against it. She put both hands over her mouth, trying to muffle the sound of her shuddering breath in the dark room. There was nothing she could do to hush the racing of her heart. One or the other was sure to wake Aunt Ruth.

After a minute or so, she felt as if she could make her way to the dresser and get her nightgown. She could undress in the dark and slip into bed and not have to make any explanations. She didn't know how to explain things to herself, much less to her aunt.

Once she had changed, she felt her way over to the bed, suppressed a cry when her bare foot made contact with the sharp high heel of the shoe she had just discarded, and climbed between the sheets.

She was just congratulating herself on her success when she felt the mattress shift beside her.

"About time you were in bed."

Madeline pressed her lips together, biting back the first response that sprang to them. "I'm sorry, Aunt Ruth. I didn't mean to disturb you."

"Not a fit time of night for decent folk."

Madeline didn't have to see her aunt's face to know the expression of disapproval that would be on it. "Drew and I were talking."

Aunt Ruth sniffed. "Must have been some mighty exciting talk to make you draw your breath that hard."

Madeline's face turned hot, she was sure it was red as fire, but she didn't say anything until she was sure she could keep hold of her temper and her sense of humor.

"We were wondering if you'd like to help us catch a murderer tomorrow." She grinned to herself as her aunt made sputtering noises from the darkness beside her.

"Me? Don't be absurd. It's bad enough for you to go chasing around Europe with not even the sense God gave billy goats without me chasing after you. What do I know about solving murders?"

"If you'll help me make a list of where we went the day of the party, all the stores we went to and where we had lunch, we might be able to find out if Freddie Bell was at any of the same places that day. Then maybe we'll figure out who put the key from the Queen Bess into my purse."

"And what does that have to do with these murders?"

"Maybe it was the murderer."

"And maybe it doesn't have anything to do with the murders. Did your supposed detective ever consider that?"

"Why would anyone besides the murderer have put it in there?" Madeline paused and then plunged ahead. "Unless whoever it was, was trying to drive me and Drew apart. Who would want to do that?"

"Besides me, you mean." Aunt Ruth snorted. "No need to

beat around the bush, missy. I think the man's a mistake, for you or for any decent American girl, but if I was going to commit murder to save you from yourself, your Mr. Farthering would be my first and only victim."

"I don't think you'd ever kill anybody, Aunt Ruth, but you didn't—"

"Don't be silly. Do you really think I'd ruin your reputation or give any young man, foreign or not, improper ideas about you?"

"No. I didn't think you would in the first place, but I don't know why someone else would, either."

There was a moment of silence, and then Aunt Ruth said, "You don't suppose you have another admirer in this den of iniquity, do you? Somebody who'd like to see you and your Englishman part ways?"

"I don't know of anyone."

"You'd better just come home with me then. That'll nip anything like that right in the bud." Aunt Ruth sighed heavily. "I know I'm just an old sourpuss sticking my nose in where it doesn't belong."

"Aunt Ruth, I never said—"

"You didn't need to say it. But somebody's got to look after you. We'd both better head on back home."

Madeline found her aunt's hand in the darkness and squeezed it tightly. "Better yet, you can help me remember everywhere we went on the day of the party. Then maybe we'll find out who's doing all this and there'll be no need for me to leave at all."

Aunt Ruth's only answer was another derisive snort, but she squeezed Madeline's hand in return. That was enormously comforting.

⊛

The next morning, telling him it was as perfect as she and Aunt Ruth could make it, Madeline gave Drew her list of shops and other points of interest. He in turn passed it on to Chief Inspector Birdsong, who gave his assurances that the proper inquiries would be made. On his way back from Winchester, remembering the telephone call he'd received from Dr. Corneau's nurse, Drew decided he would stop by Mrs. Chapman's cottage and talk to the Allen girl. When Birdsong had interviewed her earlier, she had denied ever going to the doctor's surgery. Had she lied? If so, had it been out of embarrassment due to her predicament or had there been a more sinister reason?

Arms and legs like sticks, Madeline's aunt had said. The Allen girl was tall and slim, and unlikely to be much of a match for the formidable Aunt Ruth. And Drew had made it possible for her to stay right here in Farthering St. John. Was that what had gotten Freddie Bell killed? No telling where the man had been snooping up until last night or who he'd set off.

He pulled up in front of Lilac Cottage and found the girl sitting in the garden out front, fallen asleep over a book. He couldn't help shaking his head. She looked terribly young. He took a peek at what she was reading and smiled to see it was a collection of fairy tales. Poor thing, her white knight had ended up more than a bit tarnished. Still, he could hardly blame her for wanting to bury herself in fantasy when her present reality was so very ugly.

He stayed a pace or so back, not wanting to startle her. "Miss Allen?" She didn't stir, so he raised his voice a fraction. "Miss Allen."

She lifted her head, looking about in bewilderment before settling on him. "Mr. Farthering. Oh, excuse me, I . . . I wasn't expecting anyone."

She sat up straighter, smoothing her hair and straightening the collar of her blouse.

Drew removed his hat. "Forgive my coming unannounced, but I was hoping we might have another little chat."

"Of course. Anytime. I haven't properly thanked you for letting me stay here." Her face was faintly pink, but whether that was from sleep or embarrassment, he didn't know. "I guess I've needed time to think some things over, and this has been the perfect place for that."

"I'm glad you've found it of help." He glanced at the empty end of the bench she sat on. "May I?"

"Please, sit. I take it this is more than a social call."

He bowed his head in acknowledgment as he sat beside her. "I'm afraid I'm going to have to ask you some rather difficult questions. Please believe me, I mean no disrespect by them."

The color in her face deepened. "All right."

"First off, I'd like to know where you were between nine thirty and ten last night?"

Her eyes narrowed. "Just here. Why?"

"Alone?"

"Yes. Why?"

"I don't suppose you've heard about the incident that took place at the cottage on my estate last night?"

She shook her head. "I haven't heard anything. You're the first person I've seen to talk to in two days. Has someone else been . . . ?" She bit her lip. "There's been another murder, hasn't there?"

He nodded. "Chap called Freddie Bell. American. Did you know him?"

"No. I never heard of him."

"I also found out something regarding one of the earlier murders. About Corneau."

Her eyes widened, almost imperceptibly. He'd definitely touched on something with that.

"Dr. Corneau?"

"Yes. If you recall, Chief Inspector Birdsong asked if you had ever gone to him. You claimed you hadn't."

"That's right." She worried the already worn corner of her book. "I don't have a usual doctor."

"But things weren't exactly usual for you then, were they?"

She pressed her lips together. "I don't know what you mean."

"Someone saw you there." He knew that Corneau's nurse had only thought she might have seen the girl there, but it was worth a try. "Would you like to tell me why? Or shall I tell you?"

Tears filled her eyes, and she refused to look at him. "Obviously, you already know why. Very well, yes, I did go there. Only the one time. And I didn't kill him."

"Did you tell anyone? About the baby?"

She shook her head fiercely, making her dark hair bob around her.

"Not Mr. Montford?"

Something flickered in her eyes. "No. Why would I? Mr. Montford knew nothing about it."

"I told her, by the way. Mrs. Montford. I told her what you asked me to."

"Did she believe you? Please tell me she did. I can't stand the thought that what we did might make her doubt her husband loved her."

"Oh, yes, she believed me," Drew said. "She never believed anything else." She seemed rather relieved by that. "And you told no one else about the child? Not your friend from the flat next to yours?"

Again the girl shook her head. Again she would not meet his eyes.

"Miss Allen." He waited until she finally looked up. "Did you kill Dr. Corneau?"

"No. I swear I didn't."

He hated to press her, but he had no choice. "Have you killed anyone?"

The tears in her eyes finally spilled down her pink cheeks, and she looked away again, one hand covering her decidedly flat stomach. "I swear I haven't killed any of those people you've been asking about."

"I'm sorry to have upset you," he said, getting to his feet. And he *was* sorry, sorry he'd phrased the question so stupidly. "If there's anything I can do . . ."

She shook her head again.

There was no need to confirm the nurse's assumptions about what the girl had done after visiting Dr. Corneau's office. The pain and regret was plain on her face. Drew wished he somehow knew what to say to her. She obviously needed comfort and absolution, and for that he knew of only one source.

"I hope you'll remember what we talked about before," he added gently.

"The sermon?"

"It's as good a place to start as any."

He passed her his pocket handkerchief, and she buried her face in it. He didn't know what to do but leave her with her thoughts and, he hoped, prayers. But he turned back again, wondering why he had never before thought to ask.

"One last thing, Miss Allen. You said you first met Mr. Montford when he came into your shop to buy a present for his son. Do you happen to recall what that was?"

She lifted her head, blinking at him, brow furrowed. "I, uh . . . It was a set of toy soldiers, I believe."

He nodded and, with a tip of his hat, got into his car and drove away.

By the time Drew reached the hallowed premises of Whyland, Montford, Clifton and Russ, it was after hours. But Russ, expecting him after their telephone conversation, let him in the back way, leading him past empty offices until they got to a rather large, fustily decorated one. Russ settled himself behind the oversized desk, with a file marked *Montford, Daniel* lying on it.

Drew turned the file to face himself but didn't open it. "He'll be watched, you know."

Russ merely smirked and gestured toward a chair. "Of course he will. But I don't think the inspector believes Daniel killed his father. He just hasn't got a better suspect at the moment, and he's certainly not going to let this one fly out of his grasp. No doubt as soon as Daniel was released, he arranged to put a man or two on the Montford house."

"Are you surprised? That Daniel was seeing a married woman?"

Russ shrugged. "Not uncommon, I suppose."

"But would you have thought it of him?"

"Didn't know him that well, to be honest. I mean, I'd known his father since before the boy was born, but apart from a word here or there or an occasional visit to the office, I never heard that much about Daniel."

"That's odd. Mr. Montford always seemed quite a proud father."

"Oh, I daresay he was, but I suppose I never paid all that much mind to it. Sounds rather boorish of me, I know, but other men's children, well, they're not all that interesting, eh?"

"I suppose a businessman has other things on his mind. What

about Montford himself? Did you talk much outside of office matters?"

"Not all that much, perhaps went for a drink here and there. We got on well, to be sure, but we weren't that chummy. Not on a personal level."

Drew glanced at the framed picture on the desk. It showed Russ seated beside a stylish-looking dark-haired woman and flanked by a tall girl in her early teens and a little boy holding a stuffed duck.

"Your family?"

"Yes."

Drew smiled. "Very handsome group."

"Thank you."

Drew said nothing more for the time being. He was comfortable with the silence, but would Russ be?

Russ fumbled with his cigarette case, tapping the edge of it on the desk before at last opening it. "Is there something I can do for you, Mr. Farthering?" He selected a cigarette and then lit it, discarding the match afterward with a practiced flick of the wrist. "I presume it's more about Montford."

"Yes, if it's not too much of an imposition, I have just a few more questions."

"If you like, though I really don't have much else to say about the matter. I've told the police and I've told you everything that's pertinent to the case."

"Oh, quite. Quite. I was hoping, though, that between the two of us, we could make some headway on it."

"I'll be happy to answer any questions you might have, but I doubt I know anything that would be of use to you. Cigarette?"

Drew waved away the proffered silver case. "Perhaps there's something you haven't thought to mention."

"For example?"

"Oh, I don't know. For example, what you know about Miss Allen?"

Russ half choked on his cigarette smoke. "What?"

"Miss Allen. Margaret. Meggie, I believe she's called. The one from the investigation. Do you know her?"

"Oh. Oh, yes, the girl Montford was seeing. That was a terrible thing to get into the newspapers, especially for Mrs. Montford. Shocking business, that. Does she claim to know me?"

Drew smiled. "I asked first."

Russ studied him for a long moment, his eyes narrowed and piercing. "All right. I don't suppose there's any use in denying it. Yes, I knew Miss Allen. Knew of her, at any rate."

"She was seen at Montford's hotel. Had been seen there several times before over the past few months. But you knew why he went to Winchester all along, didn't you, Mr. Russ?"

Russ crushed out his cigarette in the green marble ashtray. "He was going there to break it off. I don't know what he told the girl beforehand, but that's what he was planning to do."

"And why did he tell you this? You said the two of you were never really personal friends."

"I . . ." Russ ground his already extinguished cigarette into ash. "I had found out about her. Quite by accident, but found out all the same. I told him, man to man, that it was madness, utter madness, to ruin himself and perhaps the firm over a tawdry passion such as this one. He had a fine wife and a son to be proud of. No need to ruin them, as well."

"And he agreed?"

"He did. He said he would break with the girl at once. That's the last I knew of it."

"I see."

"Frankly I don't know how he could face her after everything, poor child as she was. I don't think I could have looked her in the eye. Seems she was quite smitten."

"Do you think so? A girl like that and a man his age?" Drew chuckled, watching the other man's eyes. "I suppose he liked to think so, anyway."

Russ looked him up and down, smiling more to himself than at Drew. "You young pups. You think that's all women want, do you? Empty-headed, vulgar little boys who think they're God's gift wrapped in gold foil? Perhaps some girls do, quite likely most of them do, but no doubt some prefer a man with poise and experience, a distinguished man who knows how to treat them properly."

"And this Miss Allen was like that?"

"Oh, yes." Russ stopped and again smiled faintly. "From what Montford told me, yes, she was."

Drew smiled back at him and then picked up the photograph of his family. "Your little boy, how old is he?"

"He turned eight this spring."

"I suppose he likes you to bring him things? Toys and games and such."

Russ relaxed a little. "Oh, yes. He's a lively child, to say the least."

"And what did you bring him for his birthday in March? Something from Hirsch's, wasn't it? Toy soldiers perhaps?"

Russ swore. He didn't raise his voice, but he repeated the oath a number of times before dropping into his chair and closing his eyes. "How long have you known?"

Drew shrugged. "I've wondered. Haven't known."

"This will ruin me. Good heavens, this will ruin me."

"Perhaps I should be going."

Drew started to get up, but Russ held him there, a look of desperation on his face.

"No. Wait. Hear me out." He took a couple of unsteady breaths. "You have to understand. Someone has to understand. I can't hold it in any longer."

Drew waited, but Russ didn't say anything more. He only sat puffing his cigarette and blinking hard.

"How did Montford figure into it?" Drew asked finally.

Russ passed one trembling hand over his brow. "He accidentally opened a letter of mine. From her. It was put in his box at the office by mistake." He smiled, his thin mustache twitching fitfully. "He was quite understanding about it. Said he'd help me if I wanted out. Before Edith found out. Before I'd spoilt everything. I knew he was right. Meggie—Miss Allen—she's a fine girl. I won't hear a word said against her, but the whole tawdry affair was already beginning to pall. The last few times, well, I met her because I didn't know how to break off with her."

"So Montford agreed to tell her for you?" What a coward the man was. "That's why the room was in his name only that once."

"Yes."

"Did you kill him?"

Russ's pale eyes widened, and then the color rushed back into his face. "No." He shoved his chair back, making it screech against the polished floor as he got to his feet again. "No, I absolutely did not kill him. I did not."

"Did she?"

"God forgive me." Russ's voice dropped to a bare whisper. "I don't know."

"Would you have thought she could? I mean, was she the type?"

"Heavens, no. I take it you've met her. She's just an ordinary little shopgirl. Tears are likely the only weapon she has at hand, and I daresay she would have bravely held those in check."

"And whose idea was it? Saying she'd been involved with Montford instead of you?"

Russ had the grace to look ashamed. "Mine. He was dead. I didn't think it would matter at that point."

The wretched coward.

"No. I can see that. How could it matter to anyone?" Drew smiled. "I mean, anyone but Mrs. Montford and young Daniel. No doubt the firm is tainted either way."

Russ glared at him, his eyes red-rimmed. "Must you twist the knife? I didn't set out to hurt anyone. It just . . . just happened."

"Oh, certainly. One day you're walking down the street, and the next you're blaming your unfaithfulness on an innocent dead man." One side of Drew's mouth twitched into a smirk. "Happens all the time."

"All right! All right! Must you torment me? I hope to God you never take a false step!"

Drew looked away, the brittle smugness inside him crumbling just slightly. Even Christ himself hadn't condemned the woman discovered in the act of adultery. Who was Drew Farthering to be casting stones? Certainly he'd taken his own share of false steps.

His expression softened. "All right, fair enough," Drew said. "There's none of us without fault. Sounds as if you at least tried to make things right. Before Montford was killed, anyway."

Russ sat down again, his head in his hands. "I swear I hadn't thought it all through. I didn't think of his family. I couldn't think of anything but keeping what I'd done out of the papers." The words were half choked. "Away from my wife."

Drew was silent for a moment, waiting for the man to pull the shreds of his dignity back around himself.

"Anything else of importance you haven't yet mentioned?" he asked finally.

Looking drained but calmer, Russ took another cigarette from his case and lit it. "Not that I can think of at the moment, no. I suppose this will all have to come out?"

"Perhaps it needn't be as bad as you think, so long as we can clear Montford of any scandal. His family deserves as much, don't you think?"

"Yes. Of course. I suppose this . . . this part of it will have to come out."

"I don't know. If it does, it won't be from me. Not so long as that's the end of your involvement with it. You should probably tell the chief inspector what you told me. As you advised Daniel."

"I didn't kill Montford, I tell you. I may be a coward and an adulterer, but I'm no murderer."

"Did you know she was pregnant? Miss Allen?"

Russ gaped at him, unable to do more than blink stupidly. "I . . . Pregnant?"

"The Dr. Corneau who was murdered, she went to see him about it. She never told you?"

"No, never. I would have . . . I mean, naturally, I would have seen to everything for her."

"Corneau wasn't that sort of doctor."

Russ glared at him, and then he looked up at the ceiling and took a deep, steadying puff on his cigarette. "I suppose we can arrange a quiet adoption. If she's determined to keep it, I'll see they're both cared for. I can't be personally involved, of course."

"That's terribly gracious of you, but you needn't trouble yourself. It seems likely she's already seen to things on her own."

Russ eyed him suspiciously. "How do you know that?"

Drew gave him only a vague shrug. There was no reason to

tell him about the confessions of Dr. Corneau's nurse or his conversation with Miss Allen.

"Well, then there's nothing more to be done." Russ tapped the ash from the end of his cigarette. "Bad business, but there's no changing it now. It would have been absolute ruin for me if she had kept it. Surely you can see that. My wife . . ." He looked up at Drew and then dropped his gaze to some spot near his shoes. "I'm not concerned for myself, you understand."

"No, obviously."

"But my wife, she'd never get over it. My children . . ." He glanced at Drew again, looking as though he was about to be sick. "You do understand how it is. These things happen, really no one's fault, and sometimes they go bad. I'll send some money along to the girl. No doubt a new start will do her a world of good."

Drew let him finish and then stood and took his hat from the corner of the desk. "I'd best be going. If you have anything else to say concerning the case, I'd be obliged if you'd let me know. You have my card."

"Yes. Yes, certainly."

Drew was glad for the long drive home and the clean wind in his face.

— Seventeen —

The lights of Farthering Place were a welcome sight that evening. Drew had spent the drive from London trying to concentrate on the facts of the case and mostly ending up thinking uncharitable thoughts about Charles Russ and then reminding himself of his own failings. It would be good to get away from the tawdriness of Russ's affairs, from the whole case in general, for an hour or two. He pulled up to the house with just enough time to dress for dinner.

Once he was properly groomed and attired, he headed down the stairs. Coming from his own quarters, Nick caught up to him.

"You look rather done in. Anything wrong?"

Drew shrugged. "Not really. The world's not a fit place to live in, but unfortunately there just aren't any other viable options."

"Cheery as always." Nick grinned. "I understand you've been up to London again. Presumably it wasn't to see the queen."

"No, I believe Tuesdays she does the ironing and isn't at home to visitors."

"Pity. All that way for nothing."

Drew stopped halfway down, turning to face his friend. "I had a rather unpleasant conversation with Mr. Russ of Whyland, Montford, Clifton and Russ, in which I learned that Russ and not Montford was involved with Miss Allen and that he did not know of her pregnancy and its subsequent termination."

Nick blinked. "Angels and ministers of grace, defend us."

"Amen." Drew dredged up a smile. "Sorry to be so grim, old man. This one's a poser, that's for certain, and more puzzling if Montford wasn't seeing the girl. Russ said Montford did arrange for a meeting with her, to end the thing on Russ's behalf, but that was the only time he ever met her."

"Perhaps she lost her temper when he said what he'd come to say. Perhaps she blamed him for convincing Russ that he shouldn't see her again."

Drew nodded. "Or perhaps it was Russ himself. Montford opened a letter from Miss Allen by mistake. Possibly he realized what was going on and threatened to tell Mrs. Russ if Russ didn't end the affair immediately. Russ didn't want to do that, couldn't have Montford telling tales out of school, and made away with him. As good a reason as any, I'd say."

"But he was in court in London that afternoon. Can't get a much better alibi than a courtroom full of people sworn to speak nothing but the truth."

Drew exhaled audibly. "Then we're back to the girl."

"I just don't see it being her. She's not the type for one thing, though she is rather tall for a girl. Whoever bashed in Montford's skull was fairly near his height. But even if it was the girl or Russ himself, why would either of them have killed Dr. Corneau or Clarice Deschner?"

"Don't think I haven't clawed through every little gray cell I possess trying to figure that one out. I suppose there's always the possibility it was neither of them."

"Person or persons unknown?" Nick gave him a friendly swat on the shoulder and headed downstairs once more. "Well, you'll have to do better than that."

"You needn't remind me." Drew padded down the steps behind him. "If the killer is moving closer and closer to me, then the only place left is here at Farthering. That means Madeline or you or Denny or even Aunt Ruth may be targeted next."

"Or you, don't forget."

"No," Drew said, "I'd hardly forget myself, though I still have to wonder. If I am the objective in this little game, why didn't the killer come for me directly? I'm still missing something. Something important."

Nick stopped and turned to him. "Something as important as *why*?"

"Precisely. I was meeting with Montford the day he was killed so I could make arrangements to change my will in Madeline's favor. Most of it anyway. Yes, I realize we aren't married yet, perhaps we'll never be, but I'd rather she have it than anyone else. At least I'd know she would never want for anything."

"She's rather well off from her uncle's estate already, isn't she?"

"True enough. Doesn't matter. I'd want her to have it, in any case. And you and Denny and Mrs. D would be seen to either way, of course."

"That's good to know. I'd hate to have to go out and find a proper job."

"Old Padgett keeps you busy enough managing the estate. Just wait till he's retired and you have it all to do yourself. You'll wish for a proper job, I expect."

"At least, if your will is as you say, it proves definitively that I couldn't be the murderer." Nick put on an exaggerated expression of relief. "I was beginning to worry."

"I'm happy to set your mind at ease, Nick, old boy, but I must admit I've long held you above suspicion in this case."

"Really?"

"Oh, by all means. Obviously our murderer is of superior intelligence and nerve. I ruled you out from the start."

The two of them had reached the door to the parlor by then, and Drew could hear Madeline and her aunt making small talk inside. But before he could join them, Nick tugged his arm, abruptly serious again.

"Perhaps someone didn't like the idea of a change. Have you considered that?"

"I have. As it stands now, besides bequests to you and Denny and Mrs. D and a couple of charitable institutions, bequests I wasn't planning to alter anyway, everything I have would go to Constance. Needless to say, since she is gone, I needed to make a change. I suppose the next to inherit, if my current will stands, are my heirs at law, whoever they may be. Some cousin four times removed or a great-aunt or someone of that ilk. Far enough off, at any rate, to know nothing about me and care even less. And if this mysterious heir did kill Montford because he didn't want me changing my will, he'd have little reason for disposing of Dr. Corneau and even less for murdering Clarice or Bell."

Nick looked down at his shoes and then back at Drew. "You don't suppose your mother, I mean your real mother . . . ?"

Drew shook his head. The French shopgirl who had been his father's mistress for a brief week? Drew didn't even know her name. Everyone he might have asked about her was dead now. In the eyes of the world, Constance, his father's wife, was Drew's mother. Even now, he thought of Constance as his mother. And the French girl?

"It would be rather a roundabout way to go about things, wouldn't it? Perhaps she's kept up with any news about me over the years, I mean, supposing she's still alive. But she'd have rather a rough go of it if, upon my death, she tried to claim any inheritance."

"I suppose you're right."

"I'd rather imagine she'd try touching me for a few bob before she'd resort to out and out murder. And my fortune as a motive, it's rather imaginative to think someone would kill poor Montford just to keep me from changing my will. Even more so to connect that to Corneau or Clarice."

"Then I suppose there's nothing in that quarter to worry about."

"I doubt it, Nick. Besides that, no one's made any sort of threat against me."

"Not yet."

Drew laughed. "Now, how about we let all this sit for the evening and enjoy our dinner with the ladies." He straightened his tie. "Everything shipshape?"

"Dazzling."

They went in to the parlor, and a few minutes later Denny announced dinner. Nick escorted Aunt Ruth out of the room, while Drew merely stood there lounging against the mantel, the firelight painting shifting shapes and shadows across the hearth as he stared into the flames.

Madeline went over to him and stood a moment in companionable silence.

"They'll be waiting for us." She slipped her arm around his waist and nestled close. "What is it, Drew? The case?"

He sighed and told her briefly about his interview with Charles Russ. "I don't know. I can't help but think of poor Meggie Allen. You wouldn't have believed old Russ even if you had witnessed the entire conversation." He squeezed her a little closer. "I know it's not my place to judge him or anyone, but I had to leave his office before I outright thrashed him. He fathered a child by her. Now it's gone, and all I could see in him was relief that his own reputation wouldn't be in jeopardy and that his wife needn't find out anything. A colder, more callous attitude I hope I never see."

"I suppose it's easy, if you don't actually see the child, not to consider what you're really doing. But God sees his heart even if we can't. It may grieve him more than he let on. After all, she was the one who made the decision about the baby, not he. From what they both say, he didn't even know about it."

"I couldn't help thinking . . ." He looked away, knowing she could hear the pain in his voice, even if she couldn't read it there in his eyes.

"Drew?"

"I couldn't help wondering if my own mother, my real mother, had thought about doing something like that with me."

"Surely not."

"There's no way of knowing, I suppose. Not now. Your uncle Mason told me she was young, that she had no family. She had to have been desperate. Frightened. And I suppose it could have crossed my father's mind just as easily. Finance 'the procedure' and there's the end of it." He gave her a brittle smile. "Nothing like paying one's way out of an embarrassment."

"But he didn't, Drew. He brought you home. And from what I've been told, he was prouder of you than anything else in his life."

He wrapped her in both arms, holding her close enough to feel her warmth and the steady comfort of her breathing. Close enough to feel the beating of her heart. "Bless you, darling."

There was so much more he wanted to say, more he would have said, but he knew somehow that it wasn't necessary.

He turned her face up to him, smiling into her eyes, knowing his smile was none too steady. "We'd better go in now. Too much treacle and I won't want my dinner."

"And that's all Russ told you last night, was it?"

The chief inspector looked more world-weary than ever in his office's harsh, unshaded electric light. It was an expression that Drew had come to realize did not always indicate suspicion.

"I didn't press him for details, if that's what you're after, Inspector. But yes, that's all he said on the matter. I am glad to know that he took his own advice and told you everything this morning."

Birdsong frowned. "At least he told me everything he told you."

"Looks as though Mrs. Montford was right about her husband after all. No reason you couldn't discreetly inform the press that someone else who shall remain nameless was involved with the Allen girl, not Montford as was first suspected. That ought to clear Montford's name without putting Russ directly in harm's way, eh?"

"I suppose that would be all right," Birdsong said. "Of course, what the press dig up in consequence is not something for which we at the police can be held responsible."

Drew gave the chief inspector a nod. "That seems more than

fair, given Russ's involvement in the situation. And so that's the end of that."

Birdsong studied Drew, his eyes narrowing. "I've a feeling there is something brewing in that inquisitive head of yours. Am I right?"

Drew smiled. "If I happen to settle on any particular theory, I promise you'll know it at once."

"Mind you do, Mr. Farthering. Don't let your meddling end you up alongside your mate Bell there, eh?"

"No, no," Drew assured him, his smile tightening a bit. "We certainly wouldn't want that."

On his way back home, Drew stopped in Farthering St. John and parked across the street from the chemist's. As he got out of his car, he saw Mrs. Harkness standing in front of The Running Brooks, talking to Mrs. Webster from the antique shop next door. He raised his hat. "Good morning, ladies."

Mrs. Harkness waved. "Hello, Mr. Farthering. You're out early this morning."

Drew crossed the street to them. It wasn't until he got closer that he saw the fresh scrape on Mrs. Harkness's cheek.

"Why, Mrs. Harkness, what happened to you?"

Mrs. Harkness smiled, coloring. "It looks worse than it really is. I should have paid better attention."

Mrs. Webster scowled. "That Mr. Llewellyn, it's a wonder he didn't break your neck. Or his own. Fancy a man of his years terrorizing the whole county round with his bicycle like that."

"Now, Gladys, he was ever so apologetic."

Mrs. Webster huffed. "Well, it sounded to me as if he was trying to put the fault of it all on you."

"To be fair, I *did* step into the street when he was coming. I thought for certain he'd seen me. And with nobody about at that time of the morning, I thought he had plenty of room to go around." Mrs. Harkness laughed. "Still, if he'd meant to turn himself black and blue, he couldn't have done a better job of it. I don't know how he didn't see me in time to stop."

Drew shook his head. "It's nothing serious, I hope."

"Only bumps and bruises, Mr. Farthering. I did feel bad for the old gentleman, though. Spry as he is, they get a bit fragile at that age."

"He wasn't hurt, was he?"

"Mrs. Christopher who does for him says it's mostly a sprained ankle, and he's got a good lump under one eye and another on his arm. Perhaps it's all for the best. He'll be off his bicycle for a while now."

"And good thing too, if you ask me." Mrs. Webster crossed her arms over her ample bosom. "Farthering St. John has grown much too rowdy these days. What's the good of living the quiet country life when there's goings-on that would make London blush for shame? It's all over the village about what happened at Farthering Place two nights ago, you know. I do hope that American lady is all right now."

Drew nodded. "Remarkably well, in fact, though I promised Madeline I'd pop round to Mr. Clarridge's to get a little something to settle her aunt's nerves. It was rather a shock."

"I can imagine." Mrs. Webster leaned closer. "Must have been terrifying for her, finding that body and having the killer spring out from the darkness."

"Oh, Gladys, stop!" Mrs. Harkness put a trembling hand to her throat. "You make my blood run cold."

"I don't think you need worry," Drew soothed. "But you

ladies make sure you lock up well at night and don't open up for anyone you don't know."

Mrs. Harkness's eyes were wide. "Sounds as if it may well be someone we *do* know."

Drew hadn't any answer for that. It seemed more and more likely that the murderer was someone nearby, someone who could go about the village and not be especially noticed.

"The police will be keeping an extra close watch out until the man is caught. Just keep your eyes open and let them know if you see anything out of the ordinary."

"I doubt I'll be able to keep my eyes closed for another week at least." Mrs. Harkness shook her head. "That poor Mr. Bell. He seemed such a pleasant fellow."

"Yes, it's a tragedy. Madeline is quite upset by it. Oh, I say, we were trying to figure out a few things about what Bell may have been up to before he was killed. You don't happen to remember when he was last in your shop, do you, Mrs. Harkness?"

"Dear me, let me think. He was in three or four times, I believe, but I'm not sure I could tell you exactly when. There was the day he and your young lady met, I remember that. He came in looking for a book on local sites, I believe. He was back that day the three of you went to the Queen Bess, as well."

"Do you recall if he was in on the day of our dinner party?"

Mrs. Harkness thought for a moment. "No. Not that day, unless I'm mistaken. I remember your young lady and her aunt coming that day. They spent some while looking at books for some relatives in America. They said they were also going up to Winchester."

"I see. Did they mention visiting any other shops here in the village?"

"Not that I remember, no. I can't say, to tell the honest truth, where all they mentioned."

"That's all right, Mrs. Harkness. I think they put down all the places they went. I just wondered if perhaps they'd forgotten one or two. It could be important."

"Really?"

"We think perhaps Mr. Bell was at one of the places they went and that's how Madeline got his room key." Drew deliberately ignored the significant glance the two women exchanged. "It's rather muddled at the moment, I'm afraid."

"Well, if I remember anything more, I'll be sure to let you know," Mrs. Harkness said. "As it is, it's a wonder I can think at all, scared half out of my wits as I've been this fortnight. I wish Annalee was still here. With her Marcus in the house, I wouldn't have to worry about anyone breaking in at night."

Drew hadn't much considered how it might be for a middle-aged lady living alone when there was a murderer about.

"Perhaps you should go for a holiday, Mrs. Harkness. I'm sure Annalee and the children would be pleased to have you."

"And who would mind my shop? Not all of us have the means to do as we please day in, day out. Me being all alone in the world, as well."

"No, no. I hadn't thought of that."

Mrs. Webster crossed her arms and smiled at her friend. "Must be nice, mustn't it? Young lord of the manor with nothing to worry him but playing detective now and again."

"I think Mr. Farthering's been a great help to the police in all this." Mrs. Harkness gave Drew an indulgent smile. "And if you ask me, the police need all the help they can get."

"The case is rather a poser, isn't it?" Drew shook his head. "Nothing quite seems to fit."

"Go on, Bobbie." Mrs. Webster gave Mrs. Harkness's shoulder a playful shove. "Tell him what you told me."

Mrs. Harkness shrugged her off. "No. I couldn't."

"Go on."

Drew smiled to himself. It was really rather charming to see her blushing like a girl at her first recital.

"Yes, do go on, Mrs. Harkness. Do you have a theory about the murders?"

"Not really a theory as such, Mr. Farthering." Mrs. Harkness glanced at her friend, who pushed her forward again. "I just couldn't help thinking, well . . ."

"What couldn't you help thinking?"

"Well, what if the murderer actually *is* someone we know? Someone from right here in our village?"

"Do you suspect anyone in particular?"

"Oh, no. It's hard to even imagine it would actually be one of us, and if it were, why he would do such things. It's almost as if he were killing people at random. And I've read enough murder mysteries to know that, unless there's some sort of method in the crimes, there's no solving them. Without logic, it's good night, Mr. Sherlock Holmes."

"True enough." He managed not to smile at the earnestness in her comments. "But I don't think it's random at all. There's a definite key to it, if we could just find it."

"Well." She stepped back a bit, looking rather abashed by her own boldness. "Of course, I wouldn't know enough about the particulars in this case to actually say."

"Mrs. Harkness! Good morning again!"

Drew turned to see Mr. Llewellyn hobbling across the road with the aid of a cane, just as battered as Mrs. Harkness had described him. He had a sheaf of pink rhododendrons cradled in one arm.

"What are you doing up and about?" Drew hurried to him and took his arm. "Oughtn't you to be in bed?"

The two women surrounded them, clucking and scolding.

"Now, now, ladies, don't fuss. I'm not quite dead yet." There was a roguish twinkle in the older gentleman's bright blue eyes. "After all, it's not how many times one's knocked down that counts, but how many times he gets up, eh?"

Mrs. Harkness shook her head. "I'm sure Dr. Wallace must have told you to take it easy for a few days."

"But that's just the trouble, ma'am. I couldn't possibly rest easy until I had offered you my apologies for yesterday morning's unfortunate occurrence." Mr. Llewellyn shifted the flowers into her arms. "I know it's no compensation for your injuries, but I trust it will assure you of my sincere regrets."

"Really, Mr. Llewellyn, you needn't have troubled yourself. I'm not really hurt. Accidents happen. You're the one who looks as if he's been caned." Mrs. Harkness smiled on the lush bouquet. "You didn't go out on that sprained ankle and cut these yourself, did you?"

"No, I'm sorry to say. Mrs. Christopher brought them in from the garden. To cheer me up, she said, and I thought you were far more deserving of them."

He made a gallant bow, and Mrs. Webster smirked. "Oooh, I think Bobbie has an admirer."

Mrs. Harkness frowned. "Do hush up, Gladys, if you're going to be silly. I'm sure Mr. Llewellyn is only being polite."

"Nonsense. I know a handsome woman when I see one." Mr. Llewellyn waggled his salt-and-pepper eyebrows at her. "I may be old and a bit out of practice, but I'm not blind."

Mrs. Harkness shook her head. "You're a flatterer, that's what you are. I know it when I hear it, though I can't say I've heard it much since Mr. Harkness took to his heels."

He grinned at her. "All's forgiven, I hope?"

"Nothing to forgive," she assured him. "It likely was all my fault, stepping out into the street without looking."

"The fault was entirely mine, madam." He took her hand and bowed over it. "But you're a lady right through, Mrs. Harkness. I don't mind who knows it."

Drew gave Mrs. Harkness a wink, and she looked away, blushing.

"You really should be lying down, shouldn't you, Mr. Llewellyn?" She wagged one finger at the old man. "What did Dr. Wallace say?"

Mr. Llewellyn made some blustery huffing noises. "You don't get to be my age lying about with your feet up."

"Please, Mr. Farthering, can't you make him see reason?"

"I can try, Mrs. Harkness. No guarantees, of course." Drew moved to take the gentleman's arm again and was immediately shaken off.

"I can get along without help, young man."

"To be sure, but I thought you might take me round to your house and show me your new bicycle. I didn't get to see it before, not up close. I hope it wasn't damaged in the collision."

A light came into the older man's eyes. "No. Not in the least. The old girl's a battle tank." He cleared his throat hastily. "I mean the bicycle, of course. Would you really like to come see her?"

"Very much." Drew raised his hat to the two shopkeepers. "If you ladies will excuse us."

"Do be careful," Mrs. Harkness called as they crossed the

road. "I'll bring you over some of my bread pudding this after-noon, shall I, Mr. Llewellyn?"

"That would be lovely," he called back, and then he stumbled over the curb and had to hold on to Drew to keep from falling. "Confounded nuisance, this ankle. It's not sprained, you know. Just turned a bit. Wallace says I'll soon be healed up and back on my bicycle."

"Ah, splendid."

"Never saw the like of it, though. Women, God love 'em, haven't a brain among the lot of them. Granted, it was hardly light yet and neither of us was expecting anyone to be about, but she stepped right in front of me. Couldn't possibly pull up in time. Heaven knows what she was thinking."

"Perhaps her mind was on opening up her shop for the day."

Mr. Llewellyn harrumphed. "Fascinating, actually, the work-ings of the human mind. Not like a well-built machine. You can count on machines. The brain, sometimes it just goes haywire. There's no accounting for it."

"I suppose not."

"If you're going to carry on playing detective, young man, you'd be wise to study up. Read a good book on abnormal psychology."

Drew glanced at him, not liking the idea that had worried its way into his head. "Funny you should say so, but Mrs. Harkness sold me the most interesting book last week."

"Really? What was it?"

"About murderesses. Lurid stuff, really." Drew watched the man's face. He was certainly battered enough.

"If he'd meant to turn himself black and blue, he couldn't have done a better job of it."

Mr. Llewellyn nodded. "Deadlier than the male. You can bank on it."

"She said someone local had ordered it and never picked it up."

"Did she? Rum luck for our lady shopkeeper, eh? Sounds a fascinating read, if you ask me."

"Yes, I thought so. A bit grim, but certainly riveting," Drew said, still watching. "Why do you suppose people kill? I mean, not the obvious ones, the ones with something to gain, but the ones who seem to do it because . . . I don't know, perhaps because it just pleases them."

"A game, I daresay," Mr. Llewellyn replied. "You take this hatpin murderer we have now. Monstrous, clever fellow, wouldn't you say?"

"Seems so at this point, anyway. You didn't happen to be about the evening before last, did you? I mean, perhaps you saw—"

"I do generally take a ride down the lane on my bicycle before turning in for the night, but I didn't see anything out of place that evening. What time did you say this last killing took place?"

"About a quarter of ten, perhaps a bit before."

"I'd just have been coming in. This hatpin blighter is likely sitting back in plain sight, having a bit of a laugh at all the fuss being made over him. Showing who's master, eh?"

"Yes," Drew pressed, "but why?"

"Not enough time out in the fresh air, if you ask me." By then they had reached Llewellyn's cottage and the flame-red bicycle leaning against the garden shed. "Cycling. It's the nearest way to a sound body and a sound mind. Now tell me you've seen a finer machine, and I'll likely ask you to leave my premises."

For the next ten minutes the older man waxed poetical about

his beloved machine, until Drew finally made his excuses and went back to his car. He still didn't like what he was thinking. The very idea was ridiculous. He wasn't going to mention it to Madeline or Nick. Certainly not to Chief Inspector Birdsong. Not till he'd had a chance to turn things over in his mind for a bit.

— Eighteen —

The next day, leaving Madeline and her aunt in the parlor with their lace making, Drew went to talk to Roger Morris again about what and, more important, whom he might have seen around Clarice Deschner's cottage the day of her murder. He drove up to the jail in Winchester and then, finding Roger had been released, dropped in at the chief inspector's office.

"Couldn't hold him," Birdsong admitted. "The incident at your cottage makes him quite unlikely to be our man."

Drew just narrowly refrained from smirking. "Quite."

The chief inspector scowled. "He's not out of the woods yet, mind you. But it may interest you to know he did identify that black-and-white belt as belonging to the Deschner girl. Said it was across the back of the sofa with the dress when he and the girl quarreled. Wasn't sure about whether it was there when he found her later."

"No," Drew said. "Mightn't be something he'd notice at that point in time. So, one less suspect, eh? Now what?"

"Two less, actually. Daniel Montford was definitely at home at the time of the murder."

"Oh, yes? Not just his mother saying so?"

Birdsong looked faintly disgusted. "From five minutes past ten until ten twenty-seven, young Mr. Montford was sitting on the doorstep in his back garden, smoking approximately two and a half cigarettes before retiring into the house. If the murder was done between nine thirty and nine forty-five, as we suspect, he couldn't possibly have gotten back to London by ten."

"More and more, I think we're on the wrong track. It's got to be someone near to hand, someone no one pays much mind, who can get in and out everywhere rather unnoticed, someone we're used to seeing about, perhaps."

Birdsong narrowed his eyes. "Anyone come to mind, Detective Farthering?"

Drew only shrugged. "Could be anyone. Nick had rather an interesting idea. He thinks the killings are somehow moving closer to Farthering Place. And yes, geographically I suppose they are."

"Does he now? What's he reckon the reason for that might be?"

"That's the question, isn't it? Maybe it's something you lads ought to have a go at. If it's convenient, of course."

Birdsong looked him over contemplatively. "You, perhaps?"

Drew grinned at him. "Modesty forbids . . ."

"Yes, well, I can't see your modesty being much use if our killer comes after you."

"As I told Nick, Inspector, I just can't see why anyone would target me. I'm nobody."

"Maybe. Maybe not. If you're the target, someone at least *thinks* you're somebody."

"But why? What would anyone gain from killing me?"

Birdsong pursed his lips. "Hard to say. Privileged young lord of the manor? All the advantages of money and position? Might breed a bit of resentment in someone not so smiled upon. Dare I say jealousy?"

"Nick and I were wondering if it mightn't be a game."

"I've wondered myself. You're rather celebrated locally, aren't you? Just at the moment, I mean. Perhaps someone, jealous again, would like to do you one better, eh?"

Before Drew could even think what to say in reply, a young constable popped his head into the room.

"Beg pardon, sir. A Miss Forest to see you. About her hat-pins."

Birdsong and Drew exchanged glances, and then they both stood at the entrance of a tiny, birdlike creature, prim and faded and wizened as an old apple. She accepted the straight-backed chair the constable offered her and peered at Drew.

"Mr. Farthering, isn't it? I've heard you've been in and out of trouble with the police for some while now, though I didn't expect to find you here in Winchester of all places."

He managed to look repentant. "Yes, ma'am, but the chief inspector here has done his best to teach me the error of my ways."

Birdsong grimaced. "Mr. Farthering is helping us in our investigation, madam. That'll be all, Parkins."

The constable vanished, and Birdsong sat down at his desk, his hands folded expectantly. "Now, how can we be of service, madam?"

"Someone broke into my shop last night, and I'd like to know what you mean to do about it."

Birdsong's gaze flickered between Drew and the older lady. "Just what sort of shop, may I ask?"

"I carry items for ladies of taste and refinement, Inspector."
Miss Forest's stern expression dared him to insinuate anything
different. "None of the trash you see in most shops these days."

"I understand, madam."

"Now, I told the young man at the desk that I had had some
things taken. I don't know why I'm required to repeat the information. Couldn't he have seen to it? I don't know why I've
been made to come up here. The officer in Farthering St. John
couldn't be bothered, I expect. He was certainly eager enough
to hand me off to you."

"I'm sorry, madam," Birdsong said. "But if you would just
bear with us, perhaps we can find the thief and your stolen
property. Just where is this shop?"

"It's the one round the corner from the church, down at the
end of the high street in Farthering St. John. Do you know it?"

"Forest's Ladies' Emporium," Drew supplied.

She nodded. "Quite right. I should like to know what you
are going to do about the theft, Inspector."

"What exactly was taken, madam?"

"I have a list here." She took a folded paper from her purse,
opened it, and smoothed it out on the table in front of her. Then
she opened her purse again and brought out her spectacles.
Those in place, she began to read. "Two antique pearl brooches,
four china teacups, a box of rhinestone Christmas ornaments,
a pair of antique hatpins, half a dozen silver bracelets, and a
lithograph of Trafalgar Square." She looked over her glasses at
the chief inspector. "That's in addition to the display case that
was damaged and the porcelain shepherd and shepherdess that
were smashed to pieces."

"Do you think the damage was deliberate?" Drew asked.

"Well, the display case was where the stolen items had been

kept, Mr. Farthering. I would say the thief was quite deliberate in breaking it to get them."

"And the porcelain?"

She pushed her glasses further down her nose, studying Drew for a disdainful moment before turning her attention to Birdsong. "Really, Chief Inspector, whether or not the act was deliberate, I have been effectively robbed of those figures."

"Certainly, madam. Have you noticed anyone unusual in your shop or hanging about in the street nearby?"

"Unusual? Hardly. I have my regular customers, respectable women, of course. A couple of other ladies with shops across the way sometimes come by for tea and a chat. I get a tourist now and again. That American girl and her aunt came in once or twice." She glared at Drew. "Never bought so much as a handkerchief."

Drew shook his head in commiseration. "But nothing out of the ordinary?"

She pursed her lips in thought. "Well, more amusing than extraordinary. That old gentleman who rides his bicycle around the village at all hours, Mr. Llewellyn, he's come in two or three times to look at some of my ladies' jewelry." For the first time there was a spark of warmth in her faded blue eyes. "I think he has a sweetheart somewhere."

Drew pressed his lips together, feeling something twisting in his insides.

The chief inspector cleared his throat. "If we could keep our discussion a little nearer the point, madam . . ."

The woman's expression once again became severe. "As you say. I want to know what you plan to do to find whoever is responsible for the damage done to my property."

"Certainly, madam. We'll do everything in our power, but at the moment we're most interested in your hatpins."

"The hatpins? They were hardly worth anything. I told the man at the desk that they didn't matter, but that was all he wanted to know about. He didn't care that my shop had been vandalized. I shall never be able to feel secure about it again. Really, Inspector, it is the most outrageous—"

"The hatpins may have been used in the hatpin murders. I'm sure you've heard about them."

She put one little claw of a hand to the cascade of lace at her throat. "Oh."

"Don't be alarmed, ma'am." Drew gave her an encouraging smile. "There's nothing to worry you about this, but you can be a tremendous help in the investigation."

Birdsong took a small box from his desk drawer, removed the lid, and held it out for the lady to see.

"Look at this closely, Miss Forest. Is it one of yours?"

She reached out as if she would take the pin from him, but faltered and instead held her hands clasped in her lap. "Certainly one of mine. I recognize the little sparrow on the end. But it couldn't have been taken yesterday. It's one of my very old ones. I keep it—kept it, I should say—and one or two others in a box in the back room of the shop."

Drew glanced at the chief inspector. "So you didn't even know it had gone missing?"

She fidgeted with her small handbag. "Most everything in the back is packed up. How could I know?"

"Of course not," Drew soothed. "And it would stand to reason that you might not know if any of the others in that box might—"

"Oh, dear. I hadn't thought. Did you say all of these dreadful murders had been done with hatpins?"

"Not the murders precisely, no. But the hatpins were used at the scene of each one."

"Used?" Her faded blue eyes flitted from Drew to the inspector and back again.

"We're not releasing that information to the public at the moment, madam," Birdsong said with a scowl at Drew. "And I will have to ask you to keep anything mentioned here in confidence, all right?"

"Oh, yes, Inspector. Certainly."

Miss Forest eased herself out of the chair, preparing to take her leave, and Drew cleared his throat. "The other pins, sir?"

"I was just getting to that, if you don't mind." Birdsong made his expression a little more pleasant as he turned from Drew to the lady. "I will have to send an officer along with you back to your shop, madam, to have a look at the box of pins you say are kept in your back room. To see if any others are missing."

"Yes, of course. But you realize I couldn't possibly have known—"

"No one is laying blame, madam." Birdsong took her elbow and ushered her to the door. "Parkins, will you see to this lady?"

The constable came back into the room, and after a few words of instruction from the chief inspector, he hurried the lady away.

"Well, well, well." Birdsong looked smugly pleased. "It's Farthering St. John again. What do you make of that, Detective?"

"What should I make of it? Clearly our man has a need for more pins."

Birdsong looked grim at the idea. "Clearly. The other things were taken just to muddle things."

Drew nodded. "And he makes his headquarters somewhere in or around the village."

"*Your* village."

"It's not as though I own it, you know, even if it was named for my family."

"Neither here nor there. The point is to find the man before he makes use of another of those pins."

"I've been wondering about something," Drew said after a moment's silence.

The chief inspector lifted one heavy eyebrow. "Yes?"

"I don't quite like to say yet. Could be nothing."

"You're to report any flashes of brilliance at once. Wasn't that our agreement?"

Drew laughed. "So it was, but I've yet to be certain this is 'brilliance' and not just badgering a perfectly innocent neighbor of mine."

"You ought to let the proper authorities decide that, oughtn't you?"

"Your concern touches me, Chief Inspector. Truly."

"You're certainly touched," Birdsong grumbled. "If you're not going to be of any use, you may as well give me my peace and quiet. Someone ought to be working on this case."

Drew put on his hat, tipping it slightly as he did. "To be sure. But I'm not giving over, either. The moment I'm sure I have my theory straight, I'll make sure and share it with you. As it is, I don't want to cast suspicion where it ought not be cast. Let me first find out one little thing, sir, before I start telling tales out of school."

"Just one, eh?"

"Just one. I bought a book the other day, one someone else had ordered and never claimed. If that someone is who I think it might be, I'll let you fellows carry on from there. Sound fair enough?"

"Maybe you'd best tell me your suspicions, just in case."

Drew shook his head. "All in good time. I'll certainly not put myself in harm's way just making certain of this one thing."

The chief inspector did not look pleased as Drew wished him farewell and left him to his work.

☉

"It's nearly time to dress for dinner. When do you suppose he'll stop his gallivanting and grace us with his presence, this young man of yours?"

Aunt Ruth peered at Madeline over her glasses, her crochet hook still for once.

Madeline gave her a determined smile. "He has a name, Aunt Ruth. A rather nice name, in fact. Ellison Andrew Farthering."

Aunt Ruth sniffed. "Fussy and foreign, if you ask me."

"Maybe it is. Is that any reason to dislike him?"

"Obviously my opinion is of no consequence."

"That's not true. I value your opinion very much. You know I do."

The older woman turned her attention to her lace. "Could have fooled me."

"Please, Aunt Ruth—"

"No, I know when to leave well enough alone."

"I just haven't decided yet. I don't know what to tell you."

"Then I'll tell you something I haven't told anyone. Not in years and years." She stopped her work again, this time laying it completely aside. "You've heard of Bert Williamson, haven't you?"

Madeline nodded. Aunt Ruth never talked about Bert or about anything that happened when she was young. "He drowned."

Aunt Ruth's mouth tightened. "He did. Two weeks before we were to be married."

"That must have been terrible for you."

"It *was* terrible. More terrible than you know. Because I had broken with him the night before."

"You had? I thought——"

"Everybody thought. Everybody thought we were going to get married and I lost him tragically. Well, that was true . . . after a fashion. We found out that his father had embezzled some money from the bank where he was a manager, and it was all going to come out in the next day or two. My mother, your grandma Milner, told me I had to break it off with Bert before the scandal broke. I still remember the look in his eyes when I told him. Poor boy, as if he hadn't had enough heartache already."

"And then he died." Madeline reached over to squeeze her aunt's hand, heedless of her unraveled stitches. "Oh, Aunt Ruth. You don't think he meant to——"

The older woman looked a little bewildered, as if the pain were a thing of yesterday. "I don't know. I know his father ended things afterward with a bullet to the brain."

"I'm so sorry."

Aunt Ruth sniffed and straightened in her seat, her expression coolly resolute. "Well, I didn't have to face the scandal with him. And I didn't have to spend my life learning to live with his imperfections and failings, so I suppose I was saved a lot of heartache myself. I thought you might want to benefit from my poor share of wisdom, but I see you know your own mind. 'Experience keeps a dear school, but fools will learn in no other.'"

Madeline dropped her head, feeling as if she were seven years old again, small and awkward. *You're a young woman, darling, not a child.* She could almost hear Drew saying it.

She looked up again. Aunt Ruth was once more peering over her glasses at her. "I do want to learn from you, Aunt Ruth." Madeline steeled herself. "I do, and I have. And one of the things I've learned is that I don't want to spend my whole life alone. What happened to Bert was terrible for you, I know, and

I don't want to end up without the man I love, either. Can't you understand that?"

The tiniest hint of a smile tugged at the older woman's mouth. "Well, I was wondering if you loved him enough to speak for him. Land sakes, girl, I wasn't going to let you marry a man you wouldn't even stand up for."

With a little cry, Madeline threw her arms around her aunt.

"You're crushing my dress, child!"

Madeline released her. "He's a good man, Aunt Ruth, truly."

"Kind of you to say so." Nick grinned at her as he came into the room. "Of course, you really shouldn't talk about me behind my back."

As usual, Aunt Ruth looked unimpressed. "Tweedle Dum and no Tweedle Dee, eh?"

Nick laughed. "Drew not home yet? I thought he'd be here for tea. Not like him to skip that. Especially not like him to miss dinner."

"I'm sure he'll be home soon." Madeline put on a smile, forcing herself to look braver than she felt.

— Nineteen —

The windows of The Running Brooks were dark, but Drew could see a little light from the first floor. Surely she wouldn't have gone to bed already. He knocked at the door, waited a moment more and then knocked again, this time a bit louder. He waited again and heard a rustling about inside. The lights came on.

"Who is it, please?"

Her voice had that touch of anxious bravado adopted by women who lived alone. No doubt she spent her evenings in her rooms above the shop, giving herself permanent waves and listening to the wireless.

"It's Drew Farthering," he called. "I hope I haven't dropped by too late, Mrs. Harkness."

She opened the door and, smiling, put down the heavy spanner she had held defensively in front of her. "Oh, Mr. Farthering, do excuse me." She put her hand to the scarf tied around her hair. "I wasn't expecting anyone. Is there something I can do for you? Do come in."

He took off his hat and followed her inside. "I'm terribly sorry to have disturbed you after closing time, but I was wondering if you could help me with something."

"If I'm able. I was just making tea. Will you join me while we talk?"

"Yes. Lovely."

She took him past the stacks of books to the back of the shop and then to the foot of the stairs.

"Excuse me a moment while I do up the lock. I don't like to leave it open after hours." She scurried to the front door, locked it, and hurried back. "Now, I hope you won't mind sitting in the kitchen. It's so much cozier."

He followed her through her shabby little parlor and into the kitchen. It wasn't much, just a sink and some cabinets and a gas ring for the kettle. A small table and two chairs finished out the room.

"It's not a proper kitchen, you know. Hardly more than a place to brew up." She smiled in apology, and he sat down.

"It'll be fine, Mrs. Harkness. Now, do you—?"

"Ah, that's the kettle." She turned around and switched off the gas. "Why don't you ask me what you want to know while I make the tea?"

"Remember when you sold me that book?" he asked as she fussed about. "The one on women who commit murder?"

"Oh, yes. Frightful thing, that. But really, I don't know all that much about it." She set two cups on the table and filled them both from the teapot. "I ordered it from a publisher in London. Not one I usually use, of course. Do take one."

Drew picked up one of the cups. "No, to be sure, but you told me you had ordered it for a customer of yours specially."

"Yes. That's right."

"Could you please tell me who it was for?"

She sat at the table opposite him. "Mr. Farthering, you know I can't. My customers would stop trusting me with their orders if I spread gossip about them. I'm sure you can understand."

"Yes, I can and I do, but this is important. I'm thinking maybe it has to do with the hatpin murders."

Her face paled. "No. You don't think so really."

"I'm afraid I do. I promise I won't say anything to anyone but the authorities, but I need to know who ordered that book from you."

"The authorities? Is it as serious as all that?"

"Well, I haven't said anything to them yet, but yes, it might be."

She drank some of her tea, her brow puckered in thought. "I don't know that it would be of any help, I'm afraid."

"Was it Mr. Llewellyn?"

"Dear, sweet Mr. Llewellyn?" She laughed. "Oh, forgive me. You like honey in yours, don't you? I'll just get it."

She stood and reached up to the shelf above the sink.

"May I get that down for you?"

"Oh, no." She came back to the table with the jar of honey. "There's rarely anything I can't reach for myself. Mother always told me I'd be grateful for my height once the awkwardness was grown out of."

"I generally find my height an advantage, but I suppose it's different for a woman." He put two generous spoonfuls of honey into his tea, stirring it in. "A bit intimidating to a certain type of man if a woman is taller than he."

"I suppose it rather is."

She passed him a plate containing slices of stale-looking

sponge cake, which he declined with a murmur of thanks. She wasn't eating any of it, either.

"No, no," she said. "I'm sure he couldn't be a murderer. He brought me flowers."

"But you said something about him intending to bruise himself up when he ran into you. Surely there would be no better way to explain away bruises that would otherwise be incriminating."

"Don't be silly. You might say the very same thing about me." She gave him a mischievous smile. "But I suppose what's really important is that you've enjoyed the investigation."

The tea was scalding, and he took more of a swallow than he had planned.

"Enjoyed it?" he asked, the question coming out with a cough.

"Oh, you know. The mystery of the thing. Putting the clues together, hearing all the delicious, tawdry details that always come out in an inquiry. Wondering who'd be killed next and when. And how. Do have some cake." She offered him the plate again and then drank more of her tea. "'How' is always one of the best bits, isn't it?"

Again he declined the cake, watching her. "I suppose if it were just a game, a book or something, you know, it'd be smashing fun. I have to admit this one's a real puzzler, too. Motives for each of the killings yet none of them related. Not really."

"Hmmm." She tapped the edge of her cup with a neat-looking fingernail. "And always some tall, thin fellow at the scene? That *is* telling."

Drew struggled to keep his expression bland. "Of course, a short woman could never pass herself off convincingly as a man, either."

She laughed. "No, I suppose not. I don't know many who'd try anything that daft, though."

"It'd be a pretty good wheeze, don't you expect, if one wanted to get in and out of a place and not be known?" He drank more, leaving the cup only half full. "Really put one over."

"I daresay Shakespeare's lovely Portia and Viola and Rosalind all found it suited their purposes to go about in doublet and hose for a time. And they've been applauded for their wit and courage all the years since and won their gentlemen's hearts to boot. Why, you yourself told me you'd take a clever woman over a beautiful one."

"True enough. I suppose whoever's done these murders is clever enough. As I said before, it would be smashing fun if it weren't for those people being killed. That rather takes the shine off the thing, don't you think?"

She smiled faintly, and there was a far-off look in her eyes. "And there was 'the woman,' Irene Adler. Even Sherlock Holmes himself was no match for her.

"'Good night, Mr. Sherlock Holmes,'" he said, and he couldn't help the quickness in his breathing.

"You didn't notice that, did you? I suppose, being such a tiny hint, it was easy to pass over without realizing." She patted the back of his hand as it rested there on the little table. "I was afraid I'd given myself away then. Still, I thought you'd figure it out in time. And you nearly did, too. I mean, you'd considered it might be a woman at least. I can tell that much."

He remained staring at her, for a moment unable to speak.

"But for the scandal, she might have been queen of them all," he managed finally. "'A Scandal in Bohemia,' of course. Not only Clarice Deschner the Bohemian, but Irene Adler who dressed as a man to outwit Sherlock Holmes." He felt oddly dizzy, as if his mind didn't want to accept the evidence laid out before him. "I suppose I ought to be flattered at the comparison."

"Don't forget the Bohemian-Tartar waiting for Falstaff to come down dressed as the old woman of Brainford from *The Merry Wives of Windsor*. I had trouble with that one, you know. Did you ever figure it out?"

He shook his head warily. "What exactly did it mean, all that about being mismatched and hot-tempered and simply waiting for greatness to be humbled?"

"'Here's a Bohemian-Tartar tarries the coming down of thy fat woman,'" she quoted, looking quite pleased with herself now. "I'm sure you remember Slender's servant Simple was the one called a Bohemian-Tartar, a mismatched comparison if there ever was one. Tartars are notorious for their tempers, aren't they? How else would Simple do anything but simply? And who could be greater than great, fat Sir John Falstaff?"

She looked at him expectantly, and he finally nodded.

"I see. And if one descends or comes down, that's a bit the same as being humbled, I suppose."

Heavens, how her mind ran in strange paths.

Her eyes sparkled. "Women dressed as men, men dressed as women, plenty for a clever young man to choose from."

"But they hadn't done you any wrong." He had to force his voice not to shake. "All those people, you hardly knew them. How could you have—?"

"Have killed them? I'd seen you in here, buying your murder mysteries, all the time eager for a new one to solve. I thought you'd rather enjoy a real one of your very own. Before, when you were involved in that investigation, the one with your mother and stepfather, it had to be difficult for you. Losing members of your own family had to have taken all the fun out of it. But these people, well, you didn't really know them, did you? And you must admit, me not really knowing them either, not having any reason to wish them harm, not benefiting from their deaths, no one would have ever suspected me of killing them, would they?"

Clearly she was mad. Drew's heart was running like a trip-hammer inside his chest. He had to keep her talking until he figured out how to get himself out of this nasty predicament. She'd left the spanner downstairs in the shop, hadn't she? They'd both had the tea. Neither of them had eaten the cake. *Lord God, you hold me in the palm of your hand.*

"No. No, that was clever of you. Quite clever."

"That first one, your solicitor in Winchester, that was the most difficult. I tell you, I was giddy as a goose when I knocked on that door. But I had my lovely marble Shakespeare in my bag, and once he'd turned his back, it was done in a twinkle. The good doctor, well, all he could think of was making a birdie on the first hole. It was nothing to come up near him with the club he'd asked for, stab him through, and then run off shouting for help."

"I suppose not. How'd you know? About him and about Montford?"

She smiled again. "One picks up the most interesting information while people are shopping. They talk about where they've been, where they're going, who they know. You and Nick Dennison had been in a week or so before, and you told him you were seeing your solicitor in Winchester and the hotel and the time you were meeting him. There's really no art to it, especially when one is invisible to one's customers."

Something chilling came into her smile. She was right. He had chatted on with Nick, with Madeline, with other customers about his activities. There had never seemed any harm in it. Not until now.

"So you decided then that you were going to . . ." He didn't quite know what to call her murderous scheme.

"Start the game? Oh, no. I'd been thinking about it for a while before then. Our Mr. Montford just happened to be the best opportunity."

"And Dr. Corneau?"

"I had him picked out some time ago. Annalee's husband was mates with the boy who usually caddied for him at your golf club. All I had to do was send a telegram to get him out of the way that day and take his place."

Drew nodded. "And I know Roger Morris was in here with Clarice the day she was murdered. I suppose that was when you slipped the cigarette case into Roger's pocket."

She giggled. The woman actually giggled.

"That *was* good, wasn't it? I never liked that snobbish little tart anyway. She was always too good to buy anything but a newspaper here. It had to be London for everything. It was nothing to drop by her cottage once she was alone and tell her I'd found the book she wanted. I slipped plenty of Veronal into her tea while she was looking at the book, then left her in good spirits."

"And left poor Roger to take the blame for it."

"What a sniveling little hedgehog he is, simpering after her the way he did. He should be glad he didn't marry the silly creature and have her lording over him the rest of his miserable life. And then there was that wretched American boy who kept on nosing around, trying to spoil everything."

"The meddler. I take it he wasn't really part of your plan."

She shrugged. "Not at first. There was only meant to be three. After all, three is just right, isn't it? Two really isn't enough, and four is a bit much, if you ask me. I merely thought our Freddie would do nicely to put a bit of uncertainty between you and Miss Lah-de-dah. She's really the only person I hate enough to kill, but doing away with her would have spoilt everything."

"Madeline?"

"The wretched little minx. I've seen her deviling you, pulling you close with one hand and driving you off with the other. How's that for a way to treat anyone, much less the man she loves? Taunting and teasing? What does a girl like that know about how to treat a man? She's had them all thrown at her all her life no doubt. What does she know about loneliness? About aching just to hear a man's voice say something kind, something that says you're a woman and not just a thing."

"I don't—"

"You were always kind to me, Mr. Farthering." Her cheeks turned pink. "Drew."

"Mrs. Harkness—"

"I knew that if I could make you see me, really see me, you'd realize how much better I was for you than she. You need someone who's as clever as you are, someone who could keep you amused. You said yourself it had been smashing fun. She's never done anything of the kind for you, has she?"

"No, she hasn't. Why didn't you kill her? I'd've thought you'd want to make away with her. Clear your own path, as it were. No?"

She smiled. "Oh, no. I couldn't have you mourning for her for ages afterward. I wanted you to hate her, not make her into a martyred saint. And if she were dead, that's what you would have done. Forever young and beautiful, she would have been your idol and still in the way. I couldn't have that, now, could I?"

"No, of course not." He sipped more of his tea, still watching her. "Perhaps you're right after all, Mrs. Harkness." He sheepishly ducked his head. "I mean, Bobbie."

"Don't!"

Drew flinched as she slammed her fist on the table, rattling her teacup in its saucer.

"Don't you ever patronize me." The pink in her cheeks had become an angry red. "I know the idea is ridiculous. Beautiful young lord of the manor and poor Mrs. Harkness, the old ratbag from the bookshop? Doesn't matter how clever she was or how many people she got the better of or how very, very much she might have loved him." Her eyes were pleading now. "Doesn't matter. Better to go now on my own terms. Better than staying here, little more than invisible to the rest of the world."

"Where are you going?"

"Far enough." She nodded and smiled again. "Far enough so I don't have to hear them talk about poor Bobbie Harkness. You never knew how it was, did you?"

"How what was?"

"Not to be everyone's darling. Not to be anything but the life of the party. Not to be surrounded by family and friends."

He tried an understanding smile. "I don't know why you'd say that. I haven't anyone much myself anymore. Not after my mother and stepfather were killed. I can understand how you—"

"Don't," she hissed again. "Don't say you know how I feel. You've got that girl simpering after you, her and a hundred more you could have in exchange for a wink. And you've got that Nick Dennison as well, salt of the earth, stout fellow, friend in all weather. Don't tell me you couldn't snap your fingers and have Farthering Place full to bursting with the best of your society crowd any moment you cared to. Don't pretend you know what it's like for someone upon whom God didn't care to rain down graces."

"But there's Annalee. Your grandchildren. They—"

"They left me. That's my thanks, mind you, for a lifetime of mothering. But that husband of hers, that Marcus, he must work at the new store in Liverpool, mustn't he? Never mind leaving the old woman to herself now. Mr. Harkness did that years ago, you know."

"I'm sorry."

"No need to be. He left, true, but he didn't get far. No farther than the garden behind the shop."

She said it as matter-of-factly as if she'd told him she had planted radishes or carrots in that garden. There was only mild speculation in her expression as she watched him, nothing more, but it sent something electric, thick and burning, coursing through his veins.

She wasn't mad; she was vengeful. She was sober and deliberate and utterly ruthless.

"So now what?"

He knew what. She'd confessed to everything. She'd have to kill him or herself. There was still that painful beating in his blood. Maybe she'd kill them both. Either way, she knew it was the end. It was written there in that fevered look in her eye.

"Look here, Mrs. Harkness, I won't bore you with my problems. I'll just say that my life isn't quite so ideal as you make it out. No one's is. No doubt you've heard it said that if we could all lay down our packs of troubles and choose the one we'd rather carry, we'd most of us take our own back again. Maybe you've had a rum go of it with everything that's happened to you. Maybe everyone has in his or her own way."

He was starting to get up when she pulled a little nickel-plated derringer from the pocket of her housecoat. "I'd rather you sat back down."

He sat back down.

She jiggled the gun in front of his face. "Oh, I know you've had your trials. It couldn't have been easy for you with what happened out at Farthering Place. That's why I thought we could both use a bit of fun. That's why I thought you and I would reach an understanding. A sympathy, if you like. Perhaps I was wrong."

"I . . . I hardly know what to say. All those people . . ."

"They were going to die eventually anyway. They were all good people, weren't they?"

"I don't know. I suppose."

"You believe in heaven, don't you?"

"Yes, I do." Where was she going with this?

There was something bitter in her eyes. "Well then, what's the harm in sending them on a bit early?"

"That's God's decision to make, not ours."

"God." She laughed. "What does He care about me? He has His favorites, and the rest of us can go to hell. Isn't that what He says?"

"No." Drew forced himself to look directly into her eyes. "What He says is that He offers all of us His forgiveness, and His love as well, no matter what we've done. All we need do is accept it."

She shook her head. "You're so very young, aren't you? I sometimes forget, but you're hardly more than a boy. Live as long as I have and see if those tales you've heard don't turn sour. But no, I'd rather you not lose that little bit of fantasy. It looks well on you. Too many handsome men are nothing but sangfroid, and they always appear as if they're sneering. I'm glad I'll never have to see you that way." Then something evil came into her eyes as she stood and placed the barrel of her pistol just behind his left ear. "Better to go now."

Dear God in heaven, she was going to kill him right here at her kitchen table.

"It's no good using that. The chief inspector knows I was coming here." Did he know? He knew Drew had gone to inquire about a book. Surely he would deduce . . . "And how are you going to explain a dead body at your table? Or my car outside?"

"No worry there. In a little while, once we're done here, I'll put on your coat and hat and drive away. Then I and my neighbors can tell your dear chief inspector we saw 'Mr. Far-thering' leave in his car. And if they find your precious Rolls in the ditch a little way up the road, I expect they'll have their own theories on how it got there and what might have happened to you."

Lord God, you hold me in the palm of your hand.

"Someone will hear the shot."

She glanced at the derringer. "I'd never use this. It's too loud. Besides, Veronal always does the trick nicely. It worked for that Deschner girl and even helped a bit with Mr. Bell. It worked for Mr. Harkness, as well. There was never a whimper out of him. This derringer was the only really useful thing I got from the marriage."

His eyes flickered to the gun once more, and she pressed it just slightly harder against his skin.

"I shouldn't have said I'd never use this. It's more that I shouldn't *like* to use it. Especially not on that handsome head of yours. But if you're foolish and try to take it from me, I suppose I'll have no choice, weak woman that I am."

"I won't take it. The Veronal, I mean. You'll have to shoot me." He did his best to look unflinchingly into her eyes. "Or let me go. Either way, what I told you is true. God will forgive you if you ask Him."

She nodded, just a touch of a sneer on her face. "And what about you?"

He closed his eyes for a moment, knowing she would instantly pick up on any hint of insincerity now. What was he prepared to do, especially now in the face of his own death? When he very well might stand before his God in the next minute or two and answer to Him for his own deeds? He couldn't force himself to feel anything charitable toward her, not with this sick terror running through him, but there was something he *could* do.

He took a shuddering breath and looked again into her eyes, his choice made. "I will forgive you, too."

She froze where she was, and for an instant he saw past the hard cynicism, past the rage and ruthlessness. Instead, in those wild, dark eyes, he saw pain and fear and the dread knowledge that there was no going back. Not for her, he could see she was certain of that. But an instant was all she would allow before the smirk returned to her lips.

"You're an absolute lamb, Mr. Farthering." She stroked his damp forehead, pushing back an unruly lock of hair. "Truly, you are. Yet as appealing as it is, no amount of bravado or sentimentality is going to help you now. You've already taken the Veronal."

He shook his head. Even that took no small effort. *Lord God, you hold me in the palm of your hand.*

"But you had tea. It was from the same pot."

His tongue clung to the roof of his mouth, and a wave of grogginess washed over him. *Lord God, you hold me . . .*

He took a couple of quick breaths, trying to fight it, but it was no use. The room was fading out of focus, and Mrs. Harkness sounded as if she were very far away.

"The honey, my precious. The honey."

Lord God . . .

— Twenty —

Aunt Ruth had just grumbled for the third time about Drew being late for dinner when the Farthering Place telephone rang.

"Calling up with some lame excuse, I suppose."

"Please, Aunt Ruth." Madeline turned to Nick, trying to keep the worry out of her eyes. "He would call, wouldn't he?"

"Oh, I'm sure. He's just had a puncture or some such thing."

Dennison came to the parlor door. "Chief Inspector Birdsong is on the telephone for you, Nicholas."

"Me?" Nick asked. "Did he say why, Dad?"

"He asked to speak to Mr. Farthering, and finding him not at home, he asked for you. I don't advise you keep him waiting."

Nick hurried off to the study. Though she knew she wasn't invited, Madeline went after him.

"Chief Inspector," Nick said, "how are you this evening?"

Madeline could hear the faint murmur of Birdsong's voice through the telephone but couldn't understand what he was saying.

"So old Llewellyn does have a sweetheart, eh?" Nick chuckled. "That explains his being out on his bicycle in the evenings, the old *roué*."

Birdsong said something else, and Nick shook his head. "No. If they were seen together the night Mr. Bell was killed, and also when Clarice was killed, I suppose that lets him off the hook, doesn't it?"

Madeline tried to tell what Birdsong said in reply, but all she could make out was "women murderers."

"Yes, he did," Nick said. "From the bookshop here in Farthering St. John. He thought whoever bought it might enjoy playing the sort of game our hatpin murderer has been involved in."

Madeline made out the words "since this evening" from Birdsong's reply, and again Nick shook his head.

"Not a word from him. Actually I was about to go hunting for him."

Again the chief inspector spoke, but Madeline heard nothing but the low tones of his voice.

"Right," Nick replied. "I'll be ready for you. And if you find the Rolls in the ditch and happen to see him walking this way, best fetch him along home, eh?"

"What did he say?" Madeline asked when Nick hung up the phone.

Nick frowned. "Drew said something to him about finding out who ordered that book on murder. Seemed to have some idea who the killer is, but wouldn't say till he'd found out for certain if it was the same person who wanted the book."

"You don't think he's in trouble, do you?"

"Good heavens, no." Nick gave her a reassuring smile. "Just a puncture or a breakdown somewhere. Old Birdsong said he'd like to find out about that book too, even if it is a bit late for making official calls. Since Drew's out, he thought I might like to go along. Maybe between the two of us and Mrs. Harkness, we can figure out what Drew was thinking."

"You mean the three of us and Mrs. Harkness."

Nick laughed. "I didn't think you'd stand for being left home. Yes, well, best tell your aunt we'll be missing dinner. Birdsong will be by for us soon. Maybe we'll find Drew and Mrs. Harkness having a nice chat and all our worries will be for nothing."

"There's the Rolls," Nick said when the chief inspector stopped in front of the bookshop. "See? Probably just having a chat and forgot the time."

Madeline half dragged him out of the car. "I'll feel better when I know for sure."

Nick bounded up to the shop and tried the door. "Bolted tight." He gave the door four or five solid raps. "Anyone there?"

Only silence answered him.

"Mrs. Harkness?" Birdsong pounded the door with his fist. "Hello?"

More silence, followed by a single gunshot.

With a cry, Madeline rattled the door in its hinges, trying to push both men aside. They wouldn't let her.

"Stay back, miss." Birdsong pulled off his overcoat, wrapped it around his hand and forearm and then punched through the window nearest the door. Then he reached through and released the bolt. In another instant the three of them were inside.

"Drew! Drew, are you here?" Madeline's voice was thin and quavery in the dim stillness of the shop.

Birdsong shrugged back into his overcoat and strode past

the bookshelves and into the back room. "Mrs. Harkness? Mr. Farthering?"

"Are you here, old man?" Nick called.

"Upstairs," Birdsong directed, but Nick was ahead of him. He took the steps two at a time with the chief inspector right behind. Madeline tried to wedge herself past them, but the passageway was too narrow and Birdsong was holding her back.

"Best let us get the door open, miss."

"Drew!" Again and again, Nick threw his shoulder against the door. "Drew, can you hear me?"

"Drew!" Madeline's voice cracked and choked in her throat until she could only whisper. "Please be all right. Dear God, please let him be all right." She clung to Birdsong's battered sleeve, biting her lower lip, tasting blood.

"Get it open, man!" the chief inspector barked, and just then there was a splintering of wood and the door slammed back against the wall.

Madeline tore past the two men into the parlor and then stood frozen in the doorway to the bedroom, her hands over her mouth. Mrs. Harkness lay on the narrow bed, her eyes wide and staring. Her right arm sprawled onto the floor, with her hand resting alongside a small nickel-plated derringer. And close by Mrs. Harkness lay Drew. His face was still, pale, and spattered with blood. A note was fastened to his chest with a long lion-headed hatpin.

The words screamed in Madeline's head, but came out only as a pitiful whisper: "Please, God, no . . ."

Nick made a strangled sound low in his throat.

Stepping around Nick and Madeline, Birdsong went to Drew and felt for a pulse. He turned to Nick. "Go get a doctor."

Nick blinked stupidly.

"Get a doctor!" Birdsong roared. "Now!"

Nick bolted out of the room and clattered down the stairs.

Birdsong glanced at Drew's chest, taking a moment to scan the note's message.

"Oh, Drew." Madeline fell to her knees beside the bed and took him into her arms, away from . . . from *her*.

From the bookshop below she could hear Nick shouting into the telephone, demanding to be connected to Dr. Wallace at once. She held Drew tightly against her, begging for God's mercy in sobs more than words.

After a few minutes she could feel the tiniest beating in his chest. But he remained limp against her, and his lips were bluish and cold. She breathed his name against them while Birdsong grabbed his wrist, slapping it rapidly.

"Come on, boy." He pulled Drew up and gave his cheek a smart slap, and at last Drew stirred. "Wake up, Detective Farthering! No lying down on the job."

Drew muttered something unintelligible and then sank back against Madeline's shoulder.

"Here now, there will be none of that," Birdsong ordered.

He lifted Drew to his feet, shaking him, and then lowered him into the sagging old armchair in the corner. Madeline knelt on the floor beside it, glad to see the chief inspector pull a sheet over the gruesome remains on the bed.

"Drew," she coaxed. "Drew, darling."

At that, Drew's eyes opened halfway. "Oh, hullo."

His smile was unfocused and one-sided, but she thought it was the most wonderful thing she'd ever seen. "Hello."

"Where, uh . . ." He moved his hand, rustling the note that was still pinned to his shirtfront. "What's this?"

The chief inspector removed the hatpin and stuffed the paper

307

into the pocket of his overcoat. "Time enough for that after we've got you properly awake."

Between the two of them, he and Madeline got Drew on his feet and walked him into the parlor. Then, after shutting the bedroom door, Birdsong urged them over to the sofa and sat them down on it.

"How are you feeling?" Madeline asked once Drew was comfortably settled against her shoulder.

"A bit groggy," he admitted. "Not quite sure I'm right in the head yet." There was a tenderness in his eyes now. "I didn't know if I'd see you again, and I didn't care much for that thought."

"Me either," she admitted, feeling the heat rise in her face, this time not caring.

"Ahem." Birdsong pulled Mrs. Harkness's note from his pocket. "I suppose we may as well give this a look, if you feel you're up to it, Detective. And then you can tell me what's been going on here."

The note was different from the others. Instead of the Elizabethan script on antique parchment, it had been scrawled hastily on what looked to be a corner torn from a paper bag.

The chief inspector read it aloud. "'From Helena at the end of her epistle and the beginning of her pilgrimage.'"

"What . . . ?" Drew wrinkled his brow, then shook his head, covering his eyes with one hand. "Poor woman. I don't suppose it all ended well for her."

"What do you mean?" Birdsong asked, and then he raised the note. "What does *she* mean?"

Drew shrugged. "It doesn't matter now. Just a final clue. It doesn't matter."

Understanding nothing but that he hadn't been taken from her, Madeline wrapped him more tightly in her arms and covered his forehead with grateful, unashamed kisses.

Birdsong cleared his throat. "I'll just go see what's keeping that rascal with the doctor."

"You've shocked the old boy," Drew said when Birdsong disappeared down the stairs, but she didn't care. She didn't care in the least.

She pressed her lips again to his forehead. "When are you going to marry me, darling?"

"I don't know. Never?" He grinned slightly. "Or now."

Relief coursed through her veins. "Please mean it, Drew. You do, don't you?"

"The doctor could marry us. No, I suppose that's only parsons and registrars and sea captains." He nestled closer to her and squeezed her hand. "Soon, darling. Not so quickly that we shock the village or give dear Auntie the vapors, but soon. Besides, you'll want some ostentatious affair that they'll splash all over the society pages here and in the States, won't you?"

She caressed his cheek and traced her fingers over his handsome lips, glad to see a tinge of color in them now. "I'd marry you right here, this minute, and in my bathrobe if I had to."

"Why, Miss Parker! What *would* Aunt Ruth say?"

Tears sprung to her eyes. "She'd say not everyone gets a second chance and I'd be a fool not to realize it."

She brought her lips to his, unaware of the passage of time until she heard a discreet cough. She looked up to see Nick at the parlor door.

"Dr. Wallace is on his way." He was smiling even if his face was pale, and his tawny hair looked as if he'd spent the past little while raking his hands through it. "Though it seems, old man, you're doing quite nicely without him."

Drew nodded. "Better than you know, Nick. Our Miss Parker has agreed to stay on at Farthering Place in an official capacity."

"Oh, well done." Nick took the opportunity to shake Drew's hand and clasp his shoulder and, Madeline suspected, assure himself Drew was still solidly with them. "You might have found a less dramatic way of getting the girl to accept you, though."

"I'll have you know it was she who asked me."

Madeline flashed her eyes at him. "Drew!"

"Were you or were you not even now begging me to marry you?"

"Begging? After months of you positively throwing yourself at me, now you say *I* was begging?"

He gave her that mischievous grin she thought she might never see again, and she threw herself into his arms once more.

She was vaguely aware of Nick's laugh, the brush of his lips against her hair, and a quiet charge to take care of his friend.

Then there was the sound of the door closing behind him, and she quickly forgot everything but the steady beating of Drew's heart against her cheek.

After Dr. Wallace had pronounced Drew "disgustingly fit" and prescribed only that he refrain from any future foolishness, Birdsong sent him home.

"We have plenty to discuss, Detective Farthering, but it'll keep until tomorrow. Looks as if we needn't fret over our hatpin killer any longer. My men will see to everything here. You'd do best to have a bit of sleep and perhaps a prayer of thanks that you didn't end up with anything worse than a scare."

Drew assured him he would do just that. He and Madeline climbed into the Rolls and, with Nick at the wheel, drove back to Farthering Place. Once there, they found Denny and Aunt Ruth equally adamant that they all make an early night of it.

Mrs. Devon, of course, insisted on a soothing cup of tea for everyone first. Drew even managed to drink his, though for once he declined to add any honey.

Drew woke up rather late the next morning and then only at the knock on his bedroom door.

Denny came in with his breakfast tray, not his usual job, and a message. "Chief Inspector Birdsong would like to know when he might conveniently call upon you, sir."

Drew stretched and smoothed the hair back from his forehead. "Is my bath ready?"

"Yes, certainly, sir."

"Very well, tell him anytime is fine, provided he gives me a half hour to eat and dress."

"I'll let him know, sir," Denny said with a bow.

Precisely thirty minutes later, the chief inspector presented himself at Farthering Place. Drew was waiting in the library to receive him. Having Nick at his side and Madeline's hand in his made it easier to bear as, at Birdsong's request, he recounted his final conversation with Mrs. Harkness. He was shaken more than he liked to show by how nearly he'd brushed death the night before.

Birdsong was rather grim-faced as he took notes, asking for clarification here and there, but mostly letting Drew tell the tale. Afterward, the chief inspector held out a familiar-looking piece of parchment with delicately penned letters on it. "One of my men found this in her wastepaper basket. I don't know what it means, but she clearly changed her mind at the last moment."

Madeline took it from him. "'With as much resolve as was

in the bandit from Cairo before he died.' What does it mean? Who's the bandit from Cairo?"

Drew frowned in thought. "She liked plays on words. And it's no doubt something from Shakespeare. 'Bandit.' Hmmm. Could be outlaw, thief or robber."

"'Cairo,'" Nick mused. "Egypt perhaps? Africa?"

"Egyptian maybe. Egyptian thief? Good heavens . . ." Drew paled a little. "You know the one, Nick. From *Twelfth Night*."

Nick nodded grimly.

Birdsong looked from one to the other of them. "What's it say?"

"What is it exactly, Drew?" Nick thought for a moment. "'Why should I not, had I the heart to do it, like to the Egyptian thief at point of death, kill what I love?'"

"Oh, Drew." Madeline pressed herself to his side, tightening her grip on his arm. "She was going to kill you along with herself. How could she? If she loved you, even in such a twisted way, how could she?"

"I suppose she couldn't after all."

"But she meant to," Madeline insisted. "She planned to. What changed her mind?"

"I will forgive you, too."

He drew a shallow breath. "Just one of those little decisions we make." He smiled and kissed her hand, and Birdsong scowled at him.

"So what did the other one mean then, Detective Farthering? The one she wrote last. Who is Helena and what was at the end of her epistle?"

"As best I remember, the only one of Shakespeare's many Helenas to write about her plan to go on a pilgrimage was in *All's Well That Ends Well*." Drew indicated the volume of Shakespeare's plays that lay on the library table next to Madeline. "You'll find her letter in Act Three, darling."

Madeline picked up the book and hunted down the place he had indicated, the letter at the beginning of Scene Four. She scanned the brief lines until she reached the final two. Then she looked up at him, tears in her eyes now. "Drew . . ."

The chief inspector frowned, and she passed the book to him, pointing out the place.

> He is too good and fair for death and me,
> Whom I myself embrace, to set him free.

By lunchtime Birdsong was, at least for the time being, satisfied that he could close his investigation. That left only one bit of unfinished business.

Drew swallowed hard. Despite what Madeline had said the night before, he couldn't quite believe she had actually agreed to marry him. Sometimes he thought maybe he was still a bit muddled from the Mickey he'd taken with his tea. It hadn't occurred to him until just now exactly what her acceptance would mean. Others, formidable others, would have to be told about their plans.

Still, there was nothing to do but to face the situation head-on. Madeline gave him a gentle push forward toward the parlor door, and he knew, right or wrong, now was the time to speak. Aunt Ruth was in the parlor as usual, Mr. Chambers curled up in her lap, asleep as she did her lace making.

"Miss Jansen?"

Her lips moving as she silently counted her stitches, Aunt Ruth didn't respond.

"If I might interrupt you for a moment . . ."

She scowled, keeping her attention focused on her task. "Hold on."

Drew glanced back at Madeline, his eyes begging her to let this happen some other day, but she only beamed at him and mouthed the words *go on*.

After what seemed an eternity, Aunt Ruth set down her thread and crochet hook and fixed Drew with a steely glare. "Well?"

"I'm sorry to interrupt you, ma'am, but I have something frightfully important to talk to you about and I really cannot wait another moment."

"What's the matter? You have ants?"

That surprised a bit of a laugh out of him, but he also felt his face heat to burning. Why couldn't he keep his composure around this woman? It must run in the family.

He swallowed again, but he saw just a hint, just the tiniest glimmer of humor in her eyes, and he dared smile. "No, but I'd like to have. One aunt, anyway."

She arched one eyebrow at him. "Oh, yes?"

He glanced one last time at Madeline, and then he sat down on the sofa beside Aunt Ruth. "Look here, ma'am. I know we've been at loggerheads ever since we met, but I'd like that to change. I do love Madeline more than all the world, and I believe she loves me. I'd like your permission, and more than that, your blessing." He let himself be vulnerable and earnest before her and made bold to take her hand. "I want Madeline to be my wife, and I'd like to have your consent."

Aunt Ruth pursed her lips. "Humph. She's of age. She can do as she pleases."

"But will it please you, ma'am? As you know, I haven't any aunts myself, but I'd like to have."

Her face softened a bit. Bless her if she wasn't fighting a smile of her own. "You do have the devil's own silver tongue. I hate to think of the trouble that's going to get the both of you into."

"And out of, I hope," Drew added.

Madeline came and sat on the other side of her aunt, taking her free hand. "Please, Aunt Ruth, say yes. I know we can do whatever we want, but we want you to be happy about it, too. Happy for us."

"I suppose you'll pester me until I give in."

Madeline nodded, her eyes sparkling.

Aunt Ruth turned to Drew. "And I suppose you'll carry on with the sweet talk until you get your way. No, don't say anything else, young man. I guess I can see why a child like Madeline couldn't stand up to you for very long. And maybe, just maybe, mind you, you're actually half the wonder she thinks you are and won't make her miserable for the next fifty years. And maybe you won't get yourself killed in the next week or two. If that's the case . . ." She took their hands and clasped them together between both of hers, waking Mr. Chambers in the process. "If that's the case, you have my blessing."

"Oh, Aunt Ruth." Madeline threw both arms around her aunt's neck and hugged her tightly. "Thank you."

Drew stood up again in the extremely awkward and, for him, unusual predicament of not knowing what to say next, but both women were looking up at him expectantly.

"I'll do my very best to take good care of her, ma'am."

"Ma'am?" The older woman again fixed him with that debilitating glare, and he felt his pulse increase.

"Miss Jansen?" he offered.

"I think it's high time you called me Aunt Ruth."

He smiled. "And perhaps, with the time being particularly high just now, you ought to call me Drew."

Miss Ruth Ann Jansen
requests the honor of your presence
at the marriage of her niece
Madeline Felicity Parker
to
Ellison Andrew Farthering
on Saturday, the tenth of December
nineteen hundred thirty-two
at three o'clock in the afternoon
at The Church of the Holy Trinity and All Angels
Farthering St. John, Hampshire

Reception to follow at Farthering Place

ACKNOWLEDGMENTS

To my family, especially the feline contingent, for putting up with me.

To David Long, Luke Hinrichs, Noelle Buss, and all the fabulous people at Bethany House, just for being fabulous.

I have no words that can truly express how much I appreciate each of you.

Julianna Deering, author of *Rules of Murder*, is the pen name of the multi-published novelist DeAnna Julie Dodson. DeAnna has always been an avid reader and a lover of storytelling, whether on the page, the screen, or the stage. This, together with her keen interest in history and her Christian faith, shows in her tales of love, forgiveness, and triumph over adversity. A fifth-generation Texan, she makes her home north of Dallas, along with three spoiled cats. When not writing, DeAnna spends her free time quilting, cross-stitching, and watching NHL hockey. Learn more at JuliannaDeering.com.

More Mystery From Bethany House

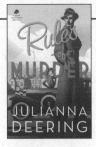

Drew Farthering loves a good mystery. So when a body is discovered on his country estate, he decides to do his own investigation. Trying hard to remain one step ahead of the killer—and to impress his beautiful American guest—Drew must decide how far to take this dangerous game.

Rules of Murder by Julianna Deering
The first DREW FARTHERING MYSTERY
juliannadeering.com

Desperate to locate her brother, Cara travels to America, where she is thrust into a web of danger. Her questions may bring her closer to her brother, but they also put her at the mercy of dangerous revolutionaries—including a man she's grown to love.

No Safe Harbor by Elizabeth Ludwig
EDGE OF FREEDOM #1
elizabethludwig.com

Melanie Ross and Caleb Nelson both claim to have inherited the mercantile. Yet even as they contest ownership, the two are forced to band together to protect their livelihood against external threats. When a body shows up on their doorstep, there's deeper trouble in store...

Trouble in Store by Carol Cox
authorcarolcox.com